Compromising the Marquess

ALL FOR LOVE
BOOK 4

WREN ST. CLAIRE

ARE YOU SIGNED UP FOR DRAGONBLADE'S BLOG?

You'll get the latest news and information on exclusive giveaways, exclusive excerpts, coming releases, sales, free books, cover reveals and more.

Check out our complete list of authors, too!

No spam, no junk. That's a promise!

Sign Up Here

www.dragonbladepublishing.com

Dearest Reader;

Thank you for your support of a small press. At Dragonblade Publishing, we strive to bring you the highest quality Historical Romance from some of the best authors in the business. Without your support, there is no 'us', so we sincerely hope you adore these stories and find some new favorite authors along the way.

Happy Reading!

CEO, Dragonblade Publishing

Prologue

London, March 1818

"THE DUKE AND Duchess of Troubridge and Lady Ava Layne," announced Lady Castlereagh's butler in stentorian accents.

"My God, I wouldn't have recognized her!" said Deodonatus, Earl of Pendrell, absently accepting the champagne glass Jerome DeVere, Marquess of Ravenshaw, pressed upon him. "Stunning, absolutely stunning."

Jerome privately agreed as he watched Ava descending the stairs flanked by her brother Robert and her mother Jocelyn. She was wearing an exquisitely tailored dress in jonquil silk under a sheer net overlay with tiny, puffed sleeves, a fashionably low cut, princess-line bodice, a blue satin sash—the exact color of her gorgeous eyes—beneath the bodice. Her shining gold hair was piled up on top of her head, revealing her elegant neck, about which a single string of pearls hung.

She was smiling, and every eye in the room had turned to watch her descent into the ballroom. This, her first official public appearance in London at the first major ball of the season, was an occasion, and Jerome, Deo, and Emrys—Robert's friends, who had all known Ava since they were schoolboys and she was a little girl—had all agreed to attend in support of the occasion.

It was hard to credit that this was the tearaway hoyden he

had rescued from numerous trees when her ambition had outstripped her capabilities; whose determination to champion the cause of strays, the unfortunate, or the ostracized landed her in numerous scrapes, several of which it had been his privilege to extricate her from; whose tender heart caused her to rescue innumerable dogs and wildlife from all sorts of threats—from cruel little boys to ferocious bloodhounds—at the risk of life and limb; and whose hair was always tumbled, dress was always torn, and knees were always scraped. But somewhere between fourteen and eighteen, she had turned into a beautiful, poised, and elegant young woman who could take a man's breath away.

Jerome had long regarded Ava in a similar light to his nieces, who were of an age with Robert's sisters, of which Ava was the eldest. But watching her now, he was overwhelmingly struck by her transformation from hoydenish schoolgirl into beautiful woman. Ava had grown up, and wrong as it was, he couldn't take his eyes off her.

Realizing Deo had addressed a remark to him, he dragged his gaze away from the golden glory that was Ava and said, "Sorry, what was that?"

"Nothing important, I was just saying I don't know why I bother with the season. In ten years, I've never met the woman I'm looking for. Probably never will." Deo looked so gloomy, Jerome patted his arm consolingly.

"Maybe this year?" Deo was taller than him by about four inches and correspondingly broad through the shoulders and chest. His size, coupled with rather harsh features and a habitually fierce expression, which were further accompanied by flaming-red hair and freckles and a socially awkward manner, tended to make him less popular with the female contingent of society.

Jerome, on the other hand, was not so socially disadvantaged. He stood just over six feet in height with an athletic frame, due to his addiction to sport. He had dark hair and blue eyes and prided himself on always being immaculately dressed. A polished manner and a reputation gained in his youth for ruining unfortunate debutantes who sought to trap him into marriage made him, paradoxically, extremely popular with the ladies. It was a mystery why a man with a shocking reputation was so attractive to the female sex, but there was a time he had taken shameless advantage of that fact. He shut down that uncomfortable train of thought before it could take him places he didn't want to go. *Especially tonight.*

Emrys Fitzgerald, Viscount Ashford, joined them at that moment, with his pretty little wife Caroline and his friend Baron Greathouse. Jerome suppressed a mild shudder at Emrys's appearance. The man was always deplorably untidy. His unruly brown hair was too long for fashion and not even neatly confined in an old-fashioned queue—which it should be if he insisted on being so out of the mode. His linen was slightly wilted, his cravat tied in a deplorable knot, and his clothes ill-fitting, as if he had shrugged himself into his coat. Emrys, unlike the rest of them, had never outgrown the scrubby schoolboy look.

"Going to be another squeeze," remarked Emrys, retrieving a glass of wine for his wife from a passing waiter.

Jerome greeted Caro and Greathouse and turned to reply to Emrys. "It is." He noted that Robert had shepherded his ladies to a spot across the room from them with a couch to sit upon and suggested, "We should show our support, don't you think?" He nodded across the room.

Robert was the second tallest of their quartet, with dark-brown hair and regular features. Like Jerome, he had been the target of ambitious damsels and their matchmaking mamas for over a decade and, having just come into his father's title last year, was an even bigger matrimonial prize now. He was also set on finding a bride this season, and owing to the parlous state his father had left the Layne finances in, his choice needed to land on a woman of substance. The lady he had an eye on was Miss Sarah Watson.

Jerome had been included in a party to Vauxhall with the Ashfords, Robert, Miss Watson, and Miss Watson's chaperone,

Lady Daphne Holbrook, last week. Jerome's role at that affair had been to distract and entertain Daphne, who proved to be a lonely widow and not at all aged. Jerome was quite good with lonely widows and had continued his acquaintance with the lady after that evening.

Robert's friends descended on him in a group and Jerome bowed over the duchess's hand and kissed it, saying, "You are looking in high force this evening, Your Grace. You will be setting a fashion with that delightful cap."

The duchess pursed her lips at him. "Your flattery will get you nowhere, Jerome."

He shrugged and smiled. "I live in hope, Your Grace." Of Robert's friends, he knew himself to be her least favorite. She remembered all too clearly his behavior in his early twenties and hadn't forgiven him—in particular, for Miss Charis Dunsenay, whose mother, Lady Mostyn, was a friend of hers. He hadn't forgiven himself either. With an internal wince he pushed thoughts of his disreputable past away. He had vowed this year that he would not dwell on what he couldn't change. He'd spent countless hours in regret, and it got him nothing but pain.

He turned his attention to Ava and immediately solicited her hand for the first dance. The duchess had made it clear Ava wouldn't be permitted to waltz until her come out ball next week, but this first dance was a quadrille, perfectly respectable.

She flushed a pretty pink when she put her gloved hand in his and allowed him to lead her onto the dance floor. Her eyes glowed with happiness, and her skin was flawless. Her features had lost their girlish roundness and developed the contours of extraordinary beauty, from her lovely, slightly retroussé nose to her lusciously kissable lips and determined chin. She was a foot shorter than him and her figure, he couldn't help noticing, had filled out becomingly. She was exquisite, and he was alarmed by the sudden thrill of heat that invaded his body when he caught a whiff of her lovely scent, rose water and something else, distinctly Ava.

"That is a very fashionable rig, Ava," he said with a teasing smile, determined to keep things on their old friendly footing.

She flashed him a sideways smile from beneath her lashes, which gave him a serious jolt. *Where did she learn that trick?*

"I thought so, too," she said. "Mama was a bit worried about the bodice, but Madame Thérèse insisted it was all the crack, so Mama gave in."

"I'm surprised Rob let you out of the house," he said frankly before he could stop himself.

She giggled, which reassured him a bit that she wasn't too grown up yet. "He didn't see it until we were about to depart, and it was too late to object."

Conversation was truncated by the steps of the dance, and he contrived to behave with perfect propriety for the duration of the number, at the end of which he returned her to her mother's side with a bow and a kiss of her hand, as befitted a grown-up young lady.

Her hand was sought for every dance after that, and he was happy to prop the wall and watch her success. Rob, who wore a harassed expression, buttonholed him at one point and said, "I'll thank you to stay away from Ava."

Jerome eyed him with a lazy smile and said, "Keep your shirt on, Rob, there is no harm in a little light flirtation. She has to try her wings sometime. Better me than some unscrupulous type."

"Since when have you had scruples?" demanded Robert.

Jerome stiffened, touched on the raw. "She is your sister, Rob. I've known her since she was a lass. I might be all sorts of a blackguard, but absolve me of that, please!"

Robert flushed and apologized. "What were you doing squiring Lady Holbrook and Miss Watson to the recital last night?"

"Daphne had a fancy to hear the performance, so I obliged."

"Daphne, is it? I know it's none of my business—"

"You're right, it isn't," Jerome snapped, nettled.

Robert raised his eyebrows at him, and Jerome flushed faintly. "Don't get your tails in a twist, it's just a harmless flirtation, nothing more. You wanted me to keep her entertained at Vauxhall, I did. Even older ladies are entitled to a little fun, don't you think? I've done nothing more than make her feel young again." *Which is perfectly true, but why do I feel the need to justify myself to Robert?* "You needn't worry about Ava. I'll keep an eye on her. You go worry about Miss Watson," he said cheerfully.

Rob smiled ruefully, acknowledging Jerome had hit the nail on the head, and went off to pursue his own agenda. Meanwhile, Jerome crossed his arms and watched Ava dancing down the line of a country dance with some pimply youth who wore a dazed expression.

Ava's effect on the male population was significant enough to cause comment, as he overheard several remarks from jealous matchmaking mamas and appreciative gentlemen alike.

AVA, ENJOYING HER first official London ball, was in a buoyant mood. Her hand had been solicited for every dance, her partners were fulsome in their admiration, and she couldn't help feeling a little thrilled by her obvious success. But even so, none of it topped the felicity of Ravenshaw condescending to dance with her as a grownup. Finally, she had the satisfaction of knowing she had caught his attention.

The man was every schoolgirl's dream, of course. Devastatingly handsome, his fashionable and perfectly fitting evening dress of plain black satin showed his excellent figure to advantage. And he had been her particular dream since she was fourteen. But he had always treated her like a little girl. Tonight, she thought, with an exhilaration that made her want to laugh for sheer joy, he finally saw her as a woman. She had caught the slight glow in his eyes, and even though he tried to hide it behind gentle teasing, she wasn't fooled. He liked the adult version of her.

She knew he had a shocking reputation, though what he was

supposed to have done to earn it she didn't know, and no one at home would tell her. But now she was in London, she could very well find out what dark secrets his past held and why he was considered too dangerous for respectable young ladies to know.

Chapter One

The Castle, Christmas 1818

I T WAS ONE of those crisp, clear winter mornings with the sun glinting off the frosted ground and the icicles hanging from the trees. There had been a light dusting of snow overnight, but not enough to make riding dangerous, and Jerome gave his stallion, Herod, his head across the rising meadow, aiming for the hedgerow on the ridge that would take them into the next field. Both his and his mount's breath puffed white in the chill air as the horse gathered itself for the jump and flew over the fence, landing neatly on the other side.

And to Jerome's horror, missing the figure kneeling in the snow on the other side by a hair's breadth.

The bonneted head looked up as the horse flew almost directly over her head and Jerome pulled Herod around to the right away from her.

"Ava! What the bloody hell—"

"Ravenshaw!" she said with relief in her voice. "Thank goodness. Please, you have to help—" Her voice was cut off by the screams of a creature in pain.

She moved, and he could see then the frantic movement of the animal caught in a trap. A badger. The poor thing was distressed, growling and shrieking, and trying to free itself. The trapped leg was bloodied.

He slid from the saddle, letting Herod's reins fall slack, and dropped to his knees beside her. "Move back out of the way," he said.

Ava moved back, uttering a small whimper at the continued shrieks and growls of the distressed beast.

"Damned gin traps!" he muttered, grasping the spring mechanism and depressing it, thus releasing the jaws of the trap. The badger, realizing it was free, sprang away from the trap and limped rapidly into the underbrush with a waddling gate.

Ava watched it go. "Will it survive with that wound, do you think?"

"I don't know. Possibly," he said, carefully disarming the trap. Once he was sure it was safe, he sat back and looked at her. Her bonnet had fallen back onto her shoulders and she had a smear of dirt on her face. He smiled and shook his head, a gentle warmth settling in his chest. This was the old Ava, the little girl he'd helped with countless rescues such as this one. If there was an injured animal anywhere in her vicinity, trust Ava to find it. All the same, he asked, "How the hell did you stumble across this one?"

"Oh," she righted her bonnet and retied the strings. "I jumped the fence just as you did and Diana shied. That's when I saw it."

He noticed her dappled mare Diana, cropping the grass a little way off beneath a tree. Herod had ambled in her direction. Rising, he looked down at his ruined breeches and helped her rise. She had stain marks on her gown, too. Fortunately Leyton, his excellent valet, was not of a highly strung nature. He would take this little incident in his stride.

Ava smiled up at him with her usual sunny grin, "Thank you, Galahad; always coming to my rescue."

"Hasn't happened for a while. I thought you had outgrown these escapades?"

"I will never outgrow rescuing animals," she said firmly. "Will you ride with me? It's a superb morning."

"It is," he agreed, leading her towards their mounts. He was about to bend to give her a lift into the saddle when she turned and put her hands on his shoulders and rising on tip toe, planted a soft kiss on his lips.

"Thank you," she said softly. The gesture was fleeting, over almost before it began, but it ignited a flame of heat in his body that made his pulse race and his mind—which he had been trying to keep from noticing things like the delicious curve of her neck, her sparkling blue eyes, and the generous curve of her breast in the bodice of her blue velvet riding dress—lost the battle with propriety altogether.

The vivid flash of her golden hair spread out on a pillow beneath him imprinted itself into his system and gave him such a jolt, he actually stepped back. Conscious of the hardened heat in his groin, he looked away a moment to gather his composure, before saying with a lightness he didn't feel, "You're welcome." He took a breath and went on with a faintly scolding tone, "You shouldn't kiss me Ava, I know it's only a gesture of affection between friends, but you're not a girl anymore. If someone saw us, you would be ruined."

She bit her lip and lowered her eyes a moment as if in contrition or disappointment, hard to tell which. Then she raised them again with that wicked sparkle of mischief in them and said, "Then you'd have to marry me! Wouldn't *that* be a disaster."

His heart, which was racing faster than it should, skipped at those words. To cover his discomposure, he bent, offering his hand for her foot which she placed in it. He tossed her into the saddle with a light quip. "Yes it would. For *you*! Imagine being tied to an old man like me with my rotten reputation."

She gasped, grabbing the pommel. "You're not old, Jerome!"

He smiled, but his cheeks ached, along with something in his chest. "I am compared to you, sweetheart. Save your kisses for a man who deserves them."

He turned away to mount Herod and said, "Race you to the next fence!" And he took off across the field. He heard the thunder of hooves behind him as Ava spurred her mare in pursuit.

London, March 1819

LADY AVA LAYNE, performing a graceful twirl under the arm of her dance partner, knew the moment Ravenshaw entered the ballroom with the Ashfords and the Earl of Pendrell. Her gaze snagged on his splendid figure, immaculate in dark blue, with pristine white linen and a perfectly tied cravat. His dark hair was cut in the rather severe Brutus style made famous some years ago by Beau Brummel and which Jerome's startling good looks carried with ease.

Ashford, his somewhat disheveled appearance notwithstanding, was one of her favorite people, and the fact that he was now married to her dear former governess, Annis Pringle, made it easy to request that her dance partner take her to them at the end of the set. Dismissing the poor man with a wave of her fan, she snagged Annis's hand and squeezed it while pressing a kiss to her cheek.

"I was hoping I would see you. You look well. When did you arrive in town?"

"Only a couple of days ago," Annis smiled. "The children all had measles in February so we had to wait until the last spot had vanished before we could come. Poor Emrys got it too and was horribly ill for a fortnight. But he is perfectly recovered now," she said with a loving look at her spouse. As if sensing her regard, Ashford turned toward her and smiled. The look of love that passed between them stabbed Ava with a deep bite of envy. *How I wish . . .*

Her gaze traveled to Ravenshaw, who was deep in conversation with the Earl of Pendrell. The great redhaired giant had scared her witless as a small child, but as she got older she learned he was nowhere near as fearsome as he looked. Just inarticulate— around females. The two men appeared to be discussing horseflesh, Jerome's favorite topic.

Insensibly, she drifted in their direction, pulled on the thread of ambient attraction that Ravenshaw exerted on her whenever he was near. Becoming aware of her presence, the men broke off their conversation to bow to her, and Ravenshaw went so far as to kiss her gloved hand. Which always gave her a little thrill.

She curtsied and wafted her fan playfully, smiling at him; and just to demonstrate that she understood exactly what they had been talking about, she said, "Tickle My Fancy is odds on to win the Guinea Stakes at Newmarket, or so I've been told."

"Have you been studying the form, Ava?" asked Ravenshaw, amused.

"No. It's Creighton, he puts the bets on for me, but don't tell Robert. I don't want to get him into trouble!" Creighton, the Layne's butler, had long been Ava's friend.

A waiter wandered past with a tray of drinks and Ravenshaw snagged one for her which she accepted gracefully, wondering how she was going to get him to ask her to dance. Another set was about to form. Pendrell transferred his attention to the Ashfords, leaving them in a bubble of their own.

"If you want advice on the turf, Ava, I'll be happy to provide it."

"Even if Rob doesn't approve?" she asked, playfully.

He grinned, which made his impossibly deep-blue eyes even more alluring, and she stifled a little sigh. "What His Grace doesn't know won't hurt him." He glanced around at the dance floor where couples were beginning to assemble. "Where is you next partner?"

Aware that her next partner was standing by her mother's side scanning the room for her, she put up her fan to shield her face and said lightly, "Oh I don't have one. It's the waltz and I was saving it for you."

He gave her a measuring stare, and said "Really? Then why is poor Haldane staring around the room like a shepherd who's lost a sheep?"

Color stained her cheeks, but she refused to be cowed and

said, "I've no idea. I'm certainly not a sheep!"

"What you *are*, is a minx!" he said darkly and offered her his arm.

She smiled and slipped her hand into it, allowing him to lead her onto the dance floor.

When he took her hand and slipped his arm round her waist, bringing her body closer to his perfectly proportioned form, she stifled another little sigh, gazing up at him through a haze of adoration, as he gracefully led her into the first movements of the dance.

At the age of fourteen, she had declared that she was going to marry this perfect ideal of a man. At the time she hadn't any real idea of what that meant. But she had nursed her adolescent crush for four long years and in her first season she'd had high hopes of bringing her long-held dream to fruition. But the season and the little season passed with no sign of her feelings being reciprocated. Ravenshaw had persistently and consistently treated her much as he always had, as a sister or a niece.

This season she was determined to prosecute her campaign mercilessly. She knew he liked her, that there was more than a degree of affection between them, that they shared many common interests, and had a personal accord she felt with no one else. And surely she wasn't the only one to feel that tingling rush of desire and longing that the touch of his hand induced in her?

Since her debut she had learned a lot more about men and their—appetites. And she was thoroughly convinced Ravenshaw was no passionless creature. His reputation was quite shocking. Not that she saw any hint of that side of him—much to her frustration. But she had a plan to winkle the rake from his protective shell.

As he guided her around the floor with effortless grace, she smiled and asked after his greys, Aphrodite and Demeter. Demeter had suffered a strained hock after Christmas when his carriage ran into a snow drift on his way back to London. A piece of intelligence conveyed to her by Robert who received regular correspondence from his friend.

"Perfectly recovered, fortunately. I was very concerned for her, but she is moving quite freely now. Have you collected any more strays?"

"Well, Rob refused to let me house old Bill McKay's donkey in the Castle stables, but Hastings was able to find alternative lodgings for Daisy with the Carrigans, who had need of a replacement for their donkey, Old Ned, who had passed on, so all's well that ends well."

"A happy tale."

He said it with a smile that made her say accusingly, "You're laughing at me!"

"No, I'm not, I swear," he said spinning her elegantly. "I'm admiring your resourcefulness."

"Well, in this case it was Hastings who was resourceful. I was at quite a stand when Rob refused my plan to put Daisy in the end stall that never gets used and is only full of rubbish and broken bits. But Rob said Daisy would upset the horses with her braying. He was probably right." She grinned. "I do hate it when Robert is right. But he often is. And when he's not, Sarah is very good at getting him to see reason. He has been much more mellow since he got married. I do adore Sarah."

"Everyone adores Sarah," he agreed.

"And I am very glad to see Annis again. She seems so happy every time I see her. And Emrys too. Between the four of them, they are excellent advertisements for a happy marriage."

"Indeed they are," he said warmly. "Our next task is to find a wife for Deo."

"Does he want a wife?" she asked, startled.

"Oh, yes, but the poor fellow despairs of ever finding the right woman. The trouble is he becomes so tongue-tied around females. I've tried to give him a few tips but he's not an apt pupil." Jerome's rueful expression made her laugh as she tried to picture him giving the awkward earl romantic advice.

"And what about you?" she asked boldly.

"Oh, I don't ever plan to marry," he said carelessly.

Her heart sank at these words and she blurted, "What, never?"

He shook his head. "Some people are cut out for marriage and some are not. I am one of the latter."

If she hadn't been watching his face so closely she would have missed the flicker in his eyes as he spoke. And the conviction that he was lying took root in her heart. Emboldened, she said artlessly, "Kenrick says that, too, but I don't believe him. He just hasn't met the right woman yet."

"That may well be true," he conceded.

"For both of you?" she pushed.

He shrugged, twirling her neatly. "I've met a lot of women," he said with an ironic smile that didn't reach his eyes. The look gave her a sudden chill and not in a good way.

"But you must marry. You've the title to consider," she pointed out.

"True." The word was curtly uttered as he brought them to a standstill and the music finished.

"It's so hot in here!" she exclaimed desperately, fanning herself. "Could we not take a stroll in the garden to cool off?"

She thought for a moment he was going to refuse and march her straight back to Mama. Her words had clearly rattled him. *Good!* She needed to get behind that polished façade he showed the world to the man beneath.

Then he offered her his arm and they threaded their way through the other couples to double doors that opened onto the terrace. After the heat of the ballroom, the air was refreshingly cool. The stars sparkled in a mostly clear sky and the crescent moon had risen. Stepping down into the garden, they strolled along the path between the trees from which colored lanterns had been suspended to provide variegated light.

"It's like fairyland," she murmured, as they moved deeper into the trees and left the other couples behind. Devonshire House had vast gardens. The scent of spring flowers mingled with the oil from the lamps and the damp of the earth, and Ava wondered if a more romantic setting was possible. *Surely . . .*

They reached a cul-de-sac where a stone bench, thoughtfully provided with a cushioned seat cover, was set beneath the lamplit branches of a large tree.

"How pretty!" she said, sitting down, and when he remained standing, looking up at the tree, she tugged at his arm. "Sit with me a moment."

He brought his attention back to her and said gently, "This is not a good idea, Ava."

"I think it is a splendid idea," she said with a wide, coaxing smile. "Come on, just sit. Where is the harm in that?"

He sat and she reached for his hand. "We are friends, aren't we, Jerome?" she said softly.

His expression had lost its playfulness, he looked slightly troubled. "Ava, you can't behave like you used to. I thought you had realized that?"

"What do you mean?"

"You're not a child anymore, Ava."

"I know that, but you persist in treating me like one!" She blinked at him, her sight suddenly wavy with unshed tears. Five years of longing for this moment threatened to overset her.

He swallowed visibly and squeezed her fingers gently. His voice was low and slightly roughened. "I know this isn't what you want to hear Ava, but that is because to me you will always be the little girl I rescued from a tree." Her heart squeezed at those words, and when she would have blurted out a protest, he raised his eyes, and even in the dark, his gaze burned her. "So you see it is futile to look at me with your heart in your eyes. I will always be your friend, Ava, but nothing more."

"Oh!" The anguish in her heart at these words burst forth in that one cry of pain, and then embarrassment and shame crashed over her in a wave that knocked the breath from her body. She ripped her hands from his grip so hard she left her gloves behind, and rising, she fled into the darkness.

"Ava!" His voice followed her, but she ran heedlessly through the trees, her only instinct to get away from the source of pain. Tears blinded her, and as she ran she left the lanterns behind and penetrated further into the darkness of the vast gardens.

JEROME ROSE SLOWLY from the seat, his heart racing and a pain in his chest. He hated himself for hurting her so, but it was for the best. She needed to understand that he wasn't the right man for her. Someone with his dark history didn't deserve the golden delight that was Ava. He had resolved last year, as soon as he fully comprehended his own feelings, that he needed to keep her at arm's length. For her own sake. But he hadn't expected it to hurt so damned much!

Realizing belatedly that she hadn't headed back toward the house, he stuffed her gloves in his pocket and moved to follow her. She might fall and hurt herself in the dark or, worse yet, encounter someone. Some unscrupulous male. The thought quickened his steps until he was running through the trees in her wake.

"Ava!" he called softly, not wanting to draw the attention of any of the other guests. If they were caught out here alone together, she was ruined.

After stumbling about in the dark for a bit he finally found her standing huddled against a tree and sobbing. He put a gentle hand on her back.

"I'm sorry, Ava." She hiccoughed on a sob, and it was so like when she cried after a fall or over a wounded animal that it was natural to draw her into his arms to comfort her. But she had curves now that she didn't have back then, and her scent and her hair were distracting and enticing. He stifled the ache of longing and sternly told his body to behave while he stroked her back gently until her sobs subsided. She drew away then and fumbled in her reticule for a handkerchief and blew her nose and wiped her face.

He didn't know what to say except that he was sorry, and that wouldn't make her feel any better. He supposed, looking back over the last year, this was inevitable, and it was better to get it over with now. She would recover from her infatuation and they could perhaps be friends again, if he could only control his own reactions.

She leaned back against the tree and sniffed. "I'll be all right. You don't need to stay."

"I'm not leaving you alone in the dark," he said firmly. "Let me walk you back to the house. There's an anteroom we can access from the garden where you can sit and let your face recover."

She hesitated and then nodded. They walked back to the house in silence and he guided her to the room he had spoken of. It was mercifully empty. He found a jug of water on the drinks tray and soaked a handkerchief for her to bathe her face. She took it with a murmur of thanks, wiped her face, and pressed the cool cloth to her eyes. After a few moments she moved to the mirror over the fireplace to inspect her appearance and with a couple of pats and repositioning of a few pins she straightened her shoulders and said, "Thank you. I'll return to the ballroom, now. Alone. Good night."

He handed over her gloves and watched her leave, her back straight and her head up. He swallowed the lump in his throat and thought he had never loved her more than he did in that moment.

Chapter Two

FOLLOWING THE HUMILIATION of Jerome's rejection, Ava threw herself into the pleasures of the season with feverish gusto, determined that no one, least of all Jerome, would know how devastated she was. Her five-year dream was shattered.

She took consolation in her many admirers, their compliments and warm glances a balm to her bruised pride. But her heart remained a bleeding thing in her breast. If she had followed its dictates, her eyes would have continued to follow Jerome around the room, her body would have drifted without volition in his direction, but in this, her pride came to her rescue.

She stiffened her backbone and refused to give into such weakness. He had rejected her, thought of her only as a silly girl. Well, she would show him she wasn't any such thing. So she kept her distance and concentrated all her attention on the various suitors who sought her hand for a dance, who invited her for a drive in the park, to a picnic, the theatre, a concert, the myriad enjoyments offered by a London season. And she tried very hard to find pleasure in them and put Jerome DeVere out of her mind.

But there was a part of her that bled a little every time he entered a room where she was and didn't approach her. A part of her that ached when, on the few occasions they stood in the same circle of company, he bowed to her formally and asked stiffly after her health. This cold, indifferent man wasn't *her* Jerome, and she wanted to corner him and shake him. But somehow the opportunity never presented itself.

He was careful never to be alone with her. He didn't ask her to dance, and if they should chance across each other in the street, or in Hyde Park, or at the theater, he exchanged the merest commonplace and moved on.

His behavior frustrated and annoyed her and drove her to flirt outrageously with whomever of her suitors offered her the opportunity, whenever he was in her vicinity. But nothing she did provoked any reaction in him and she began to realize that nothing would. Eventually she stopped trying and genuinely tried to bury her feelings for him.

Over the summer break, she was spared the sight of him as neither of them went to The Castle this year. She went with Mama to Brighton and he, she discovered through a bit of detective work, went to stay with friends in Wales.

⇜⇝

London, October 1819

AVA STRETCHED UP her hand, standing on tiptoe, to reach the book on the shelf above her head in Hatchards Bookshop and almost lost her balance when a deep familiar voice said from the other side of the shelves, "Countess, you have quite a pile there. Let me help you."

"Ravenshaw!" The Countess of Esberry's smooth contralto responded with a warmth that set Ava's teeth on edge.

The countess was a widow, probably around twenty-eight years of age, and possessed of a considerable fortune left to her by her husband. The lady was poised, elegant, sophisticated, and graceful, as well as stunningly beautiful. She had fashionably dark hair and large, long-lashed dark eyes under beautifully arched brows, a flawless creamy complexion, a perfectly straight nose, full sensuous lips, pronounced cheekbones, and a long neck that gave her an air fit for a queen. In short, a stunning beauty.

"Why thank you, my lord," she continued. "I confess I am greedy when it comes to books. You have caught me indulging my monthly passion."

"That is quite a haul," Ravenshaw said. "I see a number of titles I would recommend and some I have yet to read. You must tell me how this one strikes you."

Ava leaned, weak-kneed, against the shelves, as Ravenshaw and the countess appeared at the end of the row. Ravenshaw's attention was all on his companion and he didn't see Ava. His elegantly attired form disappeared from her sight. His voice, asking the countess if she was going to see Drury Lane's latest production of *As You Like It*, wafted back to her, leaving her clutching the shelf, her heart hammering and a stab of searing jealousy in her stomach.

Since he had told her bluntly at Devonshire House that he would forever see her as a child, and she had thought she would expire of shame and heartbreak, Ravenshaw had continued to give Ava a wide berth. She had tried, in the wake of that dire confession from him, to erase him from her heart and failed abysmally. Returning from Brighton to London for the little season, she discovered that his name was being increasingly linked with that of the countess. And here was more evidence of it. As if the sight of him dancing with the woman hadn't already underlined it. They made such an elegant couple, as if they belonged together. Tears stung Ava's eyes, and she hunted in her reticule for her handkerchief.

This was untenable! Things couldn't go on like this! She had to do something!

Miss Deborah Watson—younger sister to Ava's sister-in-law, Sarah—appeared at her elbow, and Ava said brightly, "Just got something in my eye!" as she dabbed at her cheeks and blew her nose. "Have you found the book you were looking for?"

Deborah gave her a penetrating look and then tactfully smiled and waved a copy of *The Vicar's Fireside.* "Yes, did you find yours?" Ava was grateful that Deborah pretended not to notice her agitation. She returned the other girl's smile with a rueful one of her own and tried not to mind that Deborah was another stunning beauty with fashionably dark curls and deep-blue eyes in an exquisite face. All the fashionable beauties were dark.

It was a mystery to her why Deb wasn't already married. Admittedly, she wasn't a great heiress, and her father was a vicar of respectable but undistinguished birth. But she was sister-in-law to a duke, and she was every bit as lovely as the countess—and younger to boot. It wasn't for lack of offers, either. Several gentlemen had taken a strong interest in the dark-haired beauty making her come out under the aegis of the Duchess of Trou-bridge. But it seemed Deborah was as hard to please as herself.

Now why was that? An idea began to percolate through her brain, and she vowed to do some digging. When her own affairs weren't so pressing. *Drat Ravenshaw! And double drat the countess!*

"It's up there!" Ava indicated the shelf above her head. Deborah, who was taller—everyone was taller than Ava, except her mother—reached it down for her, and the two young ladies progressed to the front desk to pay for their books.

Emerging from the shop, Ava's heart lurched at the sight of Ravenshaw, looking absolutely splendid in a perfectly fitting coat of blue superfine, pale-beige pantaloons, and exquisitely polished top boots, standing beside the countess's carriage, still conversing with her. As she and Deborah moved away from the bookshop to find Sarah and Mama, who were in a shop two doors down, the countess's carriage drew away from the pavement and Ravenshaw turned. His eyes caught Ava's and widened slightly. Something in their blue depths made her heart turn over, and a wave of longing washed through her. *If only . . .* Then he removed his hat and bowed.

"Ladies."

Both young women curtsied, murmuring, "My lord."

He replaced his hat and passed on. Ava couldn't forebear a

look at his retreating back as he strolled casually away from her. Irritation and longing warred in her breast and irritation won. *I have to* do *something!* She turned and strode out with a twitch of her petticoats, a determined line pulling her lips tight. Deborah glanced at her but said nothing.

They had only gone a few steps when a masculine voice accosted them. The Earl of Lannister stood before them, smiling and bowing. He was tall, blond, ridiculously handsome, and wholly ineligible. Despite the title, Reynard Fairbanks, 7th Earl of Lannister, was the sort of man mamas warned their daughters about and brothers forbade their sisters to know. So of course Ava made it her business to know such an irresistibly charming rake.

"Lady Ava, Miss Watson." Ava raised her eyes to Lannister's smiling face and dipped a curtsy, offering him her hand.

"My lord." She smiled warmly. His obvious pleasure at encountering them was a balm to her bruised heart. He took her hand and kissed it and offered Deborah a deep bow.

"I trust you're well?" His inquiry was directed to Deborah, who flushed faintly and inclined her head. Ava looked between the two. A blond Adonis and a dark-haired Aphrodite. *Really? Was that why . . .?*

"I am. Thank you, my lord."

⇛⇚

JEROME CONTINUED ON down the street, conscious of Ava behind him, and turned to cross the road. Looking back, his eyes landed on her exquisite little figure again, engaged in conversation with—*bloody hell! Lannister!* He gritted his teeth and crossed, dodging between riders and carriages.

Didn't she know better than to give a lecherous devil like that the time of day? Surely Rob had warned her about Lannister. The antipathy between the two men was well known, even in the wider *ton.* He'd have to have a conversation with Rob.

London, November 1819

"NOT DANCING OLD fellow?" asked Emrys wandering up to Jerome's position propping the wall and watching the dancers. Since his second marriage, Ashford's wardrobe had improved. Not to Jerome's standards, but he was generally neater, and while not in the first stare of fashion, he no longer looked like something the cat had dragged in.

Jerome dragged his attention away from the petite figure of Ava, twirling around the room in Lannister's embrace. She was here with Sarah tonight, neither her mother nor Robert was present or it wouldn't be happening.

"Pulled a hamstring with a lunge in tierce at fencing yesterday," he said with a grimace.

"Ah," said Emrys with a grin. "Probably why I don't indulge in such feats of athletic prowess."

Jerome ran his eyes over his friend's slimmed down form. "You've been exercising more though."

"Yes, but not to your level, old chap. Everything in moderation, that's my motto."

Jerome smiled. He was about to ask after Annis and the children when he noted that the music had stopped and his attention was caught by the sight of Ava slipping from the ballroom via a curtained alcove that gave onto the salons behind the main room. He would have thought nothing of it, except a quick survey of the room showed him that Lannister was nowhere in sight. A prickle of alarm raced over his skin and a sick stab of something he didn't want to identify hit his stomach.

"If you'll excuse me Emrys—" He left the sentence dangling and headed for the spot where Ava had disappeared.

Beyond the curtain was a short corridor with a series of doors off it. He tried several before he found her . . .

Standing in Lannister's embrace, her cheek resting against his chest. The tableau held him transfixed for a moment, then a searing stab of ugly jealousy speared him through the chest. Close on its heels was a red mist of rage. He retained just enough presence of mind to step into the room and close the door behind him.

"Lannister, get your hands off her, now!"

Ava opened her eyes and lifted her head in shock. "Jerome—"

He ignored her, his eyes on Lannister, who had not, as instructed, let go of Ava. If anything, his grip had tightened. The other man turned his lazy blue gaze on Jerome and said with a sardonic smile, "Such heat, Ravenshaw!"

Jerome took a threatening step towards him. "Do I have to hurt you, Lannister? Because I will. Let. Her. Go."

Lannister looked down at Ava, who placed her hands on his chest and pushed back gently. He released her and she stepped back, turning toward Jerome. "Jerome, what—"

He cut her off, his gaze still on Lannister. "Go back to the ballroom, Ava."

"I will not!" she said sharply, making him look at her.

Lannister bowed to Ava and said with an ironic smile. "I think I am rather *de trop*, my dear. I'll speak with you later." He walked past Jerome and let himself out of the room, closing the door quietly behind him.

"Ava, have you no sense?" exploded Jerome. His fury at Lannister, balked of its prey, turned on her.

She stiffened and glared back at him. "What are you so angry about?"

"It's a good thing Robert isn't here tonight. If he knew you were sneaking off to rooms with Lannister—" He stopped, catching his breath and trying to bring his temper back under control. "Surely, by now you understand that being caught alone with a man will ruin your reputation. And one with *his* reputation would ruin you beyond redemption. For God's sake, when will you grow up?"

She stepped closer and slapped his cheek with the flat of her bare hand. She had removed her gloves at some point. It stung. But not as much as the wounded anger in her eyes, which glittered with unshed tears. "How dare you! Why must you always assume the worst of me?"

His hands came up and seized her upper arms. "I don't," he said roughly. The accusation in her eyes was playing merry hell with his internal sense of right and wrong. "I'm trying to explain something to you that you seem to willfully refuse to understand! Men like Lannister can't be trusted! He's not like me or Deo or Emrys. He doesn't have a moral compass!"

"You're wrong!" she said putting her hands on his chest and leaning in, her head tilted up, her eyes fixed on his. Her intoxicating scent, the rapid rise and fall of her breasts, cupped so beautifully in her blue silk-and-net gown, inveigled their way past his defenses, his body responding in spite of every attempt to stop it.

"I am not, Ava," he said, his voice thickening. "If he hasn't shown that side of himself to you yet, be assured that he will if you allow him to."

"What side?" asked Ava, her voice suddenly breathless. Her hands sliding up to his shoulders.

He lowered his head, their gazes locked, as the madness he had been trying to contain for more than a year and a half burst its banks and he said softly, "This side," and his lips pressed to hers as his arms slid round her and pulled her lovely, soft little body tight against his.

She uttered a small moan in her throat as his lips moved over hers with devasting delight, the explosion of pleasure flooding his senses making him forget everything but holding her closer and kissing her more deeply. Her small hands plunged into his hair, and her body pressed closer as she parted her lips and kissed him back with a fervor that set fire to his blood.

The last remnants of his perception of her as a girl disintegrated. This Ava was all woman and he wanted her with bone aching desire. Another little moan of delight from her brought him back to himself with a sickening jolt.

He tore his mouth from hers and let her go, stepping back. His breathing was ragged. So was hers. And he realized he had crossed a line he could never uncross. But he had to try.

"That is what you invite from a man without scruples!" he said, trying to turn his lapse into a lesson. And then because he couldn't trust himself, he backed to the door and escaped like a coward, unable to bear the look of confusion and betrayal invading her eyes and dispersing the earlier glow of joy and desire.

London, March 1820

"GOOD GOD, AVA, I've received two dozen proposals for your hand, and you've refused every one of them! What are you looking for?" said her exasperated brother, Robert Layne, Duke of Troubridge.

Ava stood with her back to him, staring out the window of the front parlor of Layne House in Berkeley Square and clenched her hands together to suppress her urge to tell him the truth.

When she didn't answer, he went on, "You've broken the heart of nearly every eligible bachelor in London."

"Really? I think not," she replied lightly. "I simply wish to marry for love, like you did. Is that so unreasonable?"

"It's not unreasonable at all. But if two dozen of London's finest can't capture your heart, who can?"

She bit her lip. "You would never let me marry him."

"So, you've set your heart on someone unsuitable, is that it?" She felt his hand on her shoulder as he tugged her around to face him. He was frowning down at her. "Who, Ava?"

"Can't you guess?" She smiled sadly.

"Not Lannister?" Robert's expression of horror almost made her laugh. "You're right, I would never let you marry him. Put him out of your mind!"

She dropped her head to mask her expression, lest she give herself away. If he knew the truth it would be far worse.

"I mean it, Ava!" Robert put his hands on her upper arms. "He wouldn't dare approach me with a proposal in any case. He knows what I think of him. But if he's had the temerity to trifle with you—"

She burst out laughing then, unable to keep it in as she thought of what Rey would say to that.

"Oh, Rob, you are by far too easy to wind up!" she said, wiping her eyes and trying to suppress giggles. Reynard Fairbanks, Earl of Lannister, would flirt outrageously with her under Robert's nose, just to annoy him if she encouraged him to. Rob really was too serious for his own good. As much as she loved Rob dearly, his antipathy for a man she considered one of her closest friends could not but irritate her, as she and Rey had become very close over the last months of the little season. Robert's attitude forced her to conduct her relationship with the earl clandestinely. Especially after Jerome had caught her with him at Lady Bellingham's ball.

"Ava, your sense of humor—" He stopped. "Will you be serious? If it isn't Lannister, who is it?"

She just shook her head, drifting toward the door, saying lightly over her shoulder, "No one, Rob, I was just baiting you. I daresay I'll meet someone this season, or not . . ."

But his next words halted her. "I have a match to propose to you. Will you consider it?"

She turned, her heart thudding with sudden, irrational hope. "Who?"

"I've been approached by the Duke of Silverly—"

Revulsion swamped her. "Rob, he's seventy if he's a day! You wouldn't!"

"Seventy-five actually, and no, he hasn't approached me on his own behalf, but on his son's: Haldane. Apparently, he's quite smitten with you."

Her eyes widened a moment in shock. The Marquess of Haldane was a tall, well-built, and handsome man of twenty-six, with brown hair and green eyes and a kind smile. He had sought her out during the little season and become quite particular in his attentions, but then, when nothing came of it, she thought he had decided she was too lively for one of his rather staid disposition.

"He's the most eligible bachelor on the marriage mart, Ava. You're lucky to have caught his attention. Every debutante in the *ton* is on the scramble for him. And not *just* because he's wealthy, the heir to a dukedom, and of above average good looks! He's actually a nice fellow. A good man. One I would welcome as a brother-in-law." The note in his voice made her look up, and she caught the affection in his gaze. Her heart warmed. *Rob does love me so!*

"You don't need to make a decision yet. Take some time to get to know him better." Rob gave her an encouraging look.

Ava's throat closed in panic. She could feel the net tightening around her. This would be her third season. Rob had been very patient, but he was clearly wanting her to make a decision. He and Mama had discussed whether to defer their younger sister Heather's debut for one more year and decided to put it off until the little season later in the year. This must be the reason. They must be expecting her to make a match of it with Haldane this season. And on paper, he was the perfect match.

If she hadn't already given her heart to the handsomest man in London . . .

Her ideal, her Galahad. She had tried in cycles since her come out to either get over him or provoke a reaction and neither had worked until that devastating kiss at Lady Bellingham's ball. And it wasn't as if she had even tried to make that happen. Both she and Lannister had been feeling a bit blue over their respective sources of heartache and had simply gone to that room to share a hug, which they obviously couldn't do in public. Jerome was so wrong about Lannister, as Rob was, but neither of them could see it.

But that kiss had tipped her whole world sideways. And then he'd fled the room like all the devils of hell were after him. And if he had treated her with cool distance before that had happened, it had been six times worse afterward. He now seemed incapable of staying in the same room with her. He refused to look at her, let alone speak to her, unless he was forced to for the sake of politeness, and his pursuit of the wretched Countess of Esberry seemed to gain momentum.

He had said, "When will you grow up?" And kissed her like she was his heart's desire and then ruined it by telling her that was what she invited from unscrupulous men. Had he really only kissed her like that to teach her a lesson? She couldn't believe that, yet his behavior ever since did everything to convince her it was true—in particular, his pursuit of the countess.

She had lived in dread of hearing their engagement announced, but the little season had ended with no such announcement. Which gave her hope. But those had been dashed all over again when he had not come to The Castle at Christmas this past year as he used to do every year. She heard that he had again gone instead to those friends in Wales.

She recalled his emphatic denial that he would ever marry and sighed. Her vow, made six long years ago, that she would marry him when she was grown up, seemed further away than ever. Yet she couldn't let go of her impossible dream.

If distance and time were going to dislodge him from her heart, they would have done so by now. They had not. No matter how many eligible men paid court to her, they couldn't compare to Jerome. Her heart squeezed in anguish and she blinked against the sting of tears. What could she do to make him see her differently? She had thought that kiss had done the trick, but instead it had driven him further from her.

She wanted to corner him and shake him. Kiss him senseless. Test whether that lapse meant anything beyond a desire to punish her for what he saw as her willful immaturity. But he never gave her the opportunity, and now at the beginning of her third season, she feared that he never would.

I have to find a way . . . I cannot give up on my dream . . .

"Give the poor fellow a chance. For me?" Robert interrupted her thoughts and brought her back to Haldane. The man Rob wanted her to marry.

"Very well, I shall consider him," she said with a mechanical smile. Anything to keep Rob off the scent of her true desires.

But his words made her more determined than ever to find a way to change Jerome's way of looking at her before Rob started to really pressure her into a match with Haldane. But then there was the issue of getting Rob's agreement to her heart's desire. Jerome might be one of his best friends, but Rob had made no secret of the fact that he didn't consider him a suitable match for his sisters, any more than he considered Lannister a good match. It had something to do with his disreputable past, and while she had heard rumors, she didn't know the details of what he was supposed to have done that was so reprehensible.

But time was running out. Haldane was undoubtedly the most eligible of all her suitors yet. She would have to marry someone eventually or dwindle into an old maid—and she couldn't bear the thought of that. She wanted her own family, children and a loving husband. In her mind that role had always been played by Jerome. How could she see anyone else in that light? *But,* whispered the persistent voice in her head, *there is the Countess of Esberry . . .*

Ava pushed away thoughts of the countess. She was one of Jerome's flirts, yes, but surely not a serious contender for marriage, for indeed nothing had come of it last year. And Jerome had told her categorically the year before that he would not marry anyone. *Was that just to put me off? Or did he really mean it?* She didn't know, but she was determined to find out. She was not going to lose him to the Countess of Esberry! If anything the presence of a rival put her further on her mettle.

But then the vision of the countess's perfection rose in her mind's eye. So tall and elegant, a dark, luscious beauty and, perhaps most damning of all, a mature woman. She was the antithesis of Ava in every regard. Would Jerome truly consider marriage to such a woman? If she could take what he said about not wanting to marry at face value, then no. But then when she asked him if he had met the right woman yet . . . A cold feeling settled in her stomach. What if *he* thought the countess was the right woman?

No, thought Ava, *he* is *going to marry me! I refuse to give up.*

Chapter Three

White's Gentlemen's Club, London, March 1820

JEROME SAT STARING into the fire, a glass of whisky in his hand and half an ear on his friend's conversation. He was in a nostalgic, slightly melancholy mood. Two years ago, he and his friends Robert, Emrys, and Deo had sat like this in White's before the fire and Robert had bemoaned his need to marry an heiress, to make a so-called *marriage of convenience*, instead of the love match he craved.

All three of them were married now, happily as it turned out, albeit, in Emrys's case, to a different wife than the one he'd had on that night in March 1818. Robert had married his heiress, but it had turned into a love match after all. Deo was the real surprise. Who could have foreseen that the giant, awkward redhead would find the love of his life through an advertisement, of all things?

Jerome was the only bachelor among them now. If he was honest, he envied them their marital happiness but couldn't quite bring himself to believe that he could also enjoy the wedded bliss they seemed blessed with. He didn't deserve it, and the woman he wanted wasn't for him. Despite that lapse last year when he'd kissed her.

No, when it came time, and that time was rapidly getting closer—he would turn thirty-four this year—he would make a marriage of convenience. Choose a lady who understood the rules of such an arrangement. *The undoubtedly beautiful Countess of Esberry, for example . . .*

He was jerked out of his thoughts by Robert's voice. ". . . match for Ava."

His heart kicked and thudded, and his hand tensed on his glass of whisky. He raised it and swallowed a mouthful of the fiery spirit, trying to mask his reaction at the mere mention of her name.

"Who?" asked Emrys, casting a glance at Jerome that seemed to see through the deliberately nonchalant air he was trying to cultivate.

"I know you fellows will keep it to yourselves, for nothing is official yet, but I've been approached by the Duke of Silverly—"

"He's seventy-five!" Jerome's appalled tone was impossible to disguise as he stared at Robert horrified.

Rob shook his head. "He approached me for his son, Haldane."

Jerome subsided back into his seat. The Marquess of Haldane was one of London's most eligible bachelors, *and the absolute perfect match for Ava.*

A heaviness sat in his gut at the news, and he tried to shake it off, but it persisted. *What did I expect? I've known this day would come. I should be happy for her.*

"Has Ava consented?" asked Emrys.

"Not yet, but I'm hopeful she will," said Robert. "I couldn't ask for a better match for her, and what reason would she have to refuse? She promised me she would think about it. She has certainly been allowing him to squire her about town. I think we will have the thing settled in a couple of weeks."

He swallowed more whisky and joined the others in offering Robert congratulations on the match.

"What about you, Jerome?" asked Deo. "Is this your year?"

Jerome reached for the decanter and refilled his glass. He was going to make his usual reply that he wasn't cut out for marriage, but the words that came out were quite different. "Yes, I think it is." He smiled and offered his glass in a toast. "I know the Countess of Esberry knocked you back Rob—"

"Yes, thank God, or I'd never have married Sarah," said the duke. "Are you thinking of tilting at that windmill?"

"I am," said Jerome, with a smile that made his jaw ache.

"To your success!" Robert raised his glass, and the others echoed his sentiments. "You know," he added, "Sarah said something to me about your interest in the countess. Let's hope your address is a damned sight better than mine."

"Of course it is," said Deo with one of his rare smiles. "When did Jerome ever fail at anything?"

"True," said Rob topping up their glasses from the decanter on the small table beside them.

Emrys threw Jerome a penetrating look, one eyebrow raised. Jerome met it blandly and drank.

JEROME LEFT WHITE'S some hours later. He was foxed. Very foxed. Not that that was unusual lately, he reflected, given the thoughts that were increasingly plaguing him, so he'd taken to having a few before bed. Even so, he'd outdone himself this time, he thought, with the vague smugness of the very inebriated.

He was not quite falling-down drunk, but he was close. The pavement under his feet had a tendency to dip and sway, and the gaslight from the nearest lamppost was damned bright and kept flickering in a most disturbing way.

He had ignored Deo's and Emrys's attempts to put him in a hackney carriage—Rob had gone home not long after their toast to his success—and left the club to walk home. He had hoped the cool night air would clear his head a little. So far, all it had done was make it spin. He stopped by the lamppost and grasped it with a gloved hand to steady himself and consider his direction. *Am I going the right way? Does it matter?* Deciding that it didn't, he continued on.

The night sky above him was unusually clear, and the stars winked at him with a cold, indifferent light that seemed to mock him. *Have they discovered me for the fraudster that I am? Most likely.* For some unfathomable reason, the notion seemed amusing. *Are the stars the eyes of God? Can they see into my soul and lay bare the secrets that I keep hidden there?*

It would be an inestimable relief to share those secrets with someone, but that was a luxury he couldn't afford. Emrys had come close to guessing at least one of his secrets by the looks he kept throwing at him. How Jerome had kept his countenance when Rob announced the match between Ava and the Marquess of Haldane, he didn't know, but he must have succeeded, because nobody said anything.

It was a piece of devastating news that just confirmed what he had already decided over Christmas: that he needed a nice, safe marriage of convenience. The beautiful Isabella Mortimer, Countess of Esberry, was the perfect candidate for the role, if he could only bring himself to the sticking point. He hadn't meant to blurt out his intentions in that direction, but the news about Ava and Haldane was the final impetus he needed to take action. And telling his friends of his intention made it that much harder for him to back away from it.

He stopped at the end of the street and discovered he had reached Hyde Park Corner. *Definitely the wrong direction.*

A nice metaphor for his life, really, he reflected, turning right to skirt the park. *At this rate, by the time I get home, I might have sobered up.*

Would he be sober enough to call upon the countess tomorrow? Or had he got himself so successfully soused he'd have to put it off one more day? He sighed, weaving on the pavement in an attempt to avoid a pile of dog detritus and almost stepping in it anyway. *Another metaphor.* The thought provoked a drunken chuckle.

The chuckle evaporated in a flood of melancholy, and he

plunged on. Even if he did put it off, it wouldn't alter the fact that he needed to marry. While he wasn't in his dotage, he owed it to his lineage to beget an heir. He had ignored his duty long enough. If not the countess, then someone else.

The image of Ava Layne swam in his inner vision, golden, glorious, vivacious, joyful, adorable, Ava, and his heart clenched with an ache of longing he didn't usually allow himself to feel. *That's the problem with alcohol. It lets the feelings in.*

He took a breath to ease the ache and swallowed, his throat tight. He shoved the longing down.

But it could never be Ava for him. Not when she had a chance of happiness with Haldane.

"No." He spoke aloud to emphasize the point and shook his head. "Not Ava. Anyone but Ava." *That kiss had been such a mistake.*

He came to another stop at the Grosvenor Gate entrance to the park. The park was in darkness beyond, and the lodge was also just a black square shape. The trees of the avenue rustled in a breeze that had picked up and brought with it the scent of flowers and cut grass, to overlay the ever-present coal-smoke laden air of London's streets, even here in the clean part of the city. Something about the trees beckoned to him, and on impulse he climbed the gate and dropped over the other side with the ease of an athlete, drunk though he was.

He ventured up to the nearest tree, a large oak, like its sisters, marching in a straight line of two and two on either side of the wide, grassed avenue. *Even the trees are in pairs . . .* He hugged the great trunk, leaning his cheek against the rough bark, and smelled the resin. He laughed, retaining just enough self-awareness to picture how ridiculous he must look.

Overcome suddenly with weariness, he settled under the tree's canopy, his back against the trunk and went to sleep.

The Marques of R. was found asleep under a tree in Hyde Park by a groundsman at six am on Wednesday morning. The groundsman was mystified how he got there as the gates were all locked overnight, and the gentleman was clearly the worse for wear. It is whispered that the marquess is on the verge of offering for the Countess of E. Has he just ruined his chances with the lady, or will the gentleman's other attributes outweigh a lapse of this kind? The Chronicle waits with bated breath to see the sequel to this unfortunate incident. We are reminded of certain indiscretions of his youth. The man is, after all, a lady-killer . . .

Ava dropped her toast with a cold wash of horror as her eyes read this tidbit from the gossip columns of *The Chronicle*, which confirmed what she had been fearing since last year. Her stomach swooped as she reread the fatal words. *It is whispered that the marquess is on the verge of offering for the Countess of E.*

The Countess of E. Esberry. Ava conjured the willowy form of the tall, dark-haired beauty with a violent stab of jealousy that made her feel sick.

She could present no stronger contrast with Ava, who was short, blonde, generously curved, and vivacious, rather than serenely elegant. It would seem that the countess did indeed embody the type of woman he admired. They certainly made a striking couple, both dark and beautiful. Her eyes stung as a wave of unaccustomed inadequacy swamped her. Ava was wont to think of herself as attractive, not simply because of her blonde prettiness, but because of her joyful, warm personality. *But if Jerome is truly attracted to an entirely different style of woman—what hope do I have?*

She swallowed the lump in her throat. *Did that kiss at Lady Bellingham's ball really mean nothing? Gentlemen kiss easily, you ninny! It might have turned your world upside down but it wouldn't have even caused a ripple in his. I have been living in a dream, refusing to face the truth, always believing that with time he would see me differently. And now it is too late! I have run out of time to convince him that I am the right woman.*

Chapter Four

JEROME CLIMBED THE steps of the Countess of Esberry's Conduit Street house with mixed feelings in his breast. As the two of them occupied the same social circles, they came across each other on a regular basis, and somewhere in the last twelve months they had developed a friendship of sorts. A mildly flirtatious one, conducted as much for their mutual amusement in keeping the *ton* guessing as anything else.

Since he was known to conduct discreet liaisons with widows, the polite world had concluded this was another. But the refusal of both parties to admit to it and the longevity of their continued acquaintance had set tongues wagging in a different direction toward the close of the little season last year.

Jerome, sensitive to what was said of him, despite his carefully cultivated air of indifference to public opinion, had for so many years set his face against marriage that it took a while for the gossips to suspect that the untrappable marquess might have met his match. It was over this last Christmas that he gave serious thought to the need to finally knuckle under and marry.

He had been unconsciously holding off, he realized, until Ava was satisfactorily settled. With the news of her impending engagement to Haldane, the last of his excuses were washed away. He had to marry, and he needed a wife who would understand the rules of a marriage of convenience, for he wasn't free to offer anything else.

The woman he wanted, he couldn't have. He'd made up his mind to that two years ago when he realized he'd fallen in love with the unattainable. Ava. And that disastrous lapse at Lady Bellingham's ball had only confirmed in his mind that he must stay away from Ava. His loss of control, on that occasion, shamed him. The discovery he had made in her second season that she had long nursed a girlish infatuation for him made it worse, for it underlined just how young and innocent she was; and that kiss would have confused her even more. It was cruel. Recalling it made him feel sick with shame. For she was in love with an illusion, with the façade of perfection he projected to the world. If she knew what lurked behind that façade, she would run a mile in terror and revulsion.

The fact that Ava had half of London's eligible bachelors at her feet did not give him any comfort. She could have had her pick last year. He had lived in daily expectation of one of them securing her mercurial interest. And he had prayed that that someone would be closer to her own age, someone steady and reliable, who would love her as she ought to be loved. Haldane seemed to fit the bill perfectly.

He'd found, however, that knowing Haldane was her perfect match didn't stop him from longing for her, being consumed with jealousy. Adorable, irrepressible, joyful, rebellious, and willfully stubborn Ava. He was as well acquainted with her faults as her virtues, and he loved all of both. But she wasn't for him, he reminded himself yet again. He was too old for her, for one thing. For another, he'd been like a brother to her all her life. But the most immutable objection was one she knew nothing of. And he hoped, for vanity's sake, she never would. For he would die a kind of death to see her admiration of him wither and be replaced by revulsion and horror.

He shook off the melancholy thoughts. He must put Ava out of his mind and concentrate on the woman he had come here today to see. Isabella deserved that. He might not be able to offer her his heart, but he could offer her everything else. His admiration and esteem, his respect, his title, his wealth, and the protection of his name. In return, he hoped she would offer him an heir and companionship as he slipped (somewhat rebelliously) into middle age.

She received him in her front parlor with her companion Miss Esme Cartwright, a cousin of some sort who had come to live with her once she became a widow. Miss Cartwright was in her forties, a diminutive mouse of a woman with a propensity to chatter. He supposed if Isabella accepted his proposal, he would need to address what to do with Miss Cartwright. He didn't wish to have her living with them, but perhaps they could put her in the dower house. His mother had been dead since he was twelve, so there was no one to live in it now, and it was in a parlous state. Along with the rest of the estate. Another thing he had long neglected.

The ladies rose at his entrance and dropped him graceful curtsies. Or at least Isabella's was graceful; Miss Cartwright's was more of a bob.

"To what do we owe this pleasure, my lord?" asked Isabella in her soft contralto.

He smiled his charming smile and bent over her hand. "I was hoping for a few moments of your time. Alone?"

Isabella was no fool, and she gave him an assessing look before she said, "Esme, could you see about the tea, please?"

"Of course, Bella," said Esme with another bob and a look in her eyes that Jerome found hard to read. *Was it fear?*

"Please have a seat, my lord," she said, resuming hers on the sofa. He debated whether to take the seat opposite lately occupied by Miss Cartwright, and decided a more intimate approach was required, given his mission. Seating himself beside Isabella, he said, "I think you can guess the reason for my call?"

She cocked her head, which showed her long neck to advantage, and smiled a soft smile. "I might, but I think it would be immodest to admit it."

"Can I venture to say we have formed a kind of friendship these last twelve months?"

"You can," she said composedly.

"Then I can be frank with you."

"I hope you will be."

Never at a loss socially as a rule, he was finding this harder than he had thought it would be. But there was really no point in beating around the bush. "I wonder if you would do me the honor of becoming my wife?"

She watched his face as he spoke, and he wondered what it revealed, for she dropped her eyes to her lap where her hands smoothed the fabric of her gown over her knees. It was the only sign of her agitation. She was as good at masking her feelings as he was.

Returning her gaze to his face she asked, "Why me and not a young miss?"

"I think you know the answer to that. I don't want a young miss."

She pursed her lips knowingly and said, "The gossips are all touting a match between Ava Layne and Haldane. But no doubt you've heard all about it from Troubridge?"

He flushed in spite of himself but said as composedly as he could, "Yes, it will be an excellent match for Lady Ava. I've known her since she was a child, and I wish her every happiness. Haldane is a good man."

"Why the sudden desire to marry now?" she asked.

"It's not sudden. I've been thinking of it for some time."

She nodded and said carefully, "I'll ask again. Why me?"

"We deal well together, I think?"

"We do."

"You have all the attributes any man could want in a wife, Isabella. Beauty, birth, grace, intelligence, wit, and strength of character. I admire you a great deal and I would hope we wouldn't bore each other to death."

"No, I don't think we would bore each other, Jerome. But I've yet to hear anything that would tempt me to change my current state. I'm quite happy as I am, you see."

"You're not lonely?"

"I am not. I have friends to ameliorate that, you see. I counted you as one of those. Will you withdraw your friendship if I reject your offer?"

"I'm not so churlish," he said, his heart sinking at the trend of the conversation. "But what can I say to persuade you to consider my offer?" He reached for her hand, and she let him take it. "As husband and wife, we would be more than friends. Does that prospect hold no allure for you? Do you not miss that intimacy that comes with marriage?"

She flushed, her eyes dropping, and he was aware of a subtle vulnerability in her that he had not detected before. "Does it make me unnatural to say no, I do not?"

"It suggests to me that you did not find the felicity you deserved in your previous marriage and are therefore wary of entering into another contract."

"That is a fair assessment," she admitted. His pulse quickened with a spurt of anger. Had her husband used her badly? Were all men beasts? Himself included? No, for his friends were not, as evidenced by their happy marriages.

"Forgive me, I am going to be indelicate." He paused and squeezed her hand lightly. "Isabella, I can safely say you would enjoy intimacy with me, for I would make sure it was so." He added, "You must know that my reason for entering into a marriage contract is the need for an heir. I cannot offer you a celibate marriage, and frankly, I would not wish to. I would hope to offer you motherhood. Is that not something you desire?"

"It is," she admitted. "Although I had thought to give up any hope of it after five years of trying and failing. Given your desire for an heir, I am not the best choice for you, my lord. I am likely unable to bear children."

"The fault may have lain with your husband. He was considerably older than you, was he not?"

"Yes. Since we are being so frank, he did have some difficulties in that regard. But we did persist. I suffered two miscarriages. So, you see, I may not be the wife you want at all."

He kissed her hand. "I'm sorry for your loss."

"Thank you." She looked away, but it didn't disguise the pain she suffered and kept hidden from the world.

"Will you at least think about it?" he said.

She looked at him, a slightly puzzled look in her eyes. "You would still pursue this, after what I said?"

"Yes." He paused. "There are many reasons for miscarriages that we cannot possibly know of. My mother suffered many. Yet she birthed two healthy children who lived to adulthood, myself and my sister. I would be far more concerned about our ability to have an heir together if you had never conceived at all."

A slight, wistful smile curled her lips. "Very well, I will think about it."

He nodded and kissed her hand again. And then her cheek. "I am going away for a few weeks—my estate in Northumberland requires some attention. When I return, I will hope to have a positive answer from you."

He rose just as Miss Cartwright came back into the room. With a bow to both ladies he took his leave and left the house.

He couldn't say he was happy, but he felt a little more settled. He knew what he needed to do now, and he was determined to do it. The past two years of agonized yearning for something he couldn't have were at an end. He was hopeful that Isabella would agree to his proposal when she'd had time to consider it, but even if she didn't, he was set on this course now and would find another candidate. But first he needed to put his house in order. He had neglected Ravenshaw abominably. The place held dark memories for him, and he'd been avoiding them for years. It was time he faced up to them and dealt with the past once and for all.

Chapter Five

AVA WAS RUNNING down the stairs, pulling on her gloves preparatory for her morning ride, when the front doorbell rang and Creighton, their excellent butler, opened the door to reveal the Marquess of Ravenshaw. She stuttered to a halt on the stairs, halfway down, her heart lurching and thudding at the sight of him.

He was clad in a driving coat with multiple capes over a blue jacket and fawn breeches, with spotless, white-topped boots. As always, his dress was understated, fashionably elegant, and precise to a pin.

"Good morning, Creighton, is the duke at home?" he asked, surrendering his hat and coat.

Taking the garments, Creighton said, "For you, he is, my lord. In the breakfast parlor."

At that point, Ravenshaw looked up and saw Ava on the stairs. His incredibly blue eyes held hers for a breathless moment, before he smiled with practiced ease.

She continued down the stairs to the hall, saying, "Ravenshaw, what brings you to us so early?"

"I'm leaving town for a spell. Just calling to bid you all farewell."

Leaving? He was leaving. Now? It was the beginning of the season.

"Where are you going?"

"Northumberland. My estates are sadly neglected. It is time I set them to rights."

"Oh?" Her voice sounded hollow. "What brought this on? I thought you hated the place."

"My circumstances are about to change," he said with an air of seriousness she had never seen in him before. Her stomach dropped at the implication. *The countess . . .*

"So, it's true? You're going to marry the countess?" she asked, her voice raspy with shock. *I was right—about everything! I was always, and always will be, a child to him!* It felt like another life in which he had kissed her passionately that night at Lady Bellingham's ball. Never by word or look since had she gleaned that he wished to repeat the experience.

"I've asked her," he said. "I'm hopeful of receiving a positive reply upon my return."

Ava blinked, her throat tight. An annihilating humiliation hit her in the solar plexus. This was worse than Devonshire House, worse than the Bellingham ball. Her dreams were finally and irrevocably shattered. Pride made her stiffen and reel in her emotions. *He must not see how devastated I am.*

"How could you not?" she said stiffly, her lips numb.

"I understand I'm to wish you happy as well," he said. He was smiling, but it didn't reach his eyes like his smiles usually did.

She laughed, and it had a slightly hysterical edge to it that she hoped he didn't notice.

"Why yes, though nothing is official yet. Did Robert tell you?"

"He did." He took her hand and kissed it. "I do most sincerely hope you will be happy Ava; Haldane is a good man." He kissed her cheek and walked past her to the stairs. She turned and watched him mount them with his usual casual grace. He didn't look back, and she swallowed, watching him through a mist of tears. *My heart is breaking.*

Two days later

"Rey, what am I going to do?" Ava said in despair.

"There isn't a lot you can do, my poppet" said Reynard Fairbanks, the Earl of Lannister, seating himself beside Ava on the garden bench, wither they had fled from Lady Allworthy's ballroom. "If the die is truly cast . . ."

"She hasn't accepted him yet, but why would she refuse him?"

Lannister looked slightly amused and said, "If a man knew what a woman's motivations for anything were, he would be wise indeed."

"Oh, do be serious!" she begged, slapping his arm. "I have cried myself sick for two days! The only reason I am here is to see you."

Sobering he said, "Yes, I thought you weren't looking your best. But if she hasn't accepted, then all is not lost yet."

"It hardly makes a difference; my dreams are shattered. I hoped after he kissed me at Lady Bellingham's ball that what he felt for me was stronger than affection and liking. I thought I had time to convince him I was grown up and to see me differently. I realize now that I was wrong. I feel so humiliated."

"Ah—no."

"What do you mean, no?"

"I've seen the way he follows you with his eyes. The look in them. That is not the look of indifference"

"What then?"

"The kind of passion that will drive a man to sacrifice everything for the woman he loves, even his own life." Something in Lannister's tone made the words believable. As if he knew what he was talking about.

Ava's heart leaped at these words. "You are giving me hope when I had convinced myself to have none. It is cruel!" She wiped tears from her cheeks. "He has offered for the countess."

Lannister clasped her hand tightly. "I am telling you what I have seen. I am not mistaken."

"But if that is true, why has he asked the countess to marry him? If he has changed his mind about marrying, why hasn't he approached me? Told me how he feels? He *must* know how much I care for him. I never made a secret of it."

Lannister shrugged. "I don't know his reasons for holding off. He obviously thinks they are sufficient. But as for him knowing your feelings—my dear, you are an incorrigible flirt. He is accustomed to seeing you play one suitor against another over the past year. How is he to know what is real and what is not, when half the men in the *ton* are dazzled by you?"

"But he must know he is different; I don't flirt with him." *Even if he gave me the chance.*

"No and you are not friends with him either, as you are with me."

"We used to be," she said wistfully. "Then everything changed after Devonshire House, when he made it clear I was just a little girl to him. And it got even worse after the Bellingham ball." She sighed. "I thought he finally saw me as a woman when he kissed me. But ever since then, he has been positively avoiding me."

"He doesn't look at you like he thinks you are a little girl, I can assure you of that."

"But why must he marry that woman now? He has always maintained such a set against marriage."

"I suspect because of your imminent engagement to Haldane."

"But I'm not going to be engaged to Haldane! I told Robert I would think about it, meaning to let him down gently. I should have refused outright! Rob must have taken that as my consent and told Ravenshaw it was settled."

"Presumably, yes."

"So, he was laboring under a misapprehension when he asked

her?"

"It would seem so."

"Then I must tell him it is not so! Oh, why did I lead him to think it was settled when I spoke to him before? My stupid pride! My only instinct was to cover up my humiliation!" She clasped her hands. "If only he had not already left London! He must be almost in Northumberland by now."

"You could write to him?"

"I suppose . . ." She chewed her lip and shook her head. "No. Things have progressed so far with the countess that he will feel he cannot back out now. I know such things are of importance to gentlemen, and Ravenshaw is every inch a gentleman. I must see him in person to persuade him."

"Then you will have to wait until he returns."

Ava sprang up agitated. "It may be too late by then! The countess may write to him giving her consent. I must go to Northumberland and see him."

"Ava, you can't do that!" Lannister eyes widened in shock.

She shrugged. "I can ride. It will take me what, three days?"

"Are you mad? You can't ride all the way to Northumberland on your own!"

"I can. I am perfectly capable of doing that." Ava jutted her chin stubbornly. She was an excellent horsewoman, Jerome had always said so, and no better judge of horse riding could be found than the Marquess of Ravenshaw. He was a bruising rider and a member of the Four Horse Club.

"But think of the scandal, my dear girl! Troubridge would have an apoplexy! And rightly so." *If even Lannister thinks my scheme too wild . . .* She sank down on the seat beside him again, momentarily defeated.

"It is too dangerous by far for you to make a such a journey on your own. Particularly on horseback." Lannister went on.

"Urgh!" Ava drummed her heels in irritation. "It is so frustrating to be a female!"

"Now promise me you won't do something so harebrained!"

She wriggled uncomfortably under his minatory gaze. Rey was seldom serious, but when he was, one got the feeling he could do things one would regret. He confirmed that with the next words. "If you do, I will tell your brother."

"You wouldn't! He would shoot you!"

Lannister's lips twitched. "I am almost tempted, just to see him try. He has been threatening to shoot me for two years."

"Oh, do be serious. You wouldn't betray me to Rob."

"If you attempt to go off on your own, I will be forced to, for your own safety; or go after you myself."

"Would you?"

"Of course I would!" he said roughly.

"Oh Rey, you're so sweet!" She played with her handkerchief a moment, her thoughts a jumbled mess. Then an idea struck her. Sitting up, she fixed him with an anxious stare. "If you won't let me go on my own, would you escort me?"

"Good God, that's just as bad, Ava! It's a three-day trip at minimum, probably four by coach—"

"We wouldn't go by coach. We could take your curricle, couldn't we?"

"No, not for a journey of that distance," he said firmly.

"Oh, very well . . ."

"And how would we explain ourselves? I'm known on the North Road, Ava. I would be recognized."

"I could wear a veil so no one shall see my face. It would not be out of character for you to be seen with a veiled female, would it?"

"No," he admitted reluctantly.

"Well then—" She placed a hand on his arm and leaned in pleadingly. "Please Rey! My happiness depends upon it!"

"But what happens when we get there? Even if your brother doesn't murder me, Ravenshaw will. If we're caught, you'd have to marry me, not Ravenshaw, you realize that?"

"We won't be caught," she insisted. "And if we were, I should just refuse. Rob can't make me marry you."

"Well thank you my sweet, but you're overlooking a minor point of honor. I would be obliged to marry you whether we liked it or not. And as much as I adore you, I'd rather not be forced into marriage at gunpoint. Even with your enchanting self."

She went on as if he hadn't spoken. "For I won't have Haldane now. How dare Rob set it about I had already accepted him! I'm so furious with him. It will serve him right to be worried about me when I vanish."

"You don't mean to tell him where you are going?"

"Of course not. He would come after me and stop me. I must reach Ravenshaw before he does so."

"If he figures out we are both missing, he is likely to think we have eloped. You do realize that?"

"Oh yes, that would be famous, for it will put him off the scent!"

"Ava, you are incorrigible."

"Yes, I know," she said smugly. She felt much better now she had a plan of action. She would make this one last effort to secure her future happiness, and if it failed—her heart quailed at the notion—if it failed, she would know she had tried. But she had to believe it would succeed, for if it didn't, her life would not be worth living anyway.

Chapter Six

Ravenshaw, Northumberland

JEROME STOOD ON the cliffs overlooking the German Sea, the gusty wind blowing his dark hair back and piercing his shirt with icy fingers. The clouds were gathering, bringing a storm. The water crashed and roiled against the rocks below, sending sea spray high into the air. Droplets peppered his skin, and the smell of salt, seaweed, and imminent rain filled his nostrils.

Behind him, the sprawling wreck of Ravenshaw faced the sea's buffeting salt-laden wind. The row of second floor double doors with their balconies looked black and sightless from here. His eyes strayed to one balcony in particular and a shiver, unprovoked by the wind, skated over his skin. He dragged his gaze away and shook himself. He faced out to the sea once more, where the louring storm beckoned. The setting sun broke through the clouds on the horizon, sending shards of pale-golden light over the greenish-gray, storm-tossed waves.

He'd spent the past three days here with his steward, Kelham, going over all the things that needed to be done to bring the house back to what it once was. He felt its heavy gray stone behind him. The weight of it pulled at him, the place taunting him with memories he'd spent his lifetime trying to forget. Layer on layer of imperfection, guilt, regret. *The problem with memories is that they never leave you. Even if you banish them to a corner of your mind under lock and key, their presence remains like a festering wound, gathering nastiness in the dark.*

Part of him wanted to flee south again, but the knowledge that the time had come to stop running held him fast. He had to face this down, once and for all. The constant quarreling between his parents that had tainted his childhood. The suspicions that had haunted his adolescence. The guilt that nearly destroyed his young adulthood. Why he would choose to do it now, when he was at his lowest ebb, he didn't know. It was madness. Yet, in the depths of his despair, he found a source of strength he didn't know he had.

Ava was lost to him, and that was as it should be, for her happiness was worth far more than his own. In surrendering her to Haldane's care, he found a kind of melancholy peace. An easing of the ceaseless ache of wanting what he couldn't have, that had dogged him for two years. If she was happy, he would find the strength to sort out his own life and make of it what he could with the fractured pieces that remained.

Turning his back on the sea, he was drawn irresistibly to the place beneath that balcony where he was told his mother's shattered body had lain, soaked with rain from the storm that shook the house that night. He'd not been here, not seen any of it. He only had his father's clipped account of what happened. And he had been haunted ever since by the question *What if?*

What if I had been here? Could I have prevented it?

He made himself walk over the bit of ground where she must have landed, but it was covered now in a tangle of ground creeper, weeds, and long grass. There was nothing here or in the house to indicate what had happened on that long ago night, and no one to tell him.

After his mother's death, the existing servants had been dismissed by his father, replaced by a caretaker couple, the McClellans, new to the area, and the house shut up to all intents and purposes. When his father was killed falling from his horse, in Jerome's seventeenth year, he'd not reversed that decision, only making sure that the tenants were looked after properly by the steward he appointed and the home farm kept in order.

He chose to spend his holidays at friends' houses, and only when he left Cambridge did he take up residence in his London townhouse in Hanover Square. He would post up quarterly to meet with Kelham and inspect the home farm and tenants and expected fortnightly reports from the man on their condition. But the house had remained shut up and neglected. Until now.

The wind whipped at his jacket and sliced through his shirt.

He trudged back to the house, in through the large entrance hall with its soaring atrium ceiling, and up the broad stairs to the first floor where the library was situated. He'd made this his headquarters since he'd arrived. The McClellans, thrown into a spin by his unexpected appearance, had scrambled to make a bedroom usable for him and took the holland covers off the furniture in the breakfast room and the library.

Kelham, learning that the marquess was soon to be wed, had been given instructions to hire as many staff as would be needed to clean the place up and to throw an army of workmen at the ruined stables in the west wing and the portion of the east wing that had lost its roof. Gardeners were also to be employed to transform the tangled forest that had once been the surrounding green, the south lawn, and rose arbor into something resembling a garden once more.

The windows in the library looked out on the sea and rattled with the rising wind, which was beginning to howl around the gray stone building. The light was fading fast, and he rang for candles and a fire, pouring himself a whisky from the decanter on the sideboard.

While the fire and candles were attended to, he paced to the window and watched the heavy gray storm clouds approach. The golden light from the westering sun was almost gone now. The panes of glass, lashed by rain and hail, soon obscured what was left of the view, and he turned away to a lit fire and a room made cozy by several candelabra and one of the new maids bobbing a curtsy.

"Will that be all, my lord?"

"Yes, thank you." He smiled.

"Mrs. McCelland said dinner would be ready by six, my lord, if it pleases you."

"My thanks to Mrs. McClelland. It does," he said and watched her move toward the door. She was barely sixteen, he thought. One of the village girls, no doubt, and ecstatic to have a job at the big house. Something in the cast of her features seemed vaguely familiar. On impulse he said, "Just a moment."

She turned. "My lord?"

"What is your name?"

"Lucy, my lord. Lucy Miller," she said with another bob.

He frowned in an effort of memory. "Are you related to Ellen Miller by any chance?"

"That'd be my gran, sir. Who was my lady's own abigail back in the day."

"Yes, I remember her. Is your grandmother still alive?"

"No, sir." Lucy's face took on a melancholy expression. "She died before I was born, but my da spoke of her highly. I wished I could have known her."

His heart skipped. "How did she die?"

"She contracted the influenza the winter my lady died. Da said she was never the same after your lady mother passed and your father dismissed all the servants and shut up the house. When she lay dying herself, he swore she tried to tell him something about it all, but whatever it was he couldn't catch it."

"Where does your father live Lucy? Could I speak with him?"

She shook her head. "He took bad with a stroke last year and never recovered. He passed in his sleep."

"I'm sorry to hear that," he said. *Is there no one left with living memory of what happened the night my mother died?*

"Tell me, Lucy, are any of the servants my father dismissed still around here?"

She frowned. "Well, there's old Mrs. Pennyweather, who was married to the head gardener, Pennyweather, but she's blind and deaf and most people say she ain't right in the head no more."

"Where does she live?"

"On the promontory, hard by Hartley Common, my lord. Her daughter, Elspeth Nancarrow, looks after her."

"Thank you, Lucy."

"You're welcome, my lord." She bobbed another curtsy and left him to some dark thoughts.

He would pay a visit to Mrs. Pennyweather tomorrow. It was time he faced the truth. He could no longer live with suspicions. He had to know what really happened that night.

He had several whiskies before he went to bed, but it didn't stop the things that haunted him from surfacing in the dark, jerking him from sleep in a cold sweat of horror and guilt.

Chapter Seven

MRS. PENNYWEATHER'S COTTAGE was a picturesque one, made of mellow stone and thatched roofed, with roses climbing around the white painted door and a riot of color in the well-tended garden.

A pump middle-aged woman in a serviceable gown of gray worsted and a striped pinafore, with a broad brimmed straw hat on her head, was digging in the garden when he arrived at the gate. She looked up in surprise when Jerome addressed her.

"Good day to you, ma'am, would you be Mrs. Pennyweather's daughter?"

She rose awkwardly to her feet, stripping off her gardening gloves and straightening her hat. "Good heavens, sir, you startled me! Yes, I am." She blinked her myopic blue eyes as she drew closer, and her mouth fell open. "My lord!" She dropped a curtsy.

"May I come in?" he asked with a smile. "I was wishful to speak with your mother if I could?"

"Of course, my lord," she said, moving to lift the latch and open the gate for him. "Though Mam is blind and almost stone deaf. You'll have to shout for her to hear you. And even if she does hear you, there's no guarantee she'll understand what you want. She's old, and her mind wanders a bit."

His heart sank at these tidings, but he had to at least try.

"Well, I won't take up too much of her time. I just have a couple of questions for her."

"Come in, my lord. Would you like a cup of tea or some of my rosehip wine?"

"Tea would be splendid," he said with another smile, standing aside for her to precede him into the house. It was a small house with a two-up, two-down configuration and as neat and well-kept as the garden.

The door opened straight into the stone-floored kitchen, with a large hearth and well-scrubbed table and Windsor chairs. A dresser was against the wall and an easy chair was in the corner of the room on which sat a fat, black-and-white cat, one leg stuck in the air while it cleaned a haunch.

"My husband Will works at the glass manufactory, my lord. He'll be right disappointed to have missed your visit," she said, bustling over to the kitchen hearth to set the kettle on. "The village has been in such a flutter since Mr. Kelham set it about you was hiring again! My Elsie and Bob both applied, you know. Started yesterday they did. Elsie for a housemaid and Bob in the laboring team." She beamed at him. "You wouldn't be needing a glazier, would you? Will's a good man, hard worker, and skilled."

"Tell him to apply to Kelham. He will know what positions are still required."

She bobbed a curtsy, a faint flush to her cheeks, "I'll tell him, my lord. Now you just get yourself settled, and I'll go fetch Mam. She can't manage the stairs no more, so we have her bed set up in the parlor."

"I'll come to her if it's less trouble," he said.

"Nay, my lord!" said Elspeth Nancarrow, scandalized. "She likes to sit in her chair by the fire with old Percy there." She nodded at the chair and the cat. "I'll fetch her. You sit." She waved to the table and chairs and Jerome sat, his lips twitching. He had the feeling Mrs. Nancarrow might have quite a brood, if her managing ways were any indication.

She disappeared through the curtained archway that divided

the kitchen from the parlor, and he heard her saying loudly, "Mam, His Lordship is here to see you!"

"What's that, Elsie?" The old lady's voice was quavery.

Elspeth repeated herself louder, and the old lady said, "Lord Gareth? To see me?"

"Nay, Mam, his son, Lord Jerome himself."

"The lad? What's he want with the likes of me?"

"Come along, Mam, upsy-daisy. Here's your stick, now hold my arm!"

Jerome heard the sounds of shuffling footsteps, and the curtain parted to reveal Mrs. Nancarrow with a bent, silver-haired old woman clinging to her arm and leaning heavily on a walking stick. He rose slowly as Mrs. Nancarrow guided her mother to the chair, plucked the cat up with one arm and settled her mother deftly with the other, placing the cat on her lap. This must have been a routine, for the cat surprisingly cooperated, settling to knead and purr on the old lady's lap. Her gnarled, liver-spotted hands patting the creature soothingly as she sank back into the chair.

"There now, Mam, you'll have your tea and biscuit in a moment, but first I want to present His Lordship to you."

Elspeth nodded to him and Jerome stepped forward and bowed, even though he knew the old woman couldn't see him. Her faded-blue eyes were milky as she stared straight in front of her.

"Mrs. Pennyweather, I am delighted to make your acquaintance," he said with a firm, carrying register.

The old lady stiffened at the sound of his voice. "You're nay Lord Gareth?"

"I'm his son, ma'am, Jerome DeVere at your service."

The old lady smiled and cackled. "Well, I never. Elsie, it's the lad himself! How old are you now?"

"I'll be thirty-four in June, Mrs. Pennyweather."

"Nay! I remember you in leading strings, toddling about after your mother and that dog, the one with white-and-brown patches."

"Ah, Cedric the spaniel." Jerome smiled. The old lady seemed far more lucid than he had been led to expect.

Mrs. Nancarrow placed a cup of tea on the table beside her mother's chair and, taking her hands, showed her where it was. She offered Jerome one, too, with a stick of shortbread in the saucer. He took it gratefully and, pulling up a chair, sat nearer to the old lady and said, "Mrs. Pennyweather, I was wondering if you recall the night my mother died?"

"Aye. I do. So sad that was."

"Can you tell me what happened?"

"There was a terrible storm that night. My Tom, who was head gardener in those days, was worried about the roses being ruined by the storm. We was trying to cover them, but the wind was too fierce, and then the rain came; it was hopeless. The whole rose arbor was destroyed that night." The old lady took a sip of her tea and stared into the past.

"Do you know what happened at the house that night?" he prompted.

"The wind was howling fit to bust, but we still heard her scream!" the old lady said, her face reflecting a remembered horror that made Jerome's skin crawl.

"Did my mother jump, or was she pushed?" he asked, voicing the fear he'd lived with for twenty-two years.

The old lady shrugged. "Ellen Miller knew." She turned her head to look straight at him, her blind eyes staring right through him. "I'd swear to it. Scared stiff she was that night." She smiled. "I'm canny though. Never let on I knew anything. You never asked when he passed. Thought you didn't want to know."

Jerome swallowed. "I didn't until now. Why? Do you know why he did it?"

"Mam—" The warning note in her daughter's voice went unheeded.

Mrs. Pennyweather smiled again, and it made his blood run cold. "Did you say your name was Gareth?"

He swallowed. "I'm Jerome."

"Ah the lad! I remember you, bright little fellow you was, always quick and charming as the day was long."

She settled back with the tea, and he got nothing further from her but nonsense.

Shaken, he rose and set his cup of tea untasted down on the table. Mrs. Nancarrow had her arms crossed over her chest and she looked worried.

"She rambles," she said. "It's all nonsense."

He looked at her and shook his head. "It's not. I suspected—" He swallowed. "I suspected he had killed my mother, but I didn't know for certain. That's what she meant, isn't it?" He nodded towards her mother.

Mrs. Nancarrow smiled sadly. "We don't know. No one knows for certain. Only Ellen, and she's gone."

"But he was violent, his temper was legendary." Jerome's stomach clenched. His father's rages had terrified him as a boy. As an adolescent, he learned to keep his distance. To his mother's cost and his eternal shame. Guilt and responsibility threatened to choke him. "How did you all know I wasn't the same?"

She smiled sadly. "We remember you." She said it simply, and his eyes stung at the trust that implied. *Do I deserve it?* He'd left the place neglected for years, unable to face the dark secrets it harbored. Unable to face his own guilt. *For not being here to protect her.*

And now that you know, is it worse or better? The parallels between Mama and Charis—my God, how am I supposed to live with this?

Chapter Eight

AVA WOKE WITH a start when the coach came to a halt. Blinking, she sat up and stretched, her vision obscured by the veil over her face and the fact that the light was dim due to clouds.

"Where are we?" she asked.

"Newcastle. There's a storm brewing. We will stop here for the night and continue on tomorrow." Lannister opened the door and jumped out, offering a hand to help her alight.

"But surely if we're this close, we can press on," she protested.

"Look at those clouds!" Lannister nodded to the sky. "They are green! I'm not continuing in that. The roads will be impassable in minutes with a downpour like that. Besides, I'm hungry, aren't you?"

Dinner does sound enticing. I haven't eaten since breakfast. Perhaps if the storm clears we can continue on later. She let him help her down and into the inn, where he bespoke two bedchambers, dinner, and the private parlor for their use. The story he gave was the same they had used for the entire journey: He was escorting his sister home. Since they were both blond and blue-eyed, and since for the most part, Ava kept her face veiled in public, they had seemingly got away with it so far.

The impending storm had lowered the temperature and her hands and feet were cold. It was good to cozy up to a warm fire and remove the tiresome veil. She also removed her cloak and sat on the settle before the fire, letting its heat permeate her bones. She had gotten colder than she realized in the curricle.

Rey removed his coat, gloves, and hat and poured two glasses of red wine from the bottle provided by the landlord. He joined her on the settle and offered a toast. "To your success, my dear."

She toasted with a smile, her heart skipping. The closer they got to their goal, the more anxious she became. *What if Jerome doesn't want to see me?* He would be so angry, and he would likely take that out on Rey, which wasn't fair. *Perhaps I should go on by myself?*

Dinner arrived, and they sat down to eat. Ava realized how hungry she was with the first bite, despite her worry over Jerome's reaction to her imminent arrival unannounced on his doorstep. She pushed away the thoughts. She had already worried herself silly over it. Whatever would be, would be. She must accept that. But in her heart, she just knew she and Jerome were right for each other. *Somehow it will work out.*

Instead, she turned her thoughts to something she had been thinking about for a while. Now was probably the last opportunity she would get to ask. Putting down her fork, she reached for her glass of wine and looked at her dinner companion over the rim. He was cutting into the steak on his plate and not looking at her.

"What do you think of Miss Deborah Watson?" she asked. Her apparent non sequitur, just as he had raised his glass to drink, caught him in mid-swallow. He choked, causing him to fall into a coughing fit, which made his face red and his eyes and nose stream. Alarmed, Ava poured him some water, which he took once he could breathe again.

When he had restored himself to equilibrium, he tried to go on with his meal without responding, but Ava, on the scent, wouldn't let it go. "I think she likes you."

"Lots of women like me," he said indifferently, not meeting her eyes.

Ava narrowed her gaze at him. "You like her too."

He leaned back in his chair and raised an eyebrow, his glass once more in his hand. "I like women. All women, Ava. What are you trying to say?"

"I think there is something between you," she said with a quizzical smile. She sipped her wine. "She blushes whenever you speak to her, I've noticed. And you—"

He crossed his arms and regarded her with an overly cynical smile. "I flirt with women all the time. I flirt with you, for God's sake."

"You banter with me because we're friends. And yes, you do flirt with women. Other women. But not Miss Watson."

He shook his head with a smile, "Your romantic nature is getting the better of you, Ava."

She frowned. "It's not. I know I'm right. But you won't confide in me. Why?"

He leaned forward with his elbows on the table and looked at the light through the ruby liquid in his glass. "All right," he said at last. "But if you breathe a word of this to anyone, and I mean *anyone*, I'll murder you in your bed."

She reached out a hand and covered his where it rested on the table. "I won't," she said softly. "You have my word."

He regarded her steadily for a minute, as if trying to decide what to say. "Two years ago, I met Sarah Watson, when your brother was very ineptly trying to court her."

Ava giggled. "Rob did make an idiot of himself, didn't he?"

"Yes, he did." He frowned at the tablecloth. "I recognized in Sarah a quality—" He swallowed. "A quality I admired greatly. I fell a bit in love with her." He said it softly and his gaze drifted to somewhere and something that wasn't in the here and now.

Ava watched and waited. His face had softened from its usual cynicism.

Bringing himself back to the present, he cleared his throat. "I knew she wasn't for me. She loved your pompous ass of a brother. And in any case, I was no more worthy of her than he was. Less, in fact, by a long way; although I'd not admit that to his face." His mouth quirked up in one corner.

"And then, God damn it, in the little season after their wedding, I met her sister." He stopped and swallowed. His eyes looked glassy he'd gone there again, back in time. She knew he wasn't seeing the wall in front of him. Something in his face made her drop her fork. It clattered on her plate and jerked him back to the room.

"Suffice it to say that I am no more worthy of Miss Deborah Watson than I was of her sister."

"You have made no move to secure her affections?"

"Good God, no!"

"Why not?" protested Ava, clasping his hand.

He looked at her with a kind of helpless agony. "Because she is an angel, and I am the devil. I have nothing to offer her. Nothing."

Ava shook her head and said softly, "That isn't true."

"It is," he said quietly and with such conviction Ava was silenced. She squeezed his hand and stifled a yawn.

"Finish your dinner and go to bed," he said roughly. "You're all done in, and it won't do for you to arrive on Ravenshaw's doorstep looking like a death's head."

She slapped him playfully. "How unflattering."

He smiled, took her hand, and kissed it. "If Ravenshaw has any sense, he'll marry you in a heartbeat," he said. They resumed their meal and Rey sent her to bed, just as a loud crack of thunder rent the air, accompanied by a brilliant flash of lightning and followed by the teeming sound of rain on the roof and pavement. Wind rattled the widows and lashed the rain against the panes.

"We arrived just in time," he said with satisfaction, settling into an armchair with a glass of whisky. "Sleep well, my sweet. We will leave early in the morning when this has cleared. I'll have you safely to Ravenshaw before ten o'clock!"

She kissed his cheek. "I can't thank you enough, you know. I really am grateful. You're the best of good friends, Rey."

"Nonsense!" he said roughly. "Get your beauty sleep," echoing what he had said earlier. "You want to look your best for him tomorrow, don't you?"

She smiled and left him, climbing the stairs to her room, carrying her cloak and veil.

REY SETTLED INTO his chair, his booted feet stretched to the fire, whisky in hand, and reached for the book he was reading: *Les Liaisons Dangereuses*. But for a few moments he sat staring into the fire, his mind absorbed by the topic of Miss Deborah Watson. The usual sweet heartache he experienced when he thought of her engulfed him. He had hoped that it would lessen with time, but the opposite seemed to be true. And she was as far beyond his reach as she had ever been.

He had told no one, until Ava dragged it out of him, how he felt. And he was by no means sure that telling her was a good thing. Not because he didn't trust her not to tattle—she had given her word, and he believed her—but because saying it out loud made it just that bit more real and painful. He rubbed his chest absently. *It hurt, damn it!*

He swallowed the ache in his throat and swirled the glass of whisky. Well, he couldn't have *his* happily ever after, but Ava could. He lifted the glass in silent toast and swallowed. The fiery liquid soothed his tight throat and spread a warm glow through his stomach. He reached for his book and opened to the page he was up to, determined to push the thoughts and feelings back where they belonged: under lock and key.

Absorbed in the book, he read for several hours, half aware of the pouring rain, and glad to be warm and dry.

Close to midnight, the sounds of an arrival made him look up from his book. *Poor devils, arriving in this downpour!* He returned to his book and had just turned another page when the door to the parlor was flung open and a voice he had been dreading hearing said menacingly, "Where the bloody hell is she, you blackguard? By God, I'll kill you!"

Rey looked around at the Duke of Troubridge, who stood in the doorway fuming. His hat and coat were liberally sprinkled with raindrops, but it was obvious he had traveled by coach, for he wasn't soaked to the skin.

Putting the book aside, he rose in a leisurely fashion which disguised—he hoped—both the fact that his senses were on high alert and his very real discomfort with this situation. He was fully alive to the fact that Troubridge had every right to be annoyed with him. But the duke was also laboring under a load of misapprehensions. He just hoped he had enough time to explain and that the damned man would listen. He was not sanguine about either hope.

Troubridge stepped into the room and raised a pistol in his direction, which made Lannister bristle with annoyance. He tightened his lips, and was about to say something cutting, which would likely inflame Troubridge further, when his wife, Sarah, stepped around her spouse, shutting the door behind her on the interested staff standing gaping in the corridor, and laid a hand on the arm with the raised pistol.

"Robert, don't!" she scolded gently.

Lannister's heart softened at the sight of her. Sarah was a tall, elegant brunette, with chestnut hair and gray eyes. As he'd confessed to Ava, he'd developed a serious tendre for her two years ago, but it had mellowed now into affection.

Troubridge turned his head to look at her and the two exchanged a silent communication. That sent a stab of envy through Rey's chest, sharp enough to stop his breath. *That! That is what I want! That kind of mutual understanding.* He swallowed the raw ache in his throat and blinked eyes that suddenly stung. For a moment, a pair of lustrous blue eyes in a perfect face swam in his internal vision before he repressed the picture viciously. *She is not for me. My perfect angel.*

Troubridge lowered the pistol reluctantly and said slightly more mildly, "Where is she?"

Rey toyed with the idea of making a disingenuous quip and decided against it. "Upstairs asleep, in her own room. And before you hare off on a tangent, I suggest you listen to my explanation of why I am here."

Troubridge's hand tightened visibly on the pistol which he kept pointed to the ground, and he spoke through clenched teeth. "Go on."

"You no doubt assumed I was eloping with your sister to Gretna?"

Troubridge nodded slowly. "Though I'm mystified why you would do so via Newcastle."

"That's because we are not going to Gretna."

"You blackguard!" Troubridge raised the pistol again.

"Robert!" Sarah said sharply.

Rey raised his hands placatingly. Part of him was enjoying torturing the poor man. *God knows he deserves it!* But he was aware that if he pushed Troubridge too far he could end up with a bullet in him, and he wasn't sure that Troubridge wouldn't make it fatal. Rey had no death wish, despite his private heartache. He had two daughters who needed him.

"I am escorting your sister to Ravenshaw," he said. "And before you try to shoot me, I'm doing it because she was determined to go alone if I didn't. Which would you prefer, that she make the journey alone on horseback—for that is what she threatened to do—or that I escort her?"

"Neither! Any decent man would have informed me of such a venture!"

"Yes, but as you're at frequent pains to tell me, I'm not a decent man," said Rey with a mock apologetic smile.

As if the sense of what he had said finally penetrated, Troubridge said, "Ravenshaw? Why the bloody hell—"

"Oh dear," said Sarah, covering her mouth with one white kid-gloved hand. Her other hand tugged at Troubridge's arm making him lower it again. "Rob, it's Ravenshaw, it's always been Ravenshaw!"

"I thought she'd outgrown that schoolgirl infatuation," he said, clearly bewildered.

"I did too," confessed Sarah, her brown creased. "Ava has got very good at dissembling. How could we all not have guessed?"

"Because she knew he," Rey nodded at Troubridge, "wouldn't approve."

"You mean Ravenshaw has been carrying on a clandestine relationship with my sister under my nose?" Troubridge had changed color and he looked stricken.

Ravenshaw was a close friend of his. No wonder he looked sick. "No," said Rey quickly. "Ravenshaw has done nothing wrong."

"How do you know?"

"Because Ava confided in me. She was heartbroken that Ravenshaw had offered for Isabella Mortimer."

"And that's what prompted this mad start?"

"Yes."

Troubridge wiped his face with one hand and then uncocking the pistol, he set it down carefully on the table and said, "Give me some of that whisky and explain, because I don't understand."

Troubridge and Sarah sat down on the settle, and Rey filled a glass and passed it to the duke, who downed it in two swallows.

"Right, now tell me what the hell is going on."

"Ravenshaw loves her."

"You're certain about that? How do you know?"

"Observation." Rey filled his own glass. He also offered Sarah a glass of wine, which she accepted. "If you bothered to watch his eyes, he tracks her every movement when he thinks no one is observing him. He looks at her like a starving man looks at a meal he can't have." No need to tell Troubridge about that passionate kiss last year. No one but himself, Ava, and Ravenshaw knew about that.

"If that is true, why didn't he tell me? Damn it, the man is my friend. I love him like a brother!"

"I don't know. You'll have to ask him that. But for whatever reason, he obviously feels Ava would be better off with someone else. You know as well as I do that he's been dead set against marriage for years. If you want my guess, I would say he feels unworthy of her for some reason, possibly to do with his past."

"My God!" Troubridge sat up slowly. "That damned article in *The Chronicle*. Lady-killer . . ."

Rey nodded slowly. He looked down at his drink, took a sip, and went on, "When you told him Ava was engaged to Haldane, he offered for the Countess of Esberry—"

"He told us the night he fell asleep in Hyde Park that he was going to do that—"

"Did he already know about Haldane?"

"Yes, I'd just told him." Troubridge shook his head. "He's damned good at hiding his feelings. None of us guessed." He dropped his head in his hands. "What a damned coil! Now he's engaged to the countess. What the bloody hell was Ava thinking?"

"She told me he'd said he asked the countess to marry him but that she hadn't agreed—yet."

Robert groaned. "So, Ava came up here to try to stop him!" He clutched his hair in frustration. "If I didn't love her so much, I'd—"

"No, you wouldn't!" said Sarah, squeezing his knee most improperly. Rey looked away, his cheeks flushing. He felt like a voyeur with these two.

"No, you're right, I wouldn't," said Troubridge, kissing her hand. They exchanged another one of those looks that made Rey choke with envy.

Troubridge sighed. "Well, at least there is probably no harm done at this point. We will escort her back to London tomorrow, and no one need know anything about this little escapade. I'll speak to Ravenshaw myself tomorrow before we leave to go home." He frowned. "I can rely on your discretion?"

Rey stiffened. "I am going to pretend you didn't ask that! Of course you bloody can!" He swallowed and said, "My apologies for my foul language S—Your Grace."

Sarah smiled, amused. "No need. Haven't you heard Robert's bad language?"

"I have, but just because your husband chooses to be foul-mouthed, is no excuse for me to follow his example in front of you!"

"Point taken, Lannister," growled Troubridge. "I'm sorry, my dear," he said to Sarah, who just squeezed his hand affectionately. She then rose.

"Well, I think I had best go up to Ava. I'll spend the night in her room. You two can share the other one! That should take care of the proprieties." And she left them, and Rey rang for another bottle of whisky and a pack of cards.

The landlord had arrived with these items just as Sarah reappeared in the doorway, pale and clearly agitated. Troubridge dismissed the interested landlord, who left reluctantly. Robert shut the door in his face and said sharply, "What is it, Sarah?"

"She's not there. Her bed hasn't been slept in, I checked with one of the maids, who saw her in the corridor that leads to the back door!"

Chapter Nine

JEROME RETURNED TO the house from his interview with Mrs. Pennyweather deeply disturbed by the implications of what he had learned. He felt in his bones that his long held suspicion that his father had been instrumental in his mother's death was all but confirmed. He found himself climbing the stairs and turning to the east wing where his mother's bedchamber was located. He reached her door and paused.

The door was slightly ajar, and with a deep breath he pushed it open. The room had two big floor-to-ceiling windows that faced the sea. Between them was a large four poster bed, from which all the bedding and hangings had been stripped. The curtains had been removed from the windows too, and the wallpaper that he remembered as gold and cream was stained and peeling away from the walls. Dust coated the floor and the room had a stale, damp smell.

He was about to cross to the nearest of windows, both of which had balconies, when he noticed faint footprints in the dust leading to the bed. He trod over to the bedside and crouched down to examine the prints. And that is when he saw it: a loose floorboard, sitting up a fraction at one end, as if it hadn't been reseated properly. He pried at it with his fingers and the floorboard came up easily enough, revealing an empty space beneath.

He put his hand in and felt around only to confirm that it was empty. *Odd.* With a frown he returned the floorboard to its position and rose.

All the other furniture that he remembered from this room had been removed. Only the bed remained. He trod over to the left side window and wrestled with the latch to open the balcony doors. He inspected the deck of the balcony and decided it might be rotted, so he didn't step out onto it. Leaning against the door frame he crossed his arms and looked out at the ocean. The sea breeze was less buffeting than last night, but it was still strong enough to tousle his hair and cool his cheeks as he took in several lungfuls of salt-laden air. He closed his eyes a moment and tried to sense if his mother's spirit still lingered in this place but felt nothing.

He was not going to find absolution here. Nor was he going to get more answers than he already had. Stepping back, he shut the windows and left the room, pulling the door shut behind him. While his interview with Mrs. Pennyweather had not been absolutely conclusive, he was certain in his heart that whatever had transpired on the balcony twenty-two years ago, his father was at least partially responsible. The thought gave him little comfort.

Unable to shake off his dark thoughts, Jerome drank steadily after dinner. It was near midnight when a loud banging on the front door brought him out of a near doze in his chair by the fire in the library.

A second set of loud raps of the knocker convinced him it was the front door where the racket was coming from, not a loose casement banging in the wind or a ghost haunting him. Struggling to his feet, he made his way out of the library and downstairs. The McClellans would have retired to their cottage some hours ago and the rest of his new servants had gone home to their beds in the village. He was alone in the house, and the storm that had raged all evening was still showing no sign of abating.

He reached the bottom of the stairs and realized belatedly that he had removed his boots some time ago, as the cold marble floor struck his bare feet. He was wearing breeches and a shirt under a thick brocade banyan against the cold. His hair was mussed, his shirt creased and open at the neck. In short, he was less than his usual sartorially elegant self. *But who the devil would be banging on my door at this time of night in a raging storm anyway?*

His head was spinning from too much whisky, and he clutched a lamp to light his way across the vast entrance hall, toward the door from which a third set of bangs emanated.

"All right, I'm coming," he muttered. Reaching the door eventually, and setting down the lamp on the side table, he pulled back the latch, and the door flew backward with the force of the wind and rain, almost knocking him off his feet.

With the weather came a small, wet figure that pitched toward him with a cry, dropping a hurricane lamp clutched in one hand. He caught it against his chest and staggered. Righting himself and the shuddering body in his arms, he stared down into a dear and familiar face, white as chalk and all wide eyes glittering darkly in the poor light.

"Jerome!" she said softly and went limp in his arms.

"Ava!" *What the bloody hell? Am I asleep and dreaming?* He scooped her up and, using his shoulder, fought the door closed and shoved the latch back into place with his elbow. She was sodden and, he guessed, freezing. He grabbed the lamp and almost ran back up the stairs to his bedchamber on the second floor, where a fire was lit. That and the library were the only two rooms in the house with a fire, and he needed to get her out of her wet clothes before she froze to death.

As he set her down in the chair by the fire, she began to come around and started to shiver. She blinked at him. "J-Jerome?"

"What the bloody hell are you doing here? Like this?"

"J-Jerome!" Her face was wet from the rain, her hair plastered to her head and water dripping down her face, but he could see the tears welling up in her eyes as she stared at him. A shudder convulsed her whole frame, her teeth chattering like dice in a box.

"Never mind," he muttered. "Let's get you warm first." He stripped off her sodden cloak and set about trying to unlace her gown, but the soaked laces seemed to pull into knots. Eventually he gave up and, finding a penknife in his desk drawer, sliced through them. She sat shivering throughout as he ripped off her clothing with little thought about what she was going to wear tomorrow. His mind was fuddled with too much whisky and the conviction that this was all a dream anyway, and he would wake alone, sore, sick, and miserable in his chair in the library in the morning.

Having got her naked, he bundled her into his banyan, stripped off his shirt, and rubbed her hair with it to get the worst of the water out of it. He found the warming pan by the hearth and stuck it under the sheets to heat them. Then he scooped her up and shoved her under the covers.

"Stay there!" he said, swaying slightly. *Fuck, I am drunker than I thought.* Turning, he staggered out into the hall. *Why the fuck do I feel like the floor is moving?* He made his way back to the library, picked up the decanter of whisky and the glass, took a swig straight from the decanter and staggered back upstairs to his bedchamber.

She was still there. Huddled under the covers shivering, her pale, dear, familiar face peering at him from the depths of the bedclothes.

He approached the bed unsteadily and poured some whisky into the glass. "Oops! Bit much!" he said, grinning like an idiot and offering her the almost full glass. "Drink up! It'll warm you!"

She reached out with a small, white hand and took the glass. She swallowed several mouthfuls before he took it back. "Aye, not too much! You'll be half-seas over!" He staggered and chuckled, "Like me!" and swallowed the rest.

He set the decanter and glass down on the bedside table. Everything was a bit out of focus by now. *Ava—it is Ava, isn't it?*

Yes! My darling Ava. What the hell she's doing in my bed I don't know. Must be a dream.

He shoved down his breeches, almost losing his balance as he extricated one leg after the other. Then he climbed into the bed. A cold body moved toward him and plastered herself to him. *She's still here.* He wrapped an arm around her, pulling her closer.

"Ava?"

"Oh, Jerome," she burrowed into him, and he rolled toward her.

"Ava," he murmured with satisfaction. And kissed her.

AVA RESPONDED TO his kiss, like a plant to sunlight, curling around him, opening up, and pulling him into the best kiss she had ever experienced. Even better than the passionate kisses they had exchanged last year. Those kisses had been punishment. These were warm and giving. He tasted of whisky, and his jaw was stubbled.

He'd looked like hell when he'd opened the door to her, with his hair all tangled, his jaw darkened, and his eyes wild, his shirt gaping at the neck showing the dark hair she had always suspected would be there. But he was also the sweetest, most wonderful sight of her life. *I reached him at last.*

During the nightmare journey from Newcastle on foot in the relentless rain, the dark held back only by the hurricane lamp the stable boy had given her along with instructions on how to find Ravenshaw, she had been certain at times that she would never make it and they'd find her body in a muddied ditch by the side of the road. But she had doggedly put one foot in front of the other and kept going, and eventually she was finally there, banging on his door, sodden and frozen to the bone, but too happy that she had reached him to care.

And then the darkness had rushed in, and when she was capable of being aware again, he was ripping off her clothing. *I have fantasized about him doing that. I must be dreaming.* A shudder had convulsed her. *I am so cold!* She couldn't stop shaking. She hadn't recognized this room, and the heat from the fire paradoxically made her shiver violently, her teeth clattering madly.

She had kept fading in and out. She was in a warm bed, wrapped in a thick robe, and Jerome had gone. *I must have dreamed the whole thing.* Tears had stung her eyes. But then he was there again, shoving a full glass of amber liquid in her face. She had drunk it. Spicy, fiery. It had sent warm tendrils outwards from her stomach and she sank back into the pillows.

Then he was beside her. Warm naked flesh. She'd pressed herself against him, hungry for his warmth. He wrapped an arm around her, pulled her in.

Then he was kissing her, and it was everything and far more than she had dreamed of. *This is heaven.*

"Ravenshaw!" the voice, insistent and loud, penetrated the thick fog of warmth he was sunk in. There was a warm body snuggled into him and his eyes felt so heavy he couldn't possibly open them, even if he wanted to. And he didn't want to. He didn't want to leave this cocoon of warmth and comfort. He snuggled down into the pillows, pulling the warm body closer.

But a hand pulled at him, shaking him.

"Damn it, Ravenshaw! Wake up!"

He jerked and blinked, staring up into the furious face of the Duke of Troubridge.

Fighting to a sitting position, he stared past Robert to Sarah standing behind him, a worried expression on her face. His head was throbbing, and his stomach felt uneasy.

"Rob!" a voice said next to him, and he turned his head and stared at the tousled blonde head and sweet, familiar face of Ava.

Ava! What the bloody hell? Ava in my bed? He groaned out loud. *What the fuck is Ava doing here? Am I dreaming? No, this is more like a nightmare, with Robert glowering at me like that.* Memories of another time and place, with similar circumstances and tragic consequences, threatened to send him into a black pit of despair. *Oh, fuck no! Not again! Please let me be dead!* The horrible irony of it would have been funny if it weren't so tragic.

Ava sat up, pulling his banyan more tightly around her and pushing a tangle of blonde curls off her face.

"Rob, what are you doing here?"

"We came to take you home, Ava. Of all the crazy, stupid things you have done in your life, this has to be the worst! If we can't hush this up, the scandal will ruin your sister's chances before she has even been presented! Honestly, your thoughtless selfishness astounds me sometimes! This is not a childish prank you can beg forgiveness for!"

Jerome bridled at Robert's chastising tone toward Ava and opened his mouth to defend her when the duke turned his ire on him. "And as for you Ravenshaw, if it wouldn't make bad worse, I'd call you out for ruining my sister. I didn't know what to expect when we arrived, but to find you like this—" Words appeared to fail him, and the pain in his eyes smote Jerome to the heart. This man was like a brother to him and to have betrayed his trust like this made him feel physically ill.

Bits of last night were coming back to him. *God, what time is it?* It was still dark outside, but the storm seemed to have blown itself out at last.

"It's not what it looks like, Robert, I swear," he said wearily. At least he hoped it wasn't. If it was, he didn't remember it, and that would be a crying shame. *Fuck! Fuck! Fuck!* This was what he had dreaded, tried to avoid. Now here he was, facing the same dilemma from eight years ago. But this time surely it was different. And he could act differently. He rubbed his face and pressed his eyes with his fingers, trying to make sense of the jumble of memories from last night.

"Ava arrived soaking wet, sometime in the middle of the night. I—I had to get her out of her clothes, she was soaked to the skin and—she fainted on my doorstep." He looked up, stiffening his shoulders. "I was drunk. I honestly thought the whole thing was a dream."

"You were drunk! And that is supposed to reassure me?" Robert's voice rose and Jerome winced.

"No. No. I realize this is beyond the pale, but I didn't intend—"

"It really doesn't matter what you intended, Ravenshaw," said Robert grimly. "Do I have to force you to do the honorable thing?"

"Of course not! I'll marry her, of course I will." Ava gasped beside him. Jerome closed his eyes to stop the kaleidoscope in his head as past and present collided. His heart lurched, and his stomach rolled over ominously. Sweat broke out on his brow. *This is different. Completely different.* He fought with his stomach for a moment and then, having mastered it, he opened his eyes. "I owe Isabella an explanation of some kind. I—" He stopped and cleared his throat, conscious that Ava had stiffened beside him at the mention of the countess's name. "I should speak to her. I don't wish to break things off by letter."

Robert nodded. "Very well. You go to London and sort out that mess. I'll take Ava to The Castle. You can be married from there."

"Rob—" Ava's voice quavered.

"Get out of that bed now, Ava, and come with us. Where are your clothes?"

Ava looked to the pile of ruined garments by the hearth and Sarah trod over to pick them up.

"She can't wear these, Robert. They are ruined, ripped, covered in mud, and still wet!" She turned to Ava with one of her gentle smiles. "I have clothes you can wear, my dear. They will be too long, but perhaps we can pin the hem up and—well, we will manage somehow. Come with me."

Ava cast Jerome a look he couldn't read. Half fearful, half pleading, he thought. She slid out of the bed, clutching his banyan, and followed Sarah to the door. When the women had left, Jerome slumped back against the pillows for a moment in relief. Then he cast off the bedclothes and stood up.

"If you hurt her, I swear I will—" said Robert tightly.

Jerome cut him off, arrested in his trajectory toward the basin and ewer. "I would never hurt her. You have my word on that."

The two men stared at each other for a full minute in silence, and then Robert's rigid posture eased as if he had seen something in Jerome's eyes that reassured him. "Very well."

Jerome continued onto the dresser where he poured cold water into the bowl and dunked his aching head.

Toweling his head and face dry, he said, "This is precisely the thing I was trying to avoid, Rob. It's why I offered for Isabella."

"Do you love Isabella?"

"No. I respect and esteem her, but no, I don't love her. I hoped I would come to feel affection for her in time—" He let out a breath.

"And Ava?"

Jerome swallowed and said quietly. "I love her with all my heart."

Robert looked at him for a moment and then came and hugged him. "Then you will care for her as she should be cared for."

"I'll try my damnedest."

"You'd better, or I'll put your balls in a vice and turn the screw!"

Jerome's lips twisted in a half smile. It was an old joke. He turned back to the bowl to wash the rest of him and Robert said, "Why didn't you tell me?"

"You warned me off, remember? Two years ago." *And you don't know what happened with Charis Dunsenay. If you did, you'd not let me near your precious sister.*

"God, yes. Well, I wanted her to marry someone younger. You've been like a brother to her. It seemed obscene."

"Precisely! Do you think I haven't thought that myself? I

didn't choose it. I just—couldn't help it!" Jerome plunged the cloth in the water and rinsed it. Which was the truth he'd struggled with the for the past two years. *God help me, I tried!*

"Yes, well, it's to be hoped you can keep her from disgracing the family name, because I sure as hell can't. On refection, Haldane wouldn't have been able to either. She'd have led him a merry dance. He's by far too sweet tempered."

Jerome lathered up his chin and set the razor to his skin. He felt a strange lightness of being taking possession of his body. He'd been steeped in misery for so long. The feeling was foreign, and it took him a while to recognize it. It was burgeoning happiness. *Ava is mine.* A smile broke out across his face as he stared in the mirror. *Ava is going to be my wife.*

Chapter Ten

AVA DESCENDED THE stairs holding up the hem of Sarah's elegant silver-gray cambric gown, which was several inches too long for her and a bit tight across the bodice even though the laces were loosened at the back. She rounded the bend in the stairs and saw her brother and Jerome waiting for them in the entrance hall.

Her heart turned over at the sight of Jerome. He'd dressed and shaved. His hair, still damp, was slicked back, and he looked almost his usual elegant self. Except for his pallor and the dark circles under his eyes.

He was speaking to Rob, but she couldn't hear what he was saying. As if sensing her presence, he broke off and looked up. The smile that spread across his face at the sight of her lifted the heaviness from his shoulders and her heart. She lifted her skirts higher and ran down the remaining steps, trailed at a more sedate pace by Sarah.

"Jerome!" she said, coming to a stop before him, a hank of blonde curl coming loose from its pins and falling on her forehead. She pushed it away and stared up at him yearningly. He took her hand and kissed it formally, and she flushed, realizing that they were, of course, not alone. Her brother was scowling at her, and she dropped a curtsy and resisted the urge to fling her arms around Jerome's neck and kiss him.

"I will see you in three weeks," he said, his intense blue eyes locking with hers.

"Three weeks?"

"I have to go to London."

The countess is in London. A stab of jealous anxiety shook her usual confidence. As if sensing her attack of insecurity, he leaned down and kissed her cheek gently. "Go with Robert and Sarah. They will take care of you. I'll see you soon."

She swallowed and nodded. He escorted her to the door and down the steps to the waiting carriage. The rising sun was tinging the sky with pale bluish-gray and gold, chasing away the darkness. He handed her up into the carriage and stepped back.

She twisted to watch him until he was lost to her sight as the carriage pulled away down the drive.

London, Four Days Later

JEROME FOUND THE Countess of Esberry in her parlor writing letters. She looked up, startled at the announcement of his name. She dropped her pen and rose, a faint flush staining her cheeks.

"My lord, I did not look to see you again for some weeks. What has brought you back to London so quickly? Not some bad news, I hope?"

"I needed to see you."

"Oh!" Her color deepened, and his heart sank further. He was wretched and deeply embarrassed over this, but there was nothing for it except to tell her the truth and hope that he didn't hurt her too much. *At best, she would be deeply insulted. At worst . . .* She waved him to a seat on the sofa and they both sat. Gathering her composure, she said with commendable calm, "What is it?"

"I hope that I can rely on your discretion—"

"Of course," she frowned and then, as if sensing his distress, she laid a hand on his and said softly again, "What is it?"

"I came to tell you that my circumstances have changed. I felt that after our previous conversation, I owed you nothing less than the truth and that I should deliver it in person."

She nodded slowly, eyebrows raised.

He took a breath and plunged in. "The fact is, I am no longer free to follow through on my offer of marriage to you." His face felt flaming hot. He'd not been this embarrassed or ashamed in years. *Not since Charis.*

"I—I see." She swallowed visibly and looked down at her lap.

"I realize how insulting this is—I am sorrier than I can say to put you in this position—but through an unforeseen circumstance I find myself honor bound to offer the protection of my name to another lady."

She looked up at that, her large, dark eyes scanned his face for something—he didn't know what. Her own expression had become quite blank. As he had previously observed, Isabella Mortimer was good at masking her feelings. His own heart lurched at what that suggested about her past. This woman wasn't for him, but he found himself fervently wishing she would find a man who would love and care for her as she should be cared for.

"Do you love her?" she asked softly.

He closed his eyes. "God help me, yes."

"When you spoke with me previously, I gather you did not believe that you had any hope?"

"That is correct. I believed her to be on the verge of contracting an alliance to another."

"I see. Then I wish you every happiness, my lord." Her voice was steady as she spoke.

He took her hand and kissed it, a sense of relief coursing through him. "You are more than gracious, my lady."

He rose and bowed, and she rose and curtsied. He turned toward the door and then back to say, "I do fervently hope you will find the felicity you deserve, my dear Isabella, for you are truly an extraordinary woman. Thank you for your understanding."

She smiled then and said softly, "I hope that Lady Ava knows how very fortunate she is."

He flushed at the mention of Ava's name and said roughly, "I am the one who is fortunate. Good day to you." He left then, his heart considerably lighter than it had been prior to his visit.

Jerome went to his club in search of a meal. He had been far too agitated to eat earlier. He made his way to the dining room and found Emrys, Viscount Ashford, eating beefsteak and reading the paper. The man hadn't seen him yet, and he hesitated near the doorway, not sure if he wanted company and the questions that would inevitably come. But Ashford looked up at that moment and smiled at him and the die was cast.

Emrys waved him over, and he crossed the room to the table under the window and drew out a chair.

"What are you doing here? Thought you were ruralizing in that vast pile of yours?"

"I had to come back to town," he said cryptically, as a waiter came over at the viscount's signal.

"Want a glass?" asked Ashford, indicating the bottle of Chambertin on the table.

"Thank you, yes." The waiter produced a glass and poured for him, topping up Ashford's glass as well. Jerome gave the man his order and braced himself for questions.

"Have anything to do with the rumors?" Emrys asked, cutting into his bloody steak.

In the act of raising his glass, Jerome lowered it and said hollowly, "What rumors?"

"About Lannister and Ava."

"What?" Jerome's heart jerked and skittered.

"I'd have said it was all nonsense if Rob hadn't hared off last week, but both he and Sarah left town in a hell of a rush a week ago, and Ava hasn't been seen since the night before that.

Silverly's in a right state about it. And when it came out that Lannister was missing, too, people started speculating." Ashford caught the look on Jerome's face and put down his fork. "You know something? What is it?"

Jerome closed his eyes and shook his head to clear it. In a lowered voice he said, "I don't know anything about Lannister, but I do know where Ava is. I know I can trust you with this. In fact, I'm surprised Rob hasn't written to tell you already, but perhaps there hasn't been time."

Ashford nodded, picking up his glass and sipping it. The deep ruby liquid caught the light and glowed.

Jerome felt his face flushing as he said, "Ava got wind of my offer for the countess and—" He swallowed a mouthful of wine. It was a heavy burgundy, woody and fragrant on the palate. "She turned up at Ravenshaw in the middle of a thunderstorm. Rob and Sarah followed mere hours after. The long and the short of it is, we are to be married from The Castle in three weeks." His heart beat rapidly as he waited for his friend's reaction.

Emrys snorted. "Thank God! You finally saw sense."

"Ah—what?"

Emrys resumed eating. "Well, you might have hoodwinked everyone else, but you didn't fool me! I saw the look in your eyes when Rob announced he'd secured the match for Ava with Haldane. You were devastated. Not that I hadn't seen you looking at her like a man starving to death before that. Although," he added, "I have to admit it was Annis that twigged me to it. A very observant woman, my wife." He said this with a smug, affectionate smile. "And she knows Ava better than anyone." Being Ava's former governess, that was understandable.

Jerome's meal appeared just then, which gave him time to gather his thoughts a little. When the waiter had withdrawn, he leaned forward and said, "If you knew all this, why didn't you say anything?"

Emrys shrugged a shoulder. "Not my place to interfere. Besides, I appreciated your scruples. We all knew Ava had an inclination for you when she was younger, but lately, it was harder to tell if that were still the case. And I knew Rob wouldn't like it. He favored Haldane, which on the face of it would be an excellent match for Ava. We all thought so, you included." He paused, took a sip of wine, and added, "Everyone except Ava, apparently."

Jerome smiled wryly. "Yes. Rob seems reconciled now, though."

"Good, I'd hate to be asked to act for him to put a bullet through you."

"I suppose I'd have to ask Deo to be my second?" Jerome smiled wryly, knowing this was a joke to lighten the mood.

"Yes, sorry old chap, but Robert has a prior claim on me."

Jerome nodded. He knew the bond between Rob and Ashford was a deep one. He cut into his beef pie and chewed thoughtfully.

"The countess turned you down in the end?" asked Ashford.

Jerome contemplated telling him the truth and decided the less anyone knew about that little complication, the better, and nodded.

"Good thing, as it turned out."

"Yes." Jerome sipped his wine.

Ashford laid his knife and fork on the plate and pushed it aside. Taking up his glass, he cradled it and said, "So Lannister's absence from town was just a coincidence."

"Must have been," said Jerome.

"Peculiar, the way rumors develop. One of the stories was that they were actually seen leaving town together in his coach. But how the deuce did Ava get all the way to Ravenshaw by herself?"

Jerome stopped in mid-chew, an odd frisson of cold passing over his skin. "I don't know, actually. In the, err—curfuffle, I never asked her."

Ashford let that go without asking any more probing questions and the conversation turned to other things. But a disturbing possibility wouldn't leave Jerome alone. He tried to shake it off and joined Ashford for cards after the meal and allowed his friend to offer him a toast in honor of his coming nuptials.

"No doubt Rob will send you an invitation. Nothing is to be announced for a few more days, I understand. Rob needed time to inform Haldane and Silverly."

"They won't be pleased."

"Agreed."

Ashford eventually rose after a few rubbers and bade him farewell. "Need to get home before the children are in bed," he said with a wave and ambled off.

Left alone and not inclined to return to his empty London townhouse, Jerome settled himself by the fire in an armchair with a drink and the newspaper.

He was disturbed an hour later by someone saying, "Lannister, by God! Where did you spring from?"

Lannister stood in the vestibule between the lounge and the card room, visible to Jerome through the broad archway.

Jerome didn't hear Lannister's response to the question, but the rumors linking Lannister and Ava plucked at him, and when Lannister entered the lounge—not the card room, as Jerome would have expected—Jerome folded the newspaper with the intent of rising to accost him. To his even greater surprise, Lannister approached him.

"Ravenshaw!" Jerome rose to shake the hand being held out to him. "Didn't expect to see you here. May I join you?"

Jerome's skin prickled with premonition, and he waved the other man to a seat. "Of course. I gather you have just returned to town?"

"I have." Lannister ordered a drink and settled into his chair, throwing Jerome a look that he couldn't read. *Speculative? Concerned? Something else?* A slightly awkward silence ensued while he waited for his drink to arrive. With glass in hand, he looked at Jerome over it and said, "The question is, why are *you* here?"

"I beg your pardon?"

"Well, I gather Troubridge didn't put a bullet through you, which is something!"

Jerome's heart raced, but years of hiding his feelings from others held him in good stead, and he said with remarkable calm. "Do you care to explain that statement?"

"I did my best to ensure he wouldn't, but the man is irrational, far too likely to go off halfcocked where his women are concerned."

Jerome's hand tightened on his own glass, and he said tightly, "Cut line!"

Lannister looked down at his glass reflectively. "Since I'm not sure what you know, nor do I know what happened at Ravenshaw, I'm reluctant to say too much for fear of putting my foot in it. I gather Ava *did* reach Ravenshaw safely?"

"She did, and how the bloody hell do you know that?"

Lannister looked up. "You relieve my mind. Once Troubridge realized where she was, I wasn't sure what he would do."

Jerome waved that aside and said, "I repeat, how do you know any of this?"

"Well, I'm the one that brought her, you see. Did you think she came all that way by herself?"

"*You* brought her?" Jerome reeled under the implications. "Why?"

"She asked me to," he said simply. "And it was that or let her go on her own, and I couldn't do that."

"It's a three-night journey to Ravenshaw from London, at minimum. More likely four."

Lannister smiled ironically. "Yes, it is." Jerome's mind balked at the notion of Ava staying at an inn with Lannister—for three nights! With no one to chaperone her, protect her from—

"Where did you see Troubridge?"

"At Newcastle. We stopped there because of the storm. I had no notion she would continue on in that weather. Crazy girl!"

"She walked all the way from Newcastle in that tempest?"

Jerome said horrified. Only then realizing what Ava had actually done.

"Seemingly, yes." Lannister frowned. "Didn't she tell you any of this?"

Jerome shook his head.

"And Troubridge didn't mention me?"

"No." Jerome frowned into the fire, a notion forming in his mind that made him feel ill.

"You have surrendered any pretensions to the hand of Lady Isabella?"

"Yes," Jerome's response was clipped, even as he flushed with a mix of shame and annoyance.

Lannister nodded. "You are going to marry her—Ava, I mean—aren't you?"

Jerome stiffened, flushing further. "Of course!"

"Thank God for that!" Lannister grinned. "All's well that ends well then." He offered his glass in toast.

Jerome stared at him hard for a moment. "You never wished to marry her yourself?"

"I adore Ava, but no." His lips twisted in a slightly bitter smile, and he looked away.

"I suppose I should thank you for bringing her to me safely," said Jerome grudgingly.

Lannister offered his glass in a toast and Jerome clinked his to it.

Both men drank in silence, Jerome thinking that the first thing he was going to ask Ava when he saw her was how the hell she got from Newcastle to Ravenshaw on foot in the dark and a raging storm.

Chapter Eleven

J EROME SLEPT BADLY, haunted by Ava's journey north with Lannister and what must have been a terrifying ordeal, walking from Newcastle to Ravenshaw in the dark and during one of the worst storms he had ever witnessed. He shuddered. How she had arrived unhurt—in fact, how she had even found his house in the dark—was a mystery. But one he was profoundly grateful for.

What mystified him further was the exact nature of the relationship between Ava and Lannister, and why she, and indeed Rob, had neglected to mention the fact that she had spent a prolonged journey in his company on what must have been significantly intimate terms. As much as he tried to dismiss it, the thoughts persisted.

He woke tired and irritable at around ten from a dream that faded before he could grasp it but left him feeling unsettled and anxious. The surge of relief that he had experienced following his interview with Isabella—and the happiness that welled up in its wake when he thought of being able to claim Ava as his wife at last—had dissolved overnight.

He was drinking coffee and ignoring the plate of ham and eggs set before him when his butler presented a folded note to him on a silver salver.

"This came for you last evening, my lord."

"Thank you, Skelton," He took the folded parchment and turned it over to peruse the seal. *DeCrecy! What the hell—*

He broke the seal and spread out the single sheet.

Jerome,

If you can spare the time, I would appreciate it if you would call at Grosvenor Square.

Yours, etc.
Leticia

"Good God!" He murmured under his breath. He hadn't seen his elder sister in several years, except in passing at the odd ball or concert. For the most part, they didn't mix in the same circles. To his knowledge, she spent a good part of the year ruralizing at her husband's estate in Shropshire, and when in London, her social engagements revolved around the political calendar. What she wanted with him now, he couldn't fathom, but it was fortuitous, for it had occurred to him that he ought to inform her of what he had discovered about their parents while he was at Ravenshaw. To say nothing of his engagement to Ava.

He and Leticia had never been close, the age difference between them being almost ten years. He had been in short coats when she had her debut and married John Norwich, the Earl DeCrecy, soon after. As her husband was ten years her senior and, in Jerome's opinion, a dry stick, the two men had never formed any kind of friendship, either, and seldom ran across each other socially, despite belonging to the same club.

When he arrived later that morning at her house in Grosvenor Square, the butler conducted him to the parlor where his sister sat at a desk, engaged, he assumed, in correspondence. She abandoned this at his entrance, rising to greet him. Letty had been a beauty in her day and still had good bone structure. The birth of six children had thickened her figure and there was some gray beginning to show in her dark locks, but they otherwise shared the same coloring. She also, to his critical eye, seemed tired.

"Well, that was quick," she remarked, offering him her cheek.

"I confess it has been so long since I heard from you, I was alarmed. I thought you were still buried in the wilds of Shropshire."

"How can I be, with Sophie's debut this year?"

"Oh Lord, is it?"

She shook her head at him. "You're a terrible uncle, you know."

He rubbed his face. "Yes, I do know. I'm sorry."

"Never mind. Sit down and tell me the rumors are greatly exaggerated, and you are *not* having an affair with Isabella Mortimer."

"I'm not."

"And there is no truth to the rumor that you're going to marry her?"

"No." He swallowed. London's gossipmongers had a lot to answer for. He took refuge in irritation. "Is this what you asked me to come for? To rake me over the coals for gossip with no foundation?"

"Not primarily, but it was my most pressing question. I'm relieved it's not true. Isabella is not right for you."

"What makes you say that?" he asked, caught off guard. "I wouldn't think you know me well enough to hazard a guess as to who would suit me."

"I may not have seen you much in recent years, but I know you, little brother. Unless you have changed out of all recognition."

He regarded her with a quizzical frown. "You were so much older than me. I didn't think you paid me much attention at all."

She half smiled and shook her head. "My primary reason was in fact to apprise you of Sophie's come out, because I knew you would have forgotten, and to request your assistance."

"What do you need me for?" he asked with foreboding.

"John has been sent to America on a diplomatic mission by the wretched Foreign Secretary. It's all over this dreadful slave trade business. Certain powerful interests in the American south are angry about us policing the Atlantic and trying to enforce the abolition. All of which you would know if you got your head out of a horse's arse occasionally and paid attention to what was going on in the world! When was the last time you attended Parliament?"

"Lord, I don't know, last year some time?" he said ignoring the insult. "I would hardly pick John as the conciliatory type. What was Castlereagh thinking?"

"It might surprise you to know that John volunteered. He feels quite strongly on the subject."

"Oh. Well, all power to him. I did vote in favor of the bill, if it's of any interest to you."

"So I should hope. Appalling business. Anyway, I digress. With John away, I need a male escort. It won't do for it to appear that Sophie has no man overseeing her interests. You can chase away the fortune hunters. You know she has a substantial dowry from John's mother."

"Well, actually that might prove problematic. You see I'm getting married in a fortnight."

"What?" Leticia stared at him. "So, the rumors *were* true, just not the lady involved!" she clasped her hands. "So, who is she?"

"Lady Ava Layne," he said woodenly.

"Oh, my dear, that is marvelous! She will suit you admirably!"

That was the last thing he expected her to say. "You think so?"

"Of course!" She rose. "Now give me a hug, I'm tickled pink! Ava is a delight!"

He rose and obliged his sister with a hug and kiss to her cheek, somewhat bemused.

"I am getting an invitation to the wedding," she said resuming her seat.

"Yes, of course!" he said with a guilty start. "It's being held at The Castle, a small private ceremony, just family and close friends."

She cocked her head at him and said shrewdly. "This is all very sudden. To my knowledge there has been no notice in *The Gazette*, and in fact the rumors were that Ava was all set to marry Haldane and then that she had run off with Lannister. Which, mind you, I didn't credit. Troubridge would never allow it. There is a big juicy scandal at the center of this, I can feel it. What happened, little brother? And don't try to fob me off, for I won't believe you."

He sighed and rubbed his face.

"The long and the short of it is that I have been in love with Ava for two years, but I was of the belief that she had outgrown her schoolgirl infatuation for me." He flushed. "I was also fully aware of the age gap between us and that Robert wanted her to marry someone younger, a man without my—reputation. When he told me that he had secured a match for her with Haldane, it seemed the perfect solution. I knew I needed to marry—the title and all that. So I asked Isabella Mortimer."

"She refused you?"

"She said she would think about it, and I went to Ravenshaw to set it to rights—I've neglected the place shamefully. But Ava knew of my offer to Isabella. She followed me!" He shook his head. "She is heedless of convention, incredibly brave, and the most determined woman I've ever met—except for you, Letty. Robert and Sarah arrived almost at the same time as Ava did, and everyone decided marriage was the proper course of action. The notice should appear in *The Gazette* any day now. Robert needed time to inform Haldane first."

"What a tale! And you are happy?"

"Yes. I don't think it has fully sunk in yet. I miss her like the devil." He knew he had a foolish expression on his face, and couldn't help it. Thinking of Ava reduced him to a state of internal mush.

He wished he could remember more of what had transpired between himself and Ava between climbing into bed with her naked and being woken roughly by Robert. But the amount of alcohol he had consumed had fuddled his senses and left gaps in his memory. He did remember kissing her, but nothing else.

"Well, you can escort me and Sophie to your wedding. It won't hurt her prospects to have you respectably married now. In fact, the more I think about it, the better this seems. Ava can show Sophie the way of things, which will relieve me of my duties a little." It struck him again how tired she looked, and he frowned. *Was she ill?*

"I believe you are more than capable of chasing the fortune hunters away. Half the men in London are terrified of you, anyway," he said.

She sniffed. "If you weren't my brother, I'd box your ears for that insult!" But her eyes twinkled, and he knew she was joking.

He grinned at her. "Then I'm glad I'm your brother."

"Are you? We hardly see each other from one year's end to the next. Would you like some tea?"

"Why not?" He had no plans for later except to go to his club. He could spare another hour for the sister he never saw, as she said, *from one year's end to the next.* And he really needed to tell her what he had discovered at Ravenshaw.

She rose to go to the bellpull, and the sunlight streaking through the window drew attention to her belly through her high-waisted gown. *That would explain why she looked so tired.*

"Good God, Letty, are you increasing?" he blurted without thinking.

She turned from the bell pull and flattened the gown over her stomach. "Yes, how very observant of you, Rome!" She smiled tiredly. "A complete and unexpected surprise. I didn't discover it until John had left for America. He may have received my letter by now. Though I don't know, as I have not got anything back from him yet."

He rose and hugged her again, giving her another kiss on her cheek. "Congratulations. Are you well?"

"Yes, on the whole, just deathly tired. At my age, it's so much harder."

"Should you be gallivanting to parties at all?"

"I must. It's Sophie's chance. We had to put off her debut last year because John's sister died, and we were in black for half the year."

"You rang, my lady?" said the butler, appearing in the doorway.

"Tea, Gordon, and some of Mrs. Hallifax's egg tarts, please—I'm hungry."

"At once, my lady."

"I confess," she said when he left, "that it will be a relief to know I can rely on you and Ava to squire Sophie about if I should not be up to it some nights."

He squeezed her hand. "You can rely on us." He had an odd warmth in his chest at the notion of being of assistance to his big sister, and he was confident that Ava would relish the opportunity to assist Sophie. Letty had always been so formidably competent in his eyes. A force of nature that rushed at life with gusto and beat it into submission. In some ways very like Ava.

As she matured, Ava would likely become more like Letty and her own mother: fiercely protective of her family, strong, and determined. But also, a joyous ray of sunshine that made everyone around her love her. His heart swelled just thinking of her.

"Thank you." She smiled. "I am hoping that this is the longed-for heir. After six girls, John has been very patient. His mother was most vociferous about it. We never did get on, and she bemoaned John's choice to marry me from the moment he told her of it. Fortunately, she had a soft spot for Sophie, despite her not being a boy."

"Are you happy in your marriage, Letty?"

"Yes," she said, unequivocally.

He raised his eyebrows at her swift and emphatic response, but Gordon reappeared with one of the maids and the tea tray at that moment, and it was several minutes before conversation could be resumed.

Letty pounced on the plate of egg tarts and took two, as well as two sandwich triangles and a slice of cake. "I'm starved. Perhaps this one is a boy, if my appetite is anything to go by."

Jerome sipped his tea and ignored the food, wondering how to ask the question that had been troubling him. Before he could frame the question, Letty picked up the conversation.

"John fell in love with me at first sight. I confess it took me a little longer. I think it was well into our first year of marriage before I realized what a wonderful man he was. I didn't realize he had married me for love, you see. He is an extremely reserved man and not very good at expressing his feelings. Took me quite a while to figure him out."

"So, you didn't expect it to be a love match?"

"Not at all. I thought it was all organized between John and Papa for the usual reasons: birth, settlements, needing an heir, all that."

"Why did you accept him?" asked Jerome, puzzled.

"John was a politician, and I wanted to be a politician's wife. It seemed like the perfect match to me at the time. I had no expectations of a love match as such. I was hoping for affection and a degree of—mutual respect and acceptance? Or peace, at any rate, and John didn't seem like the quarrelsome sort."

Jerome smiled. His phlegmatic brother-in-law was indeed not the quarrelsome sort. Letty's reasons made perfect sense to him. After the strife they had both been raised in, peace was a prize to be sought and treasured. He thought of Ava and his heart leaped with hope that his marriage would be very different from that of his parents.

Letty wiped her fingers on a napkin. "I forgot," she said gently. "It was worse for you. Papa's affairs became a lot more blatant after you were born. Their tolerance for each other had worn pretty thin by then, and hostilities became much more open. He abandoned you and Mama at Ravenshaw, didn't he?"

Jerome put down his cup. "For long stretches, yes. I lived in dread of him coming home. Being sent away to school was a godsend. But then I wasn't there to protect her from him—"

"God, you don't blame yourself, do you?"

"Of course I do." He looked away. *I need to tell her what I found out. But how will she take it? It's one thing to know your father is an intemperate man and somewhat cruel, but to know he is most probably a murderer . . .*

"Rome, you were only a boy. She was ill and frail."

"Because of his abuse!" He sprang up, unable to sit still. He paced to the fireplace, staring into the flames. But it was his father's rages he saw, the barrage of verbal abuse, the violence.

"He killed her!" His hands clenched the mantle until his knuckles went white. "I always suspected, but I am almost certain of it now. And I let him get away with it." His heart thudded hard, and he felt sick. Mrs. Pennyweather's words haunted him.

"You couldn't have done anything, Rome," she said quietly. "She was his wife, and a wife belongs utterly to her husband. She has few rights, virtually no voice under the law, no separate identity apart from him. Everything she has, everything she is, he owns. If she's lucky, he's a good man. If she's unlucky—"

"There's more Letty," he interrupted her. "When Mama died, he dismissed all the servants. Did you know that?"

"No. I stayed away from him as much as possible. I'm sorry I left you to deal with it. With him." She blinked. "You were only twelve. I should have—"

"Do you remember Mama's personal maid, Ellen Miller?"

"Yes, of course. Was she dismissed, too? That would have hurt—she was devoted to Mama."

"Yes, no doubt. She died a few months later of influenza. But it seems she knew what happened to Mama that night and took the secret of it to her grave. We will never know for certain now exactly what happened, but I am as certain as I can be that he had a hand in Mama's death."

"No! Surely not. I know he was a bad man, but—"

"I stayed away, never went home in the school holidays. I'd stay at the school or go to a friend's place for the summer rather than go back there. I couldn't bear being there with him, even when she was still alive. But if I'd gone home that summer—I might have saved her!"

He rubbed his face, smearing the tears of guilt on his cheeks.

"You're no more to blame than I am," she said. "I was older Jerome, an adult, you were just a boy." She sighed. "Their arguments were horrendous." He blinked at his sister's bleak face. "I was glad to marry John just to get away. *That* was why you never saw me much. I couldn't bear to go home, any more than you could later. I buried myself in my new life and tried to forget it. But I abandoned you. I left you to deal with it. If anyone is to blame for anything, it's me. I'm sorry, Jerome." Her voice broke on a sob, and she fumbled for a handkerchief.

He crossed the room and knelt by her chair. "Don't distress yourself, Letty. I shouldn't have told you. After all, there isn't much we can do to rectify it now. Perhaps if I'd asked questions when he died—"

"What could you have done?"

"Tried to find the dismissed servants, find out what really happened."

"Would it have made any difference?" she asked sadly.

"I don't know," he admitted.

"We should have talked about this years ago." She wiped her eyes. "I'm as much a coward as you are. It's so unpleasant. I confess I still don't want to dwell on it."

"Neither do I," he said. "And we shall not. Buck up, Letty. It's not good for the babe for you to be upset."

She took a breath, wiping her eyes and blowing her nose.

"Yes, they are both gone now and can't touch us," she said with a valiant smile.

He wished that were true, but the long shadow of his father's temper haunted him, for he felt not only guilt for not saving his mother, but the fear that his father's dark soul had tainted him, too, for Gareth wasn't the only DeVere to cause the death of an innocent woman.

Chapter Twelve

AVA HAD AN uncomfortable journey from Ravenshaw to The Castle, because, while he didn't say a great deal, it was obvious that Rob was very angry with her. Or disappointed. Or both. She wasn't sure, but it hurt. Sarah was kind but a little sad, and Ava felt wretched when she ought to feel happy. She was to marry Jerome, and it was what she had wanted for so long that she really couldn't remember a time when she didn't.

She hugged to herself the kisses he had given her in his bed, whisky flavored, hot, and devouring. It had been reminiscent of those ravishing kisses in the anteroom at Lady Bellingham's ball last year, but less savagely angry, more loving. He had stroked her body and kissed her and thrust his hard cock against her flank and she had been ready to give herself to him then and there and damn the consequences. But he was very drunk, she realized, when he stared at her fuddled and dropped his head into her breast with a muttered "Oh Ava!" She'd stroked his dark head and a few moments later he was snoring!

Their arrival at The Castle triggered a flurry of activity, letters sent hither and yon. Robert sent letters to Haldane and Silverly, and one to *The Gazette* to announce her imminent marriage to Ravenshaw. Her mother and Heather were on a visit to friends in Lincoln and summoned home. Also, notes went to Hereward and

Kenrick, bidding them come home for the wedding, and invitations went to Ashford and Pendrell and their wives, Robert and Jerome's most intimate friends. He even sent for Creighton from London, along with his valet and Sarah's and Ava's maids.

Robert spoke with the local vicar and had the banns posted. The wedding itself would take place in the chapel on The Castle grounds, where Sarah and Robert had been married two years before.

Sarah set about ordering a dress for Ava from London and consulting with Smiggens about flowers to decorate the chapel and with Mrs. O'Neal, the cook, about food. Ava felt it was all happening around her, to her, and yet she wasn't a part of it. It was her wedding, but she felt like an observer.

Yes, she was marrying Jerome. It should be her perfect dream, but somehow the circumstances tainted it. He had agreed to marry her because he couldn't do anything else, given how Robert and Sarah had discovered them. But did he truly *want* to marry her?

He had been set to marry Isabella Mortimer. *Did he care for her? Was it Isabella he had really wanted to marry?* The notion tortured her with doubts and dented her normally sunny, optimistic outlook. She was conscious of a burning jealousy of the beautiful, elegant countess. She was older, more sophisticated, taller, and with an alluring, dark beauty that made Ava's blonde, blue-eyed prettiness seem insipid and girlish. *Can I compete with a woman like that?*

As much as she tried to shake it off, the worries and doubts ate at her. She longed for him to arrive. Knowing he was in London—with that woman—and not knowing what was happening drove her crazy. Ava was not normally an insecure person, but she discovered that in this, she was suddenly reduced to the state of a frightened girl, worried she had pushed the man she loved into an invidious position and that whatever warm feelings he may have had for her had been destroyed by her forward behavior. After all, she had, in essence, forced him to marry her by compromising him.

To make matters worse, when Mama and Heather arrived home, she discovered that her mother was far from happy. Mama had never liked Jerome, Ava knew this, although she didn't know why, and when she had pressed for a reason in the past, Mama had refused to discuss it, but her reaction upon learning that Ava was to marry him left Ava stunned.

Ava came down the stairs at a run to greet her mother and Heather upon their arrival to be met with, instead of the warm hugs and kisses she expected, a grim-faced dowager duchess who turned compressed lips and anguished eyes on her.

"Mama?" faltered Ava, pausing on the bottom step as the duchess removed her bonnet and refused to meet her daughter's anxious gaze.

"Tea in the drawing room, Creighton," she said, and stalked past Ava. Ava watched her go and cast a bewildered glance at her sister. Heather gave her an unhappy look and brushed past her to mount the stairs to her own room.

Ava followed her mother to the drawing room and shut the door slowly as she watched her mother pacing with unaccustomed agitation.

"Mama? What is it? What's wrong?"

Her mother turned, her expression breaking into anguished sobs. "My poor baby!" She offered Ava her embrace then and Ava was drawn into a tight hug.

"Mama, what—?"

"Oh, Ava, this is not what I wanted for you! Leopards don't change their spots, my darling. I have reason to know. You are fortunate your brother was in a position to force him to do the right thing!"

"But Mama, it wasn't Jerome's fault. It was mine. Didn't Robert tell you?"

"What?" Her mother drew back and looked at her searchingly. "What are you talking about?"

"What did Rob tell you?"

"He wrote that he had been forced to agree to a marriage between you and Ravenshaw because you were compromised!"

"He didn't tell you how—where—?"

"No." Her mother frowned. "What have you done, Ava?"

Ava swallowed and suddenly felt like she was twelve again and being chastised for her latest scrape, only this one was far worse than any of her others.

"I followed him to Ravenshaw," she whispered.

"You *what?*" The dowager duchess drew back, and it was obvious she was scandalized. "For goodness' sake, why?"

"Because he was going to marry the countess, and I couldn't bear it!"

"Oh, Ava!" Her mother covered her mouth and turned aside. "Who knows about this?" she asked in a stifled voice.

"N-no one except Robert, Sarah, me, and Jer—Ravenshaw." She decided mentioning Lannister would just make the situation worse.

Her mother's shoulders relaxed a little, and she said quietly, "Then perhaps not all is lost, but there will still be rumors." She shook her head and turned back to Ava. "You don't realize what you've done, do you?"

"Mama?" Ava stared at her, bewildered.

Her mother shook her head again sadly. "I need to speak to your brother." Mama left her and Ava sat down heavily on a chair, her knees gone weak.

ROBERT STARED AT his mother, aghast.

"I don't believe it! If there is one thing I know about Jerome, he's a man of honor. If he ruined an innocent young woman, he would have married her."

The duchess met his gaze with tight lips. "You have selective memory, then. He was notorious for it!"

"Flirtations only! Debutantes set their caps for him, tried to trap him, and he punished them a little, but nothing like what you're suggesting!"

"Your partiality blinds you, Robert."

Robert compressed his mouth into a grim line. "I shall ask him. He will tell me the truth. There are two sides to every tale and this one is surely twisted out of all recognition! God, if I thought it was true—of course I would not let Ava marry him!"

IN THE DAYS that followed, Ava's mother looked at her with sad eyes. Heather did the same, and Robert avoided her. Sarah was kind, but even her kindness was tempered by a tinge of pity that made Ava shrivel. Her usually buoyant nature thrived under the conviction that she was well-loved and that, if she made mistakes, she would be forgiven. For the first time in her life, she realized she had done something that her family couldn't forgive her for.

Five days after their arrival at The Castle, Robert requested her to attend him in his study. No doubt Robert was going to haul her over the coals. At least he had the consideration to do it in private. She straightened her shoulders and headed for the study, which was situated behind the library toward the back of the house.

She had never been afraid of her brother, but for the first time in her life, she felt a shudder of trepidation. He was not an intemperate man, but she knew of others who had been on the receiving end of his infrequent anger, and it wasn't pretty. He had never shown that side of himself to his sisters, but she believed Kenrick had seen it on occasion.

She knocked, and in answer to his summons, opened the door and stepped inside. He was not, as she expected, at his desk. Instead, he was standing in front of the fireplace with one of Em's kittens in his arms. Emerald was a stray cat he had befriended in

London two years ago and a number of her offspring had been relocated to The Castle. The kitten bore a striking resemblance to her mother, being entirely black, but instead of green eyes, this one had startlingly blue ones. Like Ravenshaw's, she thought with a pang.

"Ava." He nodded to her and set Sapphire down on the rug. The cat immediately leaped onto one of the armchairs and began kneading and purring. Ava hovered near the door, gripping her hands tightly in front of her. In the past, she would normally bounce up to him for a kiss on the cheek and a hug.

"Robert," she managed through a tight throat.

He looked at her critically for a moment. "Are you sleeping?"

"Not well," she admitted.

"I'm glad to see that you are not devoid of conscience then."

She flinched.

"I have had word from London as to what is happening. I thought you should know."

She braced herself. *Ravenshaw and the countess?*

"As you are no doubt aware, I sent a letter to Haldane and Silverly, informing them that I was unable to persuade you to accept Haldane's suit. Fortunately, few people were aware of the potential for the match, and when nothing comes of it, it will be forgotten. Not so easily dismissed are the whispers about you eloping with Lannister, however. But the notice of your impending nuptials to Ravenshaw will, I hope, silence most of those rumors."

She nodded, her shoulders relaxing.

"Naturally, it has caused quite a stir. Particularly as strong bets were being placed on his marrying the countess. However, it would seem that we have avoided the worst of the possible scandal. So, your escapade has had fewer consequences than I feared."

He paused and paced away from the fireplace to his desk. Tapping the surface with his fingers, he paused and turned. "Just because you have been lucky, I don't wish you to underestimate the damage your reckless behavior could have caused. You are fortunate that Ravenshaw is, despite everything, a gentleman. The alternative would have been Lannister, and I am not confident I could have forced him to do the right thing by you."

She opened her mouth and then shut it again. *What can I say to any of that?*

"But," he went on, "you should understand that I am deeply disappointed in you, Ava. Your selfish disregard for others is appalling. I am ashamed of you. Mama is quite devastated."

She nodded, her throat working. She wished she understood better *why* Mama was so set against Jerome. But being treated as a pariah by her family cut Ava deeply. It was unbearable. *This is awful. They all hate me!*

"Ravenshaw will arrive the night before the wedding, and I swear, if you attempt to go near him, I will lock you up!"

Her mouth fell open at this, and she gaped at him. Robert's words upset and angered her. It was so out of proportion to the situation. *Why would he say such a thing?* His color and risen, and she saw the anger he'd been keeping at bay. *Why is he so angry?*

"You have set a terrible example for your sisters, Ava, and potentially ruined Heather's chances before she is even presented. To say nothing of Ingrid's, although that is a few years off, thank goodness. If the details should ever leak out, the girls would be tarred with the same brush and considered as fast as you. Which is the most complete injustice, in particular for Heather, who is the sweetest, most biddable, and unselfish girl alive!" He stopped, his throat working.

Comprehension dawned. His partiality for Heather was showing and stabbed Ava with a jab of jealousy and guilt. Because it was true, Heather was the sweetest soul and Robert's undoubted favorite. Of course he would arch up in her defense.

"And you have all but broken Mama's heart. She did not wish this for you." He stopped again, an expression of pain crossing his features. "If I had known—but it is too late now. The notice was already in *The Gazette* when Mama—" He stopped, appearing to gather himself.

Mama knew something to Jerome's discredit. There was no other explanation. *Why will they not tell me what it is? Well, whatever it is, I am sure it is not true! I refuse to believe ill of him.* She contemplated asking what it was, but something in her shied away from knowing. She would ask Jerome himself when she had the opportunity.

Robert finally continued. "I shall speak with Ravenshaw when he arrives, and we will see what happens from there. I can only pray that it will work out well in the end, although I am not certain that any path will lead to your happiness, for if you do not marry him, you will be ruined forever, and no man will have you. And if you do marry him . . ." His face twisted with pain as his voice trailed away. Ava's heart skipped a beat, and a shiver passed over her skin. *What do they think Jerome is guilty of? It must be something bad. Or are my family just overreacting? What is going on?*

He stopped and turned away as if looking at her gave him pain. "Dinner will be served in half an hour. I suggest you go and wash your face."

Suddenly, she wanted desperately to ask him for the truth, but his expression was so forbidding she didn't dare. She took refuge in dignity and rose slowly, saying stiffly, "Yes, Your Grace."

※》》》✕《《《※

ROBERT TURNED AS she exited the room regretting immediately his callousness, "Ava—" but she either didn't hear him or chose to ignore him. He couldn't blame her. He had let his worry and temper get the better of him. He felt wrung out and exhausted. He leaned his arms on the mantelpiece and stared into the flames. The information Mama had imparted to him about Ravenshaw had shaken him.

He had considered posting back to London to confront Jerome and ask him for his side of the story. He had drafted multiple letters demanding the truth and thrown them all in the fire. Though he didn't quite believe it, he still couldn't completely shake off the fear that there was something to it. And what that something was ate at the love he bore the man who was like a brother to him. That canker of doubt was now eating at him and made him fear that he had done the wrong thing in pushing Ravenshaw to marry his dear sister. For all she might exasperate him, he loved Ava very much.

If he could have withdrawn the notice, he would have. But it was too late. There were too many rumors swirling around Ava now. He had to get her married off and quickly, or her sisters' chances would truly be ruined before they were even presented. Lannister was not to be thought of. The only acceptable candidate was Ravenshaw, who had sworn to him that he loved her. And *that* Robert did believe, because he'd seen the look in his eyes when he said it. Which meant that whatever the truth of the Charis Dunsenay affair, it couldn't be as bad as Mama thought it was. It just couldn't.

A few minutes later, the door opened quietly, and he turned his head. Sarah stood there. "How did it go, love?" she asked, moving toward him. He put out his arms, and she walked straight into them. He hugged her close.

"Awful. I was a monster. I lost my temper and just dumped the biggest load of guilt on her. And I threatened to lock her up if she went near Ravenshaw before the wedding."

"That was a bit medieval of you, wasn't it?"

"Very," he said ruefully.

"Well, you might have been a bit heavy-handed, but I'm inclined to think you did the right thing, my love. Ava has needed a lesson for some time, and you might have just administered it. She doesn't mean to be selfish, but she does tend not to understand the ramifications of her actions on others. Ravenshaw may thank you for that one day. He is the one who will have to deal with it from now on. I do hope he knows what he's in for."

"He says he loves her. I hope it's true."

"Did you tell her that?"

"No. That's for him to say. They will have to work it out between them. One thing I know: Once he's given his word, he'll stick by it. I trust him to do the right thing by her, despite—" He left it unsaid. He couldn't bring himself to dwell on what Mama had told him or sully Sarah's ears with his doubts. He must speak to Ravenshaw as soon as he arrived and learn the truth. Only then would he know peace of mind again.

ROBERT'S HARSH WORDS weighed heavily on Ava, and her only comfort in all this misery and frustration was Ingrid. Her little sister was fourteen going on fifteen, and Ava, recalling herself at a similar age, was plunged into a morass of nostalgia and pain. For it was at exactly that age that she first formed a tendre for Ravenshaw.

Unlike her, however, Ingrid was showing no signs of developing an infatuation for any male. She was still the unruly tomboy she had always been, and her forthright observations on the unfairness of older brothers who punished their sisters was somewhat of a balm to Ava's sore heart.

"I think you did the right thing!" said Ingrid. "Rob was trying to force you into marrying Haldane. You had to do something! You wanted Ravenshaw, and by all accounts he was going to marry this countess if you hadn't stopped him. I applaud you for taking control of your own destiny. Robert thinks he can control everything because he is a man and he's older. I don't plan to be controlled by a man—ever!" she said fiercely, stabbing at her cake with a fork. She and Ava were sitting in the schoolroom sharing afternoon tea. Ingrid's governess, Miss Dunne, was having a lie down. She had one of her headaches.

"Rob wasn't exactly forcing me to marry Haldane," said Ava.

"That's not what I heard," said Ingrid, licking icing off her fork. "I think you should have run off to Gretna with him. You were close enough at Ravenshaw. It's what, half a day's ride to the border? Now that would have been romantic!"

"Perhaps," said Ava wistfully. "Rob and Sarah turned up too quickly for that. Jerome was terribly drunk when I arrived. And I was soaked to the skin and freezing. It really was a dreadful storm."

"You were very brave!" said Ingrid loyally. "How ever did you find the house in the dark?"

"I got directions from the stable boy at the inn, and he gave me a hurricane lamp. I think without the lamp I would have got lost. I could barely see, what with the rain and the dark."

"Well, you have him now. You must love him a lot to go through all that."

"I do."

"And he must love you, too, for going through all that for him."

"Perhaps. I used to think he loved me, but—I'm not so sure now." Ava swallowed, her throat tight.

"I don't understand why you want him, anyway. He is so old!"

Ava flushed. "No, he's not! He's—just the right age!"

Ingrid looked at her. "You'll just have to make him love you—"

"It doesn't work like that, Ingrid!" Ava wiped tears off her cheeks. "You can't make someone love you if they don't. And I'm very much afraid I've pushed him into doing something he doesn't want to do."

"He's a man. Men don't do things they don't want to do. No one makes *them* do anything!"

"Robert forced his hand," Ava said, remembering Robert demanding that Jerome marry her.

"Gosh, he must be weak if Robert can push him around!"

"He is not weak! He's honorable!"

Ingrid snorted. "Honor or not, he wouldn't have agreed if he didn't *want* to marry you."

"I wish I knew that was true," said Ava, sniffing.

"You're so tiresome since you fell in love!" said Ingrid, disgustedly. "Write to him then and find out!"

"I can't do that. Mama has told the servants to show her any letters I want to send first."

"Really? Well, I've never known Mama to be so draconian. You really *are* in trouble, aren't you? What *did* you do, exactly?"

Ava flushed. "It wouldn't be proper for me to tell you."

Ingrid's eyes went round. "Ava! You didn't have intercourse with him, did you?"

"How do you even know what that means, you abominable child!" exclaimed Ava, not knowing whether to be shocked or laugh.

"Well, did you?"

"No! Of course not."

"But you wanted to," said Ingrid slyly.

Ava blushed scarlet, recalling her own behavior.

"Was he hard? Did he want you?"

"Ingrid!"

"Oh, I know I'm not supposed to know about such things. But I've got ears and eyes. James, the footman, and Elsie, the upstairs maid, have been having an affair for some time. I overhead some gossip between the maids."

Ava sank her head in her hands with a muffled moan.

"Well, how else am I supposed to find out? No one will tell me anything. You all think I'm still a child."

"You are, thank God!"

Ingrid ignored that and went on. "It's been most enlightening, actually. Very interesting."

"Don't, for the Lord's sake, let Mama or Robert get an inkling you know anything about it. You'll be locked up forever, and James and Elsie will lose their positions."

"Well, I'm not such a flat as that!"

"And don't use cant expressions! Where did you pick that up

from? Kenrick, I suppose?"

"Of course. Rick is the only one of you who is any fun!"

Ava shook her head. "He's usually the one in disgrace. But if you keep going like this, you'll eclipse both of us!"

Ingrid grinned at this prospect, and Ava groaned. "You little wretch, come here." Ingrid suffered herself to be hugged by her big sister and looked at her, puzzled.

"I confess I don't understand, Ava. You were always so bold and—and happy. What went wrong?"

"I was stupid. Childish and selfish. I made a mistake, and I'm paying for it now." She wiped her eyes and sniffed. "Nobody loves me anymore," she said forlornly.

"I still love you," said Ingrid loyally.

"Thank you, love," said Ava, hugging her again and kissing her blonde ringlets.

Chapter Thirteen

Three Weeks Later

JEROME DROVE HIS curricle behind his sister's chaise, escorting her and his niece to The Castle for the wedding. *My wedding!* In a couple of hours, he would come face to face with Ava again and in less than twenty-four hours, they would be married. A sensation very like panic was skirling around his veins, warring with the ache of longing in his heart to see her again and assure himself that she was well.

What was she thinking and feeling, and would he be able to tell? A younger Ava had been transparent, wearing her heart on her sleeve, but grown-up Ava had learned to dissemble, hiding behind a mask of gaiety and frivolity. That much he knew from observing her closely over the last two years. But what lay behind that mask, he had been unable to penetrate.

Arrived at The Castle at last, he helped Letty and Sophie from the carriage and turned toward the steps. Robert and Sarah stood waiting at the top, but there was no sign of Ava. His heart jolted at this absence, and he wondered what it meant.

Rob was a little stiff and hauled him off to the library immediately.

He shut the door and, turning to Jerome, said abruptly, "Tell me about Charis Dunsenay."

Jerome's heart dropped as he scanned Robert's face and saw

the tightness round his eyes. *Oh, God!* His heart squeezed. "Who told you?"

"Mama." Robert paced to the fireplace and turned. "Tell me the truth. What happened?"

Jerome took a breath. Robert was his friend, and he was marrying his sister. He deserved the truth. So, he told him.

Robert listened in silence, and at the end he said, "Mama's version is different, but then her informant is Charis's mother."

Jerome smiled bitterly. "Does Ava know?"

Robert shook his head. "We haven't told her."

"Thank you." Relief flooded Jerome's chest.

"Hopefully she need never know." Robert paused and then said quietly, "I am entrusting my sister to you. Don't let me down."

Jerome nodded, "I won't. I told you—I love her."

Robert smiled tightly. "And you learned a painful lesson."

"I did." Jerome took a breath trying to ease the iron band around his chest. "I'm sorry Rob, I never meant for this to happen."

"It's done now. It's my fervent hope it will all work out for the best."

"I certainly mean to do everything I can to make it so."

Robert stepped up to him and offered him a brotherly hug. "Welcome to the family."

Jerome closed his eyes and hugged his best friend, who had shown him more clemency than he deserved.

Jerome did not, in fact, see Ava until all the guests and family were gathered in the drawing room before dinner. He was standing by the fire talking to Emrys and Annis, who was in the last weeks of her pregnancy, when Ava entered the room. A dip in conversation alerted him, and he looked up from contemplating his boot absently and was transfixed. She was wearing her favorite color, jonquil, and she looked exquisite.

But pale, he noted, and thinner than she ought to be. The last three weeks had taken their toll on her. *Why did she look so wan and worn? Was she regretting her actions? Had Robert been harsh to her?* Even so, she stood straight backed with her chin up and a defiant expression on her face. He felt a rush of pride in her strength and a feeling of protectiveness, wanting to shield her from the hurt he could see lurking in the back of her eyes. She scanned the room and found him. Her mask almost slipped then. He saw it in the flash of emotion quickly suppressed by a brittle smile, and his heart wrenched.

He walked toward her, conscious that every eye in the room was fixed on them. They had absolutely no privacy for this first meeting after three weeks apart and so much left unsaid when she was whipped away from him at Ravenshaw, with no time to talk or for him to even reassure her that all would be well. He bowed, she curtsied, and he took her hand and kissed it.

"Ava, are you well?"

"As well as you, I expect," she said, looking up at him, with her clear-blue eyes slightly glassy. She hesitated and then said in a rush, "Did he make you do this?"

He shook his head and spoke roughly. "Of course not. In honor, I could do nothing else."

"Of course. Honor. It's all you men care about, isn't it?" Her sharp tone wasn't lost on him, and his skin prickled. *What is wrong?* He hadn't expected her to be hostile. *What happened that night?* He recalled with fuzzy warmth her eager kisses, the press of her cold body against his.

"No. Not in this case, if you believe that is my only motive—"

She swallowed visibly and blinked. "I don't know what to think."

The dinner gong sounded at that moment, and he offered her his arm to escort her to the dining room. At least it seemed they were being permitted to sit together at dinner.

Seated beside him, she said, "I understand your sister is here. I had thought you were not close?"

"We were not used to be, but she requested I deputize for her husband as escort this year for Sophie's come out—he's been sent to America. We have spent more time together in the last three weeks than we have in years," he admitted.

"Does she know?" she asked softly.

"Not all the details. She was delighted when I told her. Speak to her after dinner. She will welcome you like a sister, I promise. In fact, she would like your help with Sophie, if you would care to assist. Letty is expecting, and the pregnancy is trying at her age."

"Oh!" Ava flushed faintly and her eyes softened. "Of course, I'd be delighted."

She picked up her wineglass and swallowed a generous mouthful. His eyes followed the line of her graceful neck, and he suppressed the ache of longing to press his lips to her soft skin. He would have that right twenty-four hours from now. A flood of heat invaded his body at the thought, and all the things he had been keeping at bay threatened to breach the dam he had placed in his head to keep them out. He shoved back on it hard. He had to maintain some semblance of control. Every eye and ear around the table was no doubt straining to catch their conversation.

He offered her a dish of poached chicken in white wine sauce, and she took a small serving.

"They're all watching us, aren't they?" she murmured, her eyes on her plate.

"Yes."

"Robert is terrified I'll do something outrageous."

"Are you going to?"

She glanced up at him under her lashes, and he swallowed. His left hand was squeezing his fork so tightly, he was surprised he didn't bend the handle.

"That depends on whether I'm provoked."

"Ava—"

She smiled and reached for her wineglass again. "Don't fret, I'm just teasing. I've promised to behave. If I don't, I fear Robert will have an apoplexy. He's already threatened to lock me up!"

"He's *what*?" He kept his voice down with difficulty and watched her toying with the food. She'd barely eaten anything. Neither had he.

She smiled again and took another sip of wine.

"He never said such a thing!"

"He did. He said if I went near you before the wedding, he'd do just that. He doesn't mean for us to be alone again until after we are safely married. He doesn't trust me."

There was some sense in that. He wasn't sure his self-control could handle Ava in this mood. She wasn't the only one on a knife's edge. But he was older and should be able to control himself, even if she couldn't. "In the circumstances, that is probably sensible, but I don't like him threatening you, and I will tell him so."

She looked up at him, startled. "You would defend me?"

"Of course. You're going to be my wife, Ava. You're my responsibility now."

"Oh." She looked away, but not before he caught the glint of moisture in her eyes. She was so close to breaking down. He covered her hand with his and squeezed.

"You've been through hell, haven't you?" He spoke roughly.

"Yes." She picked up her wineglass and took another sip.

"I'm sorry," he murmured.

"It should be me that is apologizing to you, not the other way around. I forced you into this. It's my fault." She kept her chin up, but he could see what it was costing her.

He wanted desperately to take her in his arms and comfort her, but to do so on top of all that had gone before would just make bad worse.

"We will get through this together," he said quietly.

She threw him a look of such heartfelt gratitude he almost lost control of himself and kissed her. She was so damned beautiful and vulnerable and sweet. He wanted to murder Robert for treating her so.

He then asked after her mare, Diana, and taking her cue from him, she accepted the change of subject and responded that Diana was in fine fettle. And they continued to discuss horseflesh for the remainder of the meal.

RETIRING TO HER room later, Ava discovered to her fury that Robert had instructed her maid Hannah to sleep in her dressing room that night, so while he hadn't locked her up, he *had* set a guard on her.

She allowed Hannah to prepare her for sleep, and climbing into the large bed alone for the last time, she reflected on the evening.

She had been in a dangerous mood when she entered the drawing room and met Jerome.

Seeing Jerome walk across the room to her, she thought her heart would leap from her chest. He looked so heartbreakingly gorgeous, even with and despite the heavy shadows beneath his eyes that spoke of broken sleep and perhaps excess. Had he been drinking? If he had, he wasn't drunk tonight. When he took her hand, she wanted to fly apart and collapse into his arms. Instead, she took refuge in her simmering anger and forced herself to smile and pretend she wasn't falling apart.

She had not meant to tell him of Robert's threat, but she couldn't help herself. And when he said he would defend her, that they were in it together—her heart melted. Only by following his lead and talking about their shared passion for horses was she able to stop herself from breaking down altogether.

They had been afforded no opportunity for private speech, so she was unable to tax him with the thing that Robert and Mama were refusing to tell her about his past, though she remained sure it wasn't true. Indeed, Rob seemed reconciled to the marriage now, so whatever it was, Rob didn't credit it either, she must assume. The knowledge lifted the last of the heaviness from her heart.

She retired early to ward off an incipient headache, brought on by too much wine with dinner on top of all the stress and worry that came before she finally got to see Jerome and talk to him. Tomorrow couldn't come soon enough for her. Once she was Jerome's wife, she could escape from this house, which had been a beloved home and now felt like a prison of guilt and recrimination. For while Rob seemed reconciled, the same couldn't be said of Mama, who was still looking at her with sad, bruised eyes. It hurt and put a damper on what should be a happy occasion. To be out from under the disappointed gazes of her family seemed to be eminently desirable. To be Jerome's wife at last would be a dream come true, even if the circumstances under which she had achieved it were less than ideal.

She knew some nervousness. Not about the wedding night. She anticipated that with excitement; she was confident Jerome would know what to do to make the experience pleasurable for them both. No, what worried her was what came after that. Did he, could he, care for her? Or was she the spoiled, selfish child to him that she seemed to be to everyone else? Did he truly see her as a woman? A wife? His words tonight had encouraged her a little to think that he might. And could she be a good wife? She had no very clear idea of what that meant. The examples she had, her mother and Sarah, even Annis and Emily, made her afraid that she couldn't, for she wasn't like any of them.

She tossed and turned beneath the covers, afraid that she didn't know how to be a good wife, nor even what Jerome would desire in one. What was his ideal wife like? Was Isabella his ideal? If so, how very far from that picture of perfection was she?

Jerome, who never failed at anything, who was always im-maculately turned out, who excelled at all sports and who was relentlessly competitive, who had impeccable manners, whose irresistible charm had broken a dozen hearts that she knew of, who was as at home in a ballroom as he was on the hunting field—what did he want in a wife? A paragon of elegance and regal beauty like Isabella? How could she, hoydenish, bouncy Ava, measure up to his no doubt exacting standards?

She had been so focused on her desire to marry him, she hadn't thought much about what it would be like once she did, beyond a vague picture of the blissful pleasure she expected to find in his arms. They couldn't make love all the time, though she hoped they would rather a lot. So what else would their life together be?

She finally fell asleep in the middle of a muddled daydream about his kisses and touch and woke to her mother briskly pulling off her covers and commanding her to wake up.

"The wedding is at two o'clock, and we have a lot to do before then," she said.

Chapter Fourteen

"... Wilt thou love her, comfort her, honor, and keep her in sickness and in health; and, forsaking all others, keep thee only unto her, so long as ye both shall live?"

Jerome listened to the words of Robert's chaplain, and let them sink into his bones. *Forsake all others.* He, who had never been constant or faithful in his life. *But for Ava, I will.*

"I will," he responded, looking down into Ava's face as she raised it to his, her eyes shining with a light that gave him hope that this marriage, begun in such an inauspicious way, and despite his history, might have some chance of success.

"Wilt thou obey him, and serve him, love, honor, and keep him, in sickness and in health; and, forsaking all others, keep thee only unto him, so long as ye both shall live?"

Ava repeated her response in a voice that shook slightly. "I will." *Love, honor, and keep him? Did she truly love him, or was it still a girlish infatuation? Would her feelings outlast true knowledge of him behind the façade he had built to shut out the world?* The notion was terrifying.

Robert stepped forward at the command of the chaplain and put Ava's small hand in Jerome's; Jerome felt it tremble. Yet she stood straight and kept her chin up, a tremulous smile upon her lovely face, as they each repeated their vows to each other in the picturesque chapel with its stained-glass windows, white filigree decorations, polished wooden pews, and abundance of flowers. This place had born witness to each of his friends' marriages. And now it was his turn.

"I, Jerome, take thee Ava, to be my wedded wife, to have and to hold, from this day forward, for better for worse, for richer for poorer, in sickness and in health, to love and to cherish, till death us do part, according to God's holy ordinance; and thereto I plight thee my troth."

The words resonated in a terrifying way, as if he had crossed a barrier he could never step back from. He had given his word. His word to God and to Ava and to everyone present in this chapel to witness their marriage. The gravitas of the moment was imprinted on his soul.

And then it was Ava's turn. Her eyes glistened and glowed as she made her promises. "... in sickness and in health, to love, cherish..." He prayed fervently that she would, his fingers tightening on hers instinctively, battling the flutter of sick terror in his stomach. This was why he had set his face against marriage for so long. Fear. The fear that while he could fool the world, he could not fool a wife, a woman who would live intimately with him and know him better than even his best friends or his sister.

And finally, the ring, by which she was bound to him irrevocably and forever. The outward symbol of her willingness to trust in his protection and care. As he slipped it on her slender finger, he swallowed against a thickened throat.

It is done. No one can separate us now. She is mine, to love and protect and care for. God help me to do so.

LEAVING THE CHAPEL with her hand tucked into Jerome's arm, Ava felt full up to the brim with equal parts happiness and trepidation. He had spoken his vows with such purpose, his eyes so intensely blue and blazing with an inner light that set her pulse racing. Could he say those words and not mean them? *Love me, comfort me, honor, and keep me, forsaking all others . . . to love and to cherish. And the final part when he put the ring on my finger—"with my body I thee worship." Gosh, that felt positively wicked!*

Ava couldn't suppress the bubble of happiness that surfaced as they emerged from the chapel to the applause and showering of rice and rose petals in which they were doused. She was smiling so widely her eyes crinkled. Her gaze swept the assembled company and stumbled over her mother's tearful face. Mama averted her gaze, an expression of anguish in her eyes, and Ava's bubble of happiness was pricked. Why was Mama so sad? Shouldn't she be happy for her on this special day? How could Mama believe ill of Jerome? He was a good man; Ava just knew it in her bones. She looked up at Jerome, but he was being patted on the back by his friends Emrys and Deo and not looking at her.

But then he turned his attention back to her and, with a smile that lifted her heart, put an arm around her waist and shepherded her up the steps and into the house. Ava's heart filled with warmth at this proprietorial sign. She was his now. And he was hers. Nothing could come between them.

The wedding breakfast was to be held in the ballroom, followed by dancing. As was the tradition for a Layne wedding, the servants were included in the celebrations. Additional staff from the village had been hired to deputize for them in serving the food and drink.

While the whole affair had come about in a scrambling manner, the end result was so nearly like she had dreamed it would be, Ava was soon caught up in the fairy tale of it. Especially when Jerome swept her into his embrace for the bridal waltz. Circling the room in his arms, his deep-blue gaze fixed on hers, she let herself fall headlong into bliss. After the last three weeks of misery she had endured, the guilt and remorse, this felt not like vindication exactly, but perhaps a reward for penance served.

Sarah had given them the rose suite for their wedding night and moved all their belongings there. It had only one bedchamber but two dressing rooms.

When Ava rose to retire, Jerome stood with her and murmured, "I will join you in half an hour. Is that long enough?"

She nodded, blushing. Leaving the ballroom escorted by Sarah and her mother, Ava was conscious of a fluttering of anticipation in her stomach. She had endured an embarrassing conversation with her mother that morning, which, from Ava's perspective, was unnecessary. She had been shocked by her little sister Ingrid's knowledge, but it was hardly less than her own. What she couldn't do was confess to Mama that what the dowager blushingly tried to convey was not news to her. Mama's convulsive hug and tearful eyes did make her want to ask her what Jerome had done to make her dislike him so, but then Sarah had appeared, and they'd had no more privacy after that.

Ava knew very well what to expect on her wedding night and was looking forward to it immensely. She fully expected Jerome to be an accomplished lover and to enjoy the experience. *"With my body I thee worship . . ." Yes please! I cannot wait!*

Thus, by the time she had been divested of her bridal finery, washed and doused in rose water, had her hair brushed out and her body clad in a wickedly transparent white nightgown trimmed with lace, and got rid of her well-meaning maid, mother, and sister-in-law, she was in quite a fever of impatience for Jerome to appear. She dithered about where to wait for him and finally decided on the chair by the fireplace. The room was lit by three candelabra, enough to see by, but dim enough for intimacy.

He was a little late, and she began to fret, but then suddenly the door to his dressing room opened, and he was there, standing in the doorway dressed only in a robe and looking positively delicious. She sprang up from her chair and just barely restrained herself from running across the room to fling herself into his arms.

Chapter Fifteen

DURING THE CEREMONY, Jerome had refused to let all the niggles and doubts that had plagued him up to that point taint the moment. He had made a decision to embrace the occasion with all his heart and soul. He made his vows with deep purpose and intent. All the reasons he had used to persuade himself that Ava would be better off with someone else were swept away.

She is mine now. My wife to love and cherish and protect. He trembled with the power of it. He felt humbled by the responsibility of it.

He took a deep breath and let it out slowly, tightened the tie of his robe around his waist and pushed open the dressing room door and stepped into the rose-colored bedchamber.

Ava was waiting for him in a chair by the fire and stood as he entered. She checked her impetuous step in his direction as he closed the door behind him, his eyes drinking her in greedily. She was wearing a translucent white gown embellished with lace, and the rosy glow of the fire behind her outlined her deliciously curvy body through the fabric. Her blonde curls fell in a cascade around her shoulders and her blue eyes glowed; her generous mouth curved in a wide smile, her cheeks flushed a pretty pink. *She is gorgeous. And all mine.*

His memories of the night at Ravenshaw were hazy, his drunken state had left gaps and made the rest take on the aspect of a half-remembered dream. But one thing he did remember was the softness of her frozen little body pressed to his as it thawed out and stopped shaking. The memory stirred his body to life and gripped him with an ache of longing he'd been fighting for two years.

A surge of joy took possession of him as he fully and finally accepted he did not have to suppress that longing anymore.

"Jerome?" Her voice, soft and tentative, brought him back to the present with a jolt, and he stepped toward her.

"Ava." She flew to him then, landing in his arms, hers sliding around his neck, and she stood on tiptoe to offer her face for his kiss.

He bent his head and pressed his lips to hers, a soft gentle kiss.

At least that was intent. But Ava's enthusiastic response soon sent it spiraling into something far more passionate, like all their previous kisses. They seemed incapable of being sweet and tender. As if whatever pulsed between them was too hot and dark to be contained and would erupt with explosive force on the slightest provocation.

He broke the kiss to catch his breath and said gently, "Slow down, Ava."

"Why?" She pouted playfully. "I've been waiting for this forever. Haven't you?"

He hesitated to answer. *Should I admit to how long I have wanted her for?* Instead, he said softly, "How long?"

She leaned into him, pressing her breasts against his chest. "I've been in love with you since I was fourteen."

"I thought you recovered from that infatuation." He frowned.

She shook her head. "It changed. You were a storybook hero to me back then. I suppose I came to see you as a man more recently. But everyone was so horrified by my interest in you, including you, that I learned to cover it up." Her cheeks were stained pink, and a shy look entered her lovely blue eyes. "When did you see me differently?"

His face twinged, and he put up a hand to stroke a curl off her cheek. "I fell in love with you at your debut," he admitted. A smile broke out on her face and his heart turned over with love for her.

"But I knew it was wrong and tried my damnedest to resist," he added.

"Why was it wrong?" She frowned.

His lips twisted. "For so many reasons, Ava. Ones I thought were valid at the time anyway." Charis still haunted him, but he pushed that thought away. He would not let ghosts of the past ruin this.

"And now?"

"Now, I've surrendered. I love you too much to keep you at arm's length any longer, my darling."

"Oh Jerome!" She tightened her arms around him and buried her face in his robe. "I love you so much!"

He stroked her hair and pressed kisses into the top of her head, dizzy with the feelings of love and happiness washing through him.

She raised her head, and he kissed her again, a deep loving kiss that set his body aflame and made his heart overflow. Picking her up, he carried her to bed, set her down on it gently, and discarded his robe, then he climbed into the big bed with its soft pillows, white sheets, and rose-colored velvet coverlet and drapes. A perfect, pink bower for the woman who held his heart in the palm of her lovely hand.

He pushed her gown up, and she helped him get rid of it, her face alight with the warmth of happiness and adoration. Her curvy little body lay against the sheets and his eyes devoured her with desire and awe. "Beautiful," he murmured, lowering his head to kiss her again and again, his lips running over her cheeks, her jaw, her neck, and down onto the white pillows of her generous breasts.

"Ava, my Ava," he whispered, taking a perfect pink nipple

into his mouth and suckling.

She squirmed beneath him, whimpering, and her responsiveness fired his desire even more. Switching to the other breast, he inhaled her lovely scent, rose water and Ava. He felt a new kind of drunkenness. Instead of whisky, he was drunk on love. Drunk on Ava. All the feelings he'd kept suppressed welled up and flowed out as he set himself to bring his wife the pleasure she deserved.

While his mouth made a meal of her delicious breasts, his hands ran over her body, caressing and stroking. His knee pressed her legs apart and his fingers traced down her belly to the sweet spot between her legs. The wetness that met his fingers made him groan as she undulated her hips in an erotic fashion that scattered his wits. His cock pulsed, stiff and hot against her flank. *Ava, my sweet Ava.*

He stroked her, teased her with his fingers, lifting his head to watch her expression as she tossed her head, her eyes closed, her neck arched, her moans and whimpers telling him what to do to please her. Of all the women he'd pleasured—and there were many—Ava was the most responsive, the most sensuously unselfconscious. She gave herself over to pleasure with the same joyous wholeheartedness she did everything else. *God, how I love her!*

He leaned down to kiss her and slid his fingers lower, seeking the entrance to her body, to stretch her and make her ready for him. She gasped at the invasion, but she didn't flinch, pressing into his touch, eager for it. Her breath came in little pants, her eyes glazed, her expression twisted with desire, as he pulled back to watch her, his weight on one arm.

She flung her head back with a moan as his fingers explored, and his thumb teased her clitoris, that tiny bud of joy, the source of her strongest pleasure. He teased with barely there touches and circles, his fingers slippery with her arousal, inching her toward release. He coaxed and provoked responses from her that set a burning ache in his groin and made his own breath ragged.

"Ava, Ava," he rasped, her name almost a groan, as his fingers seesawed in her body, and he stroked her bud, taking her to the edge and pausing to let her savor it, pulling back a fraction, then taking her to the edge again. *How many times can I do it before she tips over?* Then he knew.

"Jerome!" Her body locked and then suddenly trembled uncontrollably, and she fell into the pleasure he'd been inducing in her body with a detectable fluttering of her flesh and tightening of her inner muscles on his fingers. Her breathless moans of delight were his reward, and he grinned, pleased with himself. Stilling his fingers, he pressed gently to let her experience the full spectrum of the pulsating pleasure.

When she lay loose-limbed and limp, he kissed her tenderly.

"Good?" he murmured.

She nodded, slightly dazed, her hands stroking his shoulders. "I knew it would be," she murmured, with a drunken smile.

"I've dreamed of bringing you pleasure," he said softly. Then he moved down her body tracing kisses over her breasts and belly until he could press his lips to her swollen nether-lips and breath in the flowery, musky scent of her, which made him groan against her flesh and open his mouth to devour her with his tongue and lips.

She cried out and pushed up into him under this treatment as he brought her swiftly to another orgasm with his mouth. Letting her ride out this second burst of pleasure against his tongue, he waited, pressing his lower body hard into the bed as his cock throbbed and begged to invade her body, take her, make her his.

Then he slowly teased her with feather-light touches of his tongue to bring her to the edge of desire, before rising up over her, and with his eyes fixed on hers he said, "Ready?"

She nodded, her arms engulfing him, a beatific smile on her face as he settled between her legs and, finding the right place by instinct, joined their bodies with a slow push.

His groan was loud and involuntary, as the tight, wet heat of her engulfed him and sent pleasure zinging up his spine and into his aching balls. He breathed through the overwhelming desire to thrust and come instantly, and let the pulsing pleasure of imminent orgasm wash through him. Clinging to the edge, he held himself still and waited out the urge. It made him ache, but the almost orgasm receded, and then he was able to move, slowly at first, and then with increasing momentum.

Ava moved with him, smiling, her lovely blue eyes fixed on his, and he linked their hands, pressing palm to palm either side of her head, as their bodies shared this sacrament of love. She lifted her legs to take him deeper, and he sped up his thrusts, unable to hold off any longer.

She panted and whimpered beneath him, and he hoped she would experience another rush of bliss, but his own trajectory was unstoppable now, and the wave rose up and engulfed him in pleasure so sharp it took his breath away. It crashed with a loud involuntary groan and rebounded through his body in eddying wavelets of ecstasy, leaving him eventually limp and dazed and so full of love for this tiny, beautiful woman beneath him that his throat clogged and his eyes misted.

Wordlessly, he kissed her gently, fiercely, and squeezed their linked hands. Her legs tightened around him, and he buried his face in her neck, fighting the wave of emotion that threatened to drown him.

Love. This is what love feels like.

Chapter Sixteen

AVA LAY STARING blindly at the canopy above her head, with Jerome's weight pinning her to the bed, his face pressed into her neck as his breathing settled, and his heartbeat slowed to a heavy thump. They were still joined, and the intimacy of what they had just shared, the beauty of it, brought tears to her eyes. She was so full up with love she couldn't contain it.

Everything she had ever hoped for or dreamed of had just come true in the most wonderful way. All her expectations were exceeded. The pleasure she had experienced took her breath away. The sensations as he slid inside her, stretching her, making her feel fulfilled and like a woman at last; the rapid thrusts that took her sensitized flesh again to the precipice of pleasure and over; the experience of feeling *his* pleasure inside her body, the warm quivering rush of his release—all this overwhelmed her with emotions she couldn't contain.

Tears welled up and leaked out of the corners of her eyes. *Tears of joy.* She gasped on a sob and Jerome moved, lifting his head, a look of alarm on his face. He released her hands and touched her face, catching tears on his fingers.

"Ava! Did I hurt you?"

She shook her head. "No! Not at all, it's just so over—whelming!" she sobbed helplessly.

"Oh, sweetheart!" he disengaged their bodies gently, and rolling onto his side, he gathered her against his chest and kissed her hair and stroked her back. "My darling Ava," he murmured, and she sobbed a bit more into his chest, her cheek against the soft dark hairs that covered it. Her hands clutched him in comfort.

She sniffed, the sobs abating as the rush of emotion receded. "I'm just so happy," she said with a sigh, nestling closer.

"So am I," he said softly, squeezing her tighter, as if he would never let her go.

"Why did you wait so long?" she asked, raising her head and resting her chin on her hand, her other hand tracing patterns on his chest.

He looked at her with a helpless expression. "I don't know, except that I thought you would be better off with another man."

She jabbed him in the chest. "How could you think that? Why?"

"I thought I was too old for you."

She shook her head and nuzzled her face into his chest and kissed it. "Never," she said fiercely.

"I've known you since you were three, Ava. It seemed— wrong!"

She shook her head again. Then lifted her face, resting her chin on her curled fist on his chest. "Were you really going to marry the countess?"

He closed his eyes a moment and then opened them. "I thought you were going to marry Haldane. It really didn't matter who I married after that. If you were happy that was all that counted."

"But how could you think I would be happy to marry anyone but you?"

He shook his head. "I was an idiot." He smiled tentatively. "Forgive me?"

She launched herself at him and kissed him. Smoothing the hair from his face—which was uncharacteristically disheveled and gave him a devilish air she rather liked—she said, "I think your idiocy requires some punishment before it can be forgiven. I cried myself sick for two days, you know."

"I'm sorry," his penitent expression made her heart turn over. "How can I make it up to you?"

She answered that by kissing him.

Some little while later, discovering his body had recovered sufficiently, she straddled his hips and boldly took him into her body, sliding down his length until she was fully seated, her eyes fixed on his as she did it.

She smiled in triumph. This position made her feel powerful, and he seemed happy to surrender the control to her as she began to move and pleasure herself on his body. His hands cupped and squeezed her breasts, his fingers sending shots of pure delight to her groin as he played with her sensitive nipples. She had discovered so much more that she hadn't known before about her own body, and she was reveling in it.

She rode him hard, panting as she chased down her own pleasure, her breasts bouncing with the movement of her body, and he touched her between her legs to help her, his beautiful blue eyes blazing with desire and love.

The pleasure rose, and she closed her eyes at the last, flinging her head back and crying out with the wave of joy as it exploded in her body, sending tingling thrills down her legs and up her spine, to the crown of her head and the soles of her feet. Panting, she collapsed forward on his chest, limp in the blissful aftermath.

His arms wrapped around her and held her against him, pressing kisses to her hair. She lifted her head and looked at him through slitted eyes, smiling in muzzy delight. "Oh, that was good!" she murmured.

He cupped her face. "You can take your pleasure of me anytime you please, my darling." He kissed her, and she responded, giving him back kiss for kiss, and in moments, the passion flared in her again.

This time he took charge, rolling her under him and moving

in her with deliberate desire. She lifted her legs and gloried in his taking of her as his mouth traced kisses down her neck, while her arms and legs hugged him close, drawing him into her body as if she never wanted to let him go.

"Ava—" He uttered her name with a low groan. "Oh God, Ava!" He came apart in her arms with a deep groan and convulsion of his body that thrilled her to her toes. She felt the rush of heat of his release deep within her and hugged him close with everything she had.

Mine! He's mine at last!

He subsided on her slowly as the tremors receded and his breath, warm and damp, puffed against her neck.

"Was that good?" she asked softly, her hands tangled in his hair.

He raised his head, resting his weight on his elbows and smiled down at her, such a light of love in his eyes, her heart swelled and overflowed. "Better than good, sweetheart." He bent his head and kissed her gently. "Wonderful." He kissed her again. "Exquisite." Another kiss. "Perfect. Like my wife."

She glowed under this praise. "Oh Jerome!" She hugged him.

He gently disengaged their bodies and tucked her into his arms as they prepared to sleep. Nestling into his body she uttered a sigh of complete contentment and let sleep take her.

They made love again near dawn and fell asleep again until mid-morning.

Chapter Seventeen

London, Three Weeks Later

"JEROME!" PROTESTED AVA with a giggle as her husband tugged her into an anteroom off the gallery and shut the door. Pressing her up against it, he kissed her fervently.

"I haven't seen you all day," he said between kisses.

Sliding her arms around his neck, Ava gave him back kiss for kiss. "I know, there is a lot to organize for a debutante's ball!"

Jerome pressed kisses along her neck and rummaged through her skirts.

"Jerome?" she questioned as he raised her skirts, sliding a hand up her inner thighs. "Ohh!" She closed her eyes as his fingers slid into her soft flesh and extracted the most exquisite sensation. "I—oh! I promised Letty I'd keep an eye on Sophie!" she said helplessly.

"This won't take long," responded her incorrigible spouse as his fingers glided inside her and his thumb pressed on that spot that made her knees threaten to give out.

"You—oh!" moaned Ava, giving into the pleasure as his mouth found hers again and stifled her groans. In the next moment he undid his falls and, lifting her up as if she weighed no more than a feather, he impaled her with his member and, pressing her firmly up against the door, hammered her body hard with his.

How he managed it she didn't know, but he had the angle just right for her and a wild few minutes of ravenous desire saw them both coming together in a heated rush.

Since their wedding night, they'd made love in all sorts of positions, passionately, slowly, lovingly, and on occasion—like this one—hard and fast.

Panting in the aftermath of the sudden explosion of bliss, her feet slowly dropped to the floor as he eased her down and disengaged their bodies. He leaned his forehead against the door above her head as he caught his breath.

He smiled down at her and cupped her face, giving her a gentle kiss. "Thank you."

She rose on tiptoe and kissed him back. "Thank *you.*"

He used a handkerchief to dab between her legs, stuffed it in his pocket and poked a pin back into place in her coiffure.

"There—beautiful as ever. I'll join you in a minute."

He stepped back from the door, and she slipped out of the room, patting her hair and grinning to herself. Being married was much more fun than being a debutante.

Jerome joined her in the ballroom a few minutes later, his appearance restored to its usual immaculate perfection. Anyone looking at them would never guess they had just made frantic love standing up against a door! Unless the flush in her cheeks and the sparkle in her eye gave her away.

The fact that her gorgeous husband couldn't keep his hands off her kept Ava in a bubble of happiness the entire night. It was Sophie's debut ball at her parents' house in Grosvenor Square, and as Jerome had promised Letty their support, Ava had spent the day helping Letty with all the last-minute preparations for the ball. For which her sister-in-law was very grateful.

Sophie was a redhead, technically strawberry blonde, with a tendency to freckle, having inherited her father's russet coloring. She was a very pretty girl, with her mother's—and uncle's—beautiful blue eyes and good bone structure.

"Are you satisfied, Letty?" asked Ava, joining the older woman on the couch where she was resting and watching her daughter dancing.

Looking up as Ava sat down, Letty dabbed her eyes with her handkerchief. "Oh yes! I was just remembering her as a tiny tot and reflecting how quickly time passes. Look at me being a watering pot! It's the baby; makes me cry at the drop of a hat," she said disgustedly. Jerome appeared with refreshments for both ladies and Ava took the glass he offered her with a warm smile just for him. *My cup runneth over!*

THREE NIGHTS LATER, Jerome propped up the wall watching his wife dancing with Ashford. Despite his sloppy dress sense, the viscount was an excellent dancer and Ava loved to dance. Jerome made her reserve her waltzes for him but let her pick her other partners as she pleased. Even so, they were already getting a reputation for being unfashionably besotted. But he found he didn't care one jot for that. If adoring his wife was a social solecism, the *ton* could drown themselves in the Thames. He had never been so happy in his life.

"You've got that grin on your face again," said Robert, joining him.

Jerome flushed slightly, but the grin didn't diminish. "Is a man not allowed to be happy?" he asked.

"Of course he is. Makes me realize how unhappy you were before. And more to the point, you're making my sister happy, so I can't complain about that. I was wrong." Robert said, with the frankness that made him such a good friend.

Jerome nodded. "Thank you. I was wrong, too. I thought she would be better off with someone else. Thank God Ava had the sense to push for what she wanted."

Robert let out a breath. "Yes, although I would still wish she hadn't chosen quite such an outrageously dangerous way to do it.

Still gives me nightmares."

"Me too," said Jerome soberly.

Robert frowned. "Lannister should have told me what she planned to do. But the devil chose to escort her instead. But at least he didn't let her go on her own. That would have been worse, all things considered. Although if they had been caught, I'd have been forcing him to marry her at gunpoint instead of you."

"You didn't need to force me!"

"No. No, I didn't." Robert sighed. "It was a messy business, but it seems to have turned out better than we'd hoped. Although I've made an enemy of Silverly again. You know he was at outs with my father over Papa's refusal to marry his daughter, Mary?"

Jerome nodded. "But surely that's water under the bridge now?"

Robert shrugged. "Silverly has a long memory. The alliance with Haldane would have been a good one for both houses."

"There's always Heather," offered Jerome.

Robert looked thoughtful. "That could have some merit. He's a steady fellow, may suit Heather, and she might suit him. He was taken with Ava's liveliness, but I think, even if Ava weren't smitten with you, she would have been too much for him in the end. I hope you're able to cope with her mad starts."

Jerome prickled at the implied criticism of his wife. "Ava will never be docile. It's not in her nature, but I'm confident she has outgrown her tendency to flout convention."

It was just then, scanning the room, he realized he had lost sight of his golden-haired goddess. The dance was finished and Ashford was back with his very pregnant wife, Annis, who was sitting on a couch by the wall with Letty. No doubt the two women were discussing babies. He excused himself from Robert and went looking for Ava. He found that any time apart from her made the invisible string between them twang.

A circuit of the ballroom confirmed that she wasn't in the room, and he wondered if she had gone out into the gardens for some fresh air. It was warm in the room, and she had been dancing. He tried not to wonder why she wouldn't come to him and suggest they take a stroll together. A sixth sense was prickling his skin and not in a good way. A hollow feeling in his stomach made him hurry toward the double doors and out onto the terrace. The gardens were a maze of trees, bushes, and wandering paths lit by a scattering of lamps suspended from branches and dotted here and there with little Greek follies, fountains, and statues.

There were several couples strolling through the trees in plain view of the terrace where he stood, but there was no sign of Ava. He hesitated, wondering if she had gone to the ladies' retiring room. Come to think of it, that was the most logical explanation. What was wrong with him?

He was about to turn back when, on impulse, he descended the steps from the terrace into the garden proper and took the path that wandered around the perimeter of the garden, which was cast in greater shadow. It was toward the back gate that gave onto the mews behind the house that he found them.

He stopped some feet away. A lamp in the tree behind them lit the shadowed space sufficiently for him to recognize immediately Ava's golden curls and her topaz satin gown. The man had his back toward Jerome, but the pair of them were seated facing each other, their hands linked and heads bowed together as if in earnest conversation.

The man's hair was as golden blonde as Ava's. With a sick sort of inevitability, Jerome recognized him. *Lannister.* A cold wash ran over his skin and that hollow feeling in his stomach solidified into a heavy lump. He had refused to think about what might have transpired between Lannister and Ava on that trip to Northumberland, and they had not discussed it. But he had caught Lannister taking liberties with Ava before. Recalling that occasion, blind fury took swift and sudden hold, and he strode toward the couple, who were so engrossed in their conversation they hadn't seen him.

"Lannister!" he said, low and fierce. "Unhand my wife!"

Ava jumped in surprise, her eyes going wide. "Jerome!"

He grabbed her arm and hauled her to her feet, his eyes fixed on Lannister, who looked tired and drawn but had a sardonic smile pinned to his lips.

"Go back to the ballroom, Ava!" Jerome said peremptorily.

"Jerome—"

"I said, go back to the ballroom. Now!"

She stiffened. "We weren't doing anything wrong!"

"Go!" he said dangerously, hanging onto his temper by a thread. He hadn't taken his eyes off Lannister.

The other man rose slowly to his feet and to Jerome's fury said gently, "It's all right Ava. I can handle irate husbands. I've had lots of practice. Go back to the ballroom, love."

Ava hesitated and said belligerently, "Don't hurt him!" before storming off.

Lannister watched him with faint amusement, which infuriated Jerome. He clenched his fists, wanting to punch the smirk off his countenance.

"I wondered when this moment would come," said Lannister. "I thought you took the whole Northumberland jaunt too well. Been eating at you, has it?"

This was so accurate a summary that Jerome flinched. "I don't know what game you think you're playing—"

"No game, Ravenshaw."

"You appear to find the whole thing amusing!"

"You are jumping to erroneous conclusions." He rubbed his face tiredly. "I simply needed someone to talk to, and Ava offered."

"I'm going to say this once and once only. You will stay away from my wife. Is that clear?" Jerome's heart thudded hard, and his breath came in short pants. He had never been so angry in his life. Nor so deadly afraid.

Lannister raised an eyebrow and bowed. "As you wish. But you're making trouble for yourself."

"What the hell is that supposed to mean?"

"Ava won't like it. If you want to make her angry, you're going the right way to do so. I can't help thinking an angry wife would be the very devil."

"I'll thank you to keep your advice to yourself. Ava is my concern, not yours. Stay away from her." He turned and stalked away before he gave into the almost overmastering urge to wipe the smirk off the damned man's face.

He walked six paces and ran smack into Ava.

"I thought I told you to go back to the ballroom."

"Jerome, we were just talking! Why are you being like this?"

"Never mind, we are going home." He seized her arm and tugged her along the path.

She reefed it out of his grip and said, "What if I don't want to go home?"

"I am not going to argue with you here. We are going home. Now!" He locked his gaze on hers and a silent battle of wills ensued. "You made a promise to obey me," he said softly. "Have you forgotten?"

She gasped, her eyes widening. "And you made a promise to cherish me!" she returned. The words hit him in the chest like arrows.

He bowed stiffly. "Very well, madam, if you won't accompany me, I shall walk home and leave the carriage for you. Good evening."

He had taken two steps when she said, "No!" Her hand landed on his arm. "I'll go with you. You're right, we can't quarrel here, and I *want* to quarrel with you!"

If he hadn't been so furious, he might have laughed at that. It was so typically Ava. His heart lurched. *God, I love her. But I have to get to the bottom of this business with Lannister, or I'll have no peace.*

Chapter Eighteen

JEROME SHUT THE bedroom door and advanced on his wife, who stood by the dressing table, removing pins from her hair. Neither had spoken during the carriage drive home, but he did not mistake her silence for anything but anger. His own white-hot fury had abated a little, but not so much that he could be conciliatory.

"What is between you and Lannister?"

"We are friends! That is all." She matched him, fists clenched by her sides, her chin up and blue eyes blazing. She was magnificently beautiful in her rage.

"I caught him hugging you before, Ava!"

"It was a comfort hug. I was upset! Over you!" Her eyes sparkled with tears, but they didn't fall.

"A comfort hug! There is no such thing! A man of his ilk doesn't hug a woman he's not interested in bedding!" He turned away and paced to the fireplace, where flames danced over a log.

"What are you suggesting?" Her voice was low and panting with fury.

He turned and faced her, braced for a truth he didn't want to hear. "Well, did he? As far as I can work out, he's had ample opportunity!"

She stood, her generous bosom in its low-cut evening gown

heaving with her emotions, and glared at him but didn't reply.

Goaded, he said, "Is he—*was* he your lover?"

She closed the space between them and slapped his face, her eyes spilling tears down her cheeks even as she said through her teeth, "Is that what you think of me? That I would play you false, follow you north but dally with him on the way? How could you?"

He pulled her close and kissed her then, no more able to resist her than a siren call.

YANKED AGAINST HIS body and kissed with savage brutality, Ava's anger transmuted to passion, and she kissed him back with equal fervor. She even bit his lip and tasted blood. It fueled her jumbled emotions further and when he dragged her to the carpet and rolled her under him, she pushed up into him like a wanton, gasping and mewling like a demented kitten. His hands pushed her skirts up and undid his falls, all the while his mouth ravished her neck and her hands tore at his neckcloth and tangled in his hair.

She wanted to hit him and kiss him and bite him and love him all at once. His weight kept her pinned to the carpet, and she gloried in his strength as one hand reached between her legs to stroke her, while the other grabbed her wrists and held them captive above her head.

She moaned at the searing pleasure of his touch, and he raised his head to stare down into her eyes. "You're wet! You want me!" His voice was thick with desire.

She wrenched at his grip to get her hands free to grab his face to kiss him and show him how much she wanted him. But his grip tightened, and she made an infuriated sound of frustration as he lowered his head and kissed her deeply.

He loosened his hold on her wrists, and she tore at his jacket to pull it off. He rose up and helped her. The cloth ripped, but he didn't even seem to notice, tossing the garment aside, and reached down to yank at the front fastenings of her dress. He bared her breasts, ripped off his waistcoat and shirt, and lowered his head to devour her breasts with ravenous need.

She whimpered and squirmed. Panting, she tugged at him, "Jerome!"

"You want me?" He leaned over her, panting, his cock hard and red jutted between them from the open falls of his breeches.

She nodded. "Please," she whispered brokenly. She was afire with a need so powerful she would expire if he didn't touch her, take her. He lowered his body onto hers and, holding her gaze with his, joined them with a swift, hard thrust that jolted her whole frame and drove a groan of delight from her throat.

She lifted her legs higher, as his deep, rapid thrusts escalated her pleasure. There was nothing gentle in this brutal mutual taking, as her hands tore at his shoulders and back, digging in her nails. She gave into the savage need to bite him and rip at him, pushing up into his downward thrusts with violent need. Pleasure spiraled up and up within her, and she cried out with each hard thrust that took her closer and closer to the ball of bliss just out of reach.

It wound impossibly tight within her. She arched up into him as he thrust down, and it exploded in a coruscating lightning blast through her body, reverberating through her so strongly she forgot to breathe.

She felt and heard the devastating violence of his own release, even though it was slightly muted by the intensity of her own. But as hers receded slowly, she became aware of him more, as he continued to move in her with a shuddering force. His eyes closed, his expression torn with the agony of release, his hands gripping her shoulders from underneath as he thrust and thrust through the dying embers of his orgasm.

Slowly his body stilled and subsided on hers, heavy with the weight of total collapse.

She lay getting her breath back, listening to him breathe, feeling his warm breath against her neck, the sweat-slicked skin between them. The heat from the fire warmed them more than they needed. Her new gown was ruined—his jacket, too—and it didn't matter. Nothing mattered but this. She wrapped her arms and legs around him and squeezed.

He raised his head slowly and kissed her gently, soft, repeated kisses to her lips, his eyes dark and slumberous. "Ava," he whispered. "My Ava."

Then he pulled back, separating their bodies and rising, he lifted her in his arms and carried her to bed. He got rid of the remnants of her dress, her petticoats, stays, and stockings.

Then he fetched a cloth to clean her with and finally crawled into bed and pulled her into his arms. She nestled in, reluctant to break the silent truce between them with speech. She tucked her head into his chest and let exhaustion take her.

JEROME HELD HER as she slipped into sleep and blinked away the tears that stung his eyes. He pressed a kiss to her hair and whispered. "I love you so much, Ava."

Chapter Nineteen

JEROME WOKE WITH his wife in his arms and recalled the brutal, wonderful passion of the night before. He loved this little woman with her indomitable spirit and stubborn will—fiercely. It was that strength he had always admired in her, even when it led her into folly, which it frequently did.

He had voiced his fear that Lannister had overstepped the boundaries with her, seduced her perhaps. Lannister was a charming man and experienced with women. He was known for seducing and ruining innocents. It was what got him banned from Almack's. Ava's reaction reassured him that his fears were exaggerated. But she hadn't denied it utterly, which made him wonder if there was some gray in there somewhere. Kisses? A bit more, perhaps? He sighed and pressed his lips to her hair.

Whatever was between them, he couldn't blame her for it. It was Lannister he wanted to murder, for daring to touch her at all. But he wouldn't tolerate this so-called friendship between them any longer. If she truly loved him, she would see how impossible it was that she continue with it. After last night's shared passion, he had little doubt of her devotion to him. Ava loved him, wanted him, as much as he loved and wanted her.

She stirred in his arms and blinked up at him, a smile breaking over her face that confirmed his thoughts.

"Good morning, my darling wife," he said with an answering smile, and kissed her tenderly.

She responded and murmured, "Morning, my dearest husband." She grinned wider, her eyes opening fully. "You know, that still gives me a thrill. I wanted to be your wife for so long. I sometimes wonder if I'm dreaming and it never really happened."

"It happened," he said, kissing her again. "But I know what you mean. I sometimes feel the same way. I thought I could live with the pain of giving you up, because it was the right thing for you."

"But it wasn't! That was why I couldn't let you do it!" she said sitting up indignantly. "How could you think I would be happy without you?"

"I am glad in retrospect that you took steps to convince me otherwise, but I do wish such drastic action had not been necessary. I blame myself for that."

She subsided onto his chest with a smile and cupped his face, kissing him. "Well, I shall never regret doing it. Every step I took in that dreadful storm was worth it."

He shuddered, recalling her arriving soaked to the skin, white as a sheet, and fainting in his arms. "I never want you to give me a fright like that again. I thought for a moment you were dead when you collapsed on me."

"I do wish Rob hadn't found us quite so soon, and you hadn't been so foully drunk," she said, with a sloe-eyed smile, that stiffened his cock with more than its usual morning wood.

"Well, I am glad," he said, giving in to kissing her again. "It was bad enough as it was, facing him. It would have been worse if I'd lost control of myself and taken you then and there, as I might well have done if I hadn't been so stinking drunk. I'm embarrassed you saw me like that."

"I didn't care. You were rather funny, actually." She giggled. "Very unlike your usual impeccably dressed and correct self. You couldn't even walk straight." She laughed at the memory, and he flushed faintly. He should be able to laugh at himself, but instead he felt embarrassed and ashamed. He swallowed, vowing she would never see him like that again.

He flung back the bedclothes and rose. "We should get dressed and have breakfast. I have an appointment at Gentleman Jackson's at ten."

He bent to pick up his discarded jacket and examined the tear in the lining. Leyton, his excellent valet, would be shocked. He'd lost the buttons off his waistcoat too, he realized, picking up that article and then bending to retrieve the scattered buttons. He found five, but the sixth eluded him. He took them through to his dressing room and rang for Leyton.

Leyton was a young man in his mid-twenties, very young for a valet, especially valet to a man of the Marquess of Ravenshaw's standing as an undoubted leader of fashion and taste. But he was levelheaded and devoted to Jerome and a master with boot polish.

An hour later, dressed with his usual care, Jerome joined his wife for breakfast in the parlor.

She was dressed in a lovely blue muslin and perusing the paper when he came in.

"My apologies for keeping you waiting," he said, bending to kiss her cheek.

She looked up at him impishly. "It was worth it. You look superb!"

"And you look enchanting. That blue becomes you," he said sedately. All this for the benefit of the servants. But his eyes should convey what he really thought: that she was good enough to eat.

With breakfast served, he dismissed the servants in order to enjoy the time alone with his wife. "What do you have planned for the day?" he asked, cutting into the ham on his plate.

Buttering toast, she said, "Shopping with Letty and Sophie. And then some morning calls in the afternoon, followed by a walk in Hyde Park at five with Sarah and Deborah. You could join us if you like."

He nodded and smiled, "Thank you, I should." He added, "Will you come riding with me tomorrow morning?"

"I would love to," she said with a warm smile and a touch of her hand across the table. A passion for riding was something they shared.

They parted after breakfast with a tender kiss and Jerome set off for his bout of boxing at Gentleman Jackson's, followed by a session with foils at Angelo's and pistol practice at Manton's. He didn't maintain his competence at sports without practice, despite his natural talents, and his physical fitness was as important to him as his undoubted prowess at every sport he participated in.

Coming out of Manton's, he ran into Deo who asked him if he would help him find a new horse. The man was so big that he needed a horse that could handle his weight. So the two of them went off to Tattersalls on Hyde Park Corner to find a suitable horse for him.

"Glad you found your lady at last, Jerome," remarked Deo, patting the fetlocks of the sixteen-hand brute before him.

"So am I," said Jerome quietly. "How is Emily?" he added, asking after Deo's wife. "I don't think I've seen her since the wedding."

"No." Deo flushed. "She's been feeling a little poorly. We discovered just recently she's in the family way." The grin on his face couldn't be suppressed.

"Congratulations, old fellow," said Jerome, grasping his hand and patting him on the back. "That is wonderful news. Have you told Emrys? He'll be over the moon for you. You know Annis is due any day now."

"I haven't seen Emrys or Robert to tell them. I was going to wait until I had you all together, but—couldn't keep it to myself," he said in a burst of unaccustomed loquaciousness. "I'm terrified, you know," he added with a rueful look. "I've not a clue how to be a father. Except I don't want to be like my own father. Em is being wonderfully calm and practical about it. Lord, I adore that woman!" His freckled face flushed, and his eyes got misty.

Jerome felt a sympathetic rush of similar emotion when he thought of Ava in a like situation, and his own trepidation around fatherhood. Bad fathers left their sons with two options: be like them or be the opposite. *But is it possible to choose to be the opposite, or is the badness bred in the bone?*

⟶⟫⟫⟫⟪⟪⟪⟵

JEROME WAS A little late to his rendezvous with Ava and her sisters-in-law in Hyde Park and arrived at the entrance to find the ladies accompanied by the Earl of Lannister. He checked a few feet away at the sight of the earl, who was taking on the guise of a nemesis in his mind. *Had the man been invited to accompany them, or had he happened upon them by chance?* Jerome had no way of knowing and, since he couldn't create a scene in Hyde Park at its busiest hour, he swallowed his ire and approached the group with a smile pinned to his lips.

Ava, as if sensing his presence, turned her head and smiled at him. He took her arm and greeted the other ladies with warmth and Lannister with stiff politeness.

The earl, damn him, smiled sardonically and bowed in his direction. The man knew he was annoyed and was enjoying it!

"Well, now we have our full complement," said Lannister, indicating that he *had* been invited. "Shall we promenade, ladies?" he asked, offering an arm each to the duchess and her sister, leaving Jerome to escort his wife, as was proper. Had Ava invited him deliberately to this walk, knowing Lannister would be here? And if she had, what did that mean?

The park was full to bursting on Rotten Row at this time of the day, and they chose a less congested path for their walk to the reservoir, past the Chesterfield Gate, through the avenue of trees that grew in pairs either side of the road. Jerome was reminded of his drunken foray into Hyde Park via the Grosvenor Gate farther to the north of this same avenue of trees, the night that he learned of Ava's supposed engagement to Haldane. He looked down at her, covering her hand with his in a tight little squeeze, so thankful his life had not taken the trajectory he had believed it would that night.

She turned her bonneted head up to his and smiled, and he lost himself in the soothing tenderness of her smile and the glow of warmth in her eyes. She was as glad to see him as he was to see her. Why had he been so insane as to think a marriage of convenience was all he could aspire to? All the troubles of his parents' marriage seemed a faint memory at this moment, when his love for Ava colored every thought and feeling that he had.

The walk passed in a pleasant blur for him as their party circled the reservoir and returned to the entrance, where he and Ava parted company with the others, taking a hackney carriage to their house in Hanover Square.

With the carriage door shut, he drew her into his arms for a kiss. "I missed you today," he said softly, dropping tender kisses on her mouth and then deepening one for a thorough kiss that left them both a bit breathless. He tugged her bonnet strings and discarded it along with his hat.

"I've never known you so careless of your clothes as you are lately," she laughed, responding to his kisses.

"They get in the way," he growled, tugging her into his lap.

"I think I like possessive you," she said, stroking his jaw.

"Is that what you think this is?"

"Isn't it? Every time you see Rey, you go all feudal. I thought you were going to snarl at him at first, but you didn't."

Jerome's heart kicked at her use of Lannister's name. "Did you know he was going to be there when you invited me?"

She pushed a lock of his hair off his forehead, meeting his eyes steadily. "Yes, I did. Because I didn't want you to hear about it afterward and think I was hiding something from you for one thing, and—"

"Who invited him?"

"He happened to be present when Sarah proposed the walk a few days ago and was naturally included. He and Sarah are friends, too, you know."

He eased her off his lap as the carriage slowed, turning into Hanover Square. "That is a matter for Robert to deal with," he said tightly. "I would be obliged if you would refrain from seeking his company in the future."

She gaped at him, snatched up her bonnet, and climbed out of the carriage before he could open the door for her. He collected his own hat and followed her into the house. She headed straight for the stairs and her own room. Since they were promised to Letty for dinner prior to a visit to the theater, that wasn't unreasonable. They both needed to dress, but he wasn't fooled that his request had been received well.

He reached her dressing room and entered without knocking. She had tossed her bonnet on a chair and was in the act of removing her pelisse.

"Did you hear what I said?" he asked, carefully.

"I did." She kept her back to him as she moved to the mirror on the dresser and started removing pins from her hair.

"Well?"

She rounded on him then, fists clenched. It was last night all over again. "Rey is my friend! I haven't asked you to give up your female friends! The countess, Daphne Holbrook, and whoever else you might count as a friend. Why should I give up someone who has been nothing but kind to me since my debut? Rey is no threat to you. You're being ridiculous! Worse than Robert! Even he has conceded Rey is not as black as he is painted."

"It is entirely different!"

"How is it different? You almost married the countess! Am I to believe you never kissed her? Thought about bedding her?" Ava panted, her face pink with fury. "Do you think I'm not jealous of her? It was rumored she was your lover for months! But have I said a word about that? No, I have not!" She dashed a hand across her cheeks. "She's dark and beautiful, elegant, sophisticated, the perfect lady! Everything I'm not!"

"My God, Ava, she doesn't hold a candle to you!" he said

appalled. "I love *you*, Ava, always and forever!"

"Do you?" She seemed to wilt a little then, swaying toward him.

He crossed the room, seizing her in his arms. "How could you doubt that?"

"How could you doubt *me?*" she asked, a tear rolling down her cheek.

"Oh, Ava!" He wiped the tear away. "I'm sorry, sweetheart!" Tightening his arms around her, he kissed her. Her arms tightened around his neck, and he rested his face against her hair as she buried her face in his shoulder. "But don't you see darling, it *is* different. I haven't seen Is—the countess since I broke things off with her before our wedding. But the gossips will have a field day if they see you with Lannister after the rumors—"

She lifted her head. "What rumors?"

"When I came back from Ravenshaw, it was all over London that you had run off with Lannister! It was only the announcement of our wedding that silenced the gossip."

"I still don't see—"

"The fact is, people don't forget things like that, and Lannister's reputation is bad enough that people will think the worst given the slightest provocation, or even none at all! I don't wish to have it whispered that my wife is cuckolding me with London's most notorious rake!"

"What difference does it make if you know it's not true?"

"Damn it, Ava, if you love me, you will stop arguing with me about this and accede to my wishes. I'm your husband! I've a right to ask you to behave with the propriety befitting your station!"

She pulled away from him, her face flushing.

"So you're ashamed of me? Is that it? You care more about what people might say than the truth?"

"No, that is not what I said—"

"It sounded like it to me!" She turned away.

"Ava—!"

"Go away!" she said with impassioned rage. "You care about

appearances more than you care about me!"

"That isn't true." He spoke quietly, but realized she wasn't of a mind to hear him. "I hope you will think about what I have asked and come to your senses. I need to dress. I will see you in an hour." He left her, an ache in his chest and a bitter kind of despair threatening to swamp him.

AVA SANK DOWN on her dressing table stool and stared at her reflection in the mirror, appalled at what had just happened. She felt as if she had been slapped in the face by a stranger. She suddenly saw Jerome in an entirely new light. He had always been someone who took inordinate pains to make a good impression. She knew that. She knew he cared about his appearance and cared about winning.

But she had always seen these things as virtues to be admired, because he was a leader of fashion and he always won everything he attempted. Other men envied him, and ladies wanted to be seen with him. Women adored him, not only because he was beautiful, but because he was accomplished, perfect!

That he would put those things ahead of her feelings made her feel as if he didn't care for her at all. His words of love were hollow. He would love her if she behaved like a perfect lady. *Like the countess!* The old stab of jealousy rose up and bit her—hard. And with it came those feelings of inadequacy she had tried to stifle.

Her maid appeared at that moment to dress her, and she pushed down her desire to indulge in a hearty bout of tears. She submitted to being disrobed, washed, having her hair done, and being dressed in one of her new evening gowns. It was made of shimmering blue silk, and she had been excited to show it to Jerome, who would appreciate it, but now that felt hollow and brittle. *How am I going to get through tonight feeling like this?*

Chapter Twenty

JEROME WAS EXCRUCIATINGLY polite, and Ava was sparklingly brittle. All evening. By the time they got home, she was exhausted and went straight to her room and, for the first time since her marriage, locked all the doors. She couldn't face another fight with Jerome, and she was afraid that was what would happen. She needed a good cry with no witnesses.

JEROME WAS DEVASTATED when he found her door locked against him and promptly left the house again and went to his club, where he played cards and drank steadily for several hours before reluctantly wending his way home again. He fell into bed half undressed at four in the morning and slept until after midday.

He had the devil of a head when he woke, and when he inquired as to Her Ladyship's movements, learned that Ava had left the house early to ride her mare. He winced at the broken appointment. They had been meant to go riding together.

He groaned, drank coffee, and took himself off to Gentleman Jackson's to sweat out some of the alcohol still swimming in his system.

When he got home, feeling more sober and clearer headed, he discovered that Ava had returned and left the house again. Skelton, his butler, couldn't hazard a guess as to where she had gone, but she had taken the carriage.

Jerome retired to the library to await her return and fell asleep in his chair. When he woke it was dark, and he was informed that Ava had gone out again.

He ate a solitary dinner and once more set himself to wait for her return. All this time alone gave him time to think. What had haunted him all day was the thought: *Was this the way my parents' marriage unraveled? An initial quarrel that divided them?* He had to find a way to rebuild a level of understanding between them. A simple apology wasn't enough. She had clearly misinterpreted what he said. Exactly what she thought he had implied by his words, he wasn't sure, and it behooved him to find out. Perhaps then he could correct it.

Something else was apparent to him also and made him feel slightly sick. Ava valued her friendship with Lannister highly. Highly enough to put her relationship with himself in jeopardy. But then, he reasoned, loyalty was one of Ava's strongest traits. She was fiercely loyal to those she cared about. It was obvious she did care about Lannister, as ill as that notion made *him* feel. She also was a fierce and stubborn champion of the lese privileged, the outsider, anyone shunned or overlooked by others, and Lannister's opprobrium in society would put him in that class in Ava's eyes.

But putting her loyalty to Lannister above her loyalty to him, her husband? He struggled with that.

By the time he heard the sounds of Ava's arrival home, he had thought himself to a standstill and he was deadly sober.

He went to the library door and opened it. Ava was crossing the entrance hall toward the stairs.

"Ava." His voice arrested her progress, and she turned at the bottom of the stairs, her hand on the newel post. "May I speak with you?"

She hesitated a moment, and then with an inclination of her head, she stepped toward him. He held the library door open for her, and she went ahead of him into the room. She was still wearing her cloak of ruched white satin over a gown of shimmering blue silk. Her hair was dressed in curls on top of her head, with fashionable ringlets at the sides. She looked like a fairy princess. No, he corrected that thought with a look at her face, an ice princess.

She clutched her reticule and her fan in tight fingers; her whitened knuckles were a clear signal of her inner turmoil, although none of it showed on her well-schooled features. She waited in silence for him to say something, and that was a surprise in itself. Ava was known for her impetuosity and impatience. A younger Ava would have burst into heated speech before this, unable to bear the silence.

He approached her carefully and took her hands in his, removing the reticule and fan and tossing them on the desk chair behind him. Holding her hands, he looked into her lovely blue eyes and said softly, "Ava, I am very sorry. It seems I have deeply offended you, and that was not my intention. Will you please explain to me how I have done so?"

She made a gasping sound, her lips parting and her eyes widening in surprise. Whatever she had thought he was going to say, it clearly wasn't that. *Had she braced herself for a scold?*

Her lower lip trembled, and her eyes welled. "I—how can you care more about what others think than for my feelings?"

He stared at her, at a loss. "I don't. Why would you think that?"

"Because you want me to give up my friendship with Rey for fear of what people might say! Even though you know that there is nothing in it to cause you concern."

"I am motivated by a desire to protect you from malicious gossip as well as myself. And I admit that I am hurt by your loyalty toward him over me. I am your husband, Ava, and I love you. Surely, I have more of a right to your loyalty than he does?"

She took a ragged breath and said wretchedly, "Yes, you do! But what hurts is your forcing me to make a choice between you!" She swallowed. "Very well, I shall hold him at a distance from now on, but will you allow me the opportunity to explain it to him?"

Relief washed through him at her capitulation, and he said roughly, "Of course."

She nodded and said, "Thank you." She turned aside, as if to go to the door, and his heart sank.

"Ava." He put his hands on her upper arms and pulled her back against him. "Ava love, please—"

With a sob she turned in his arms and pressed herself against his chest, her arms going around his waist. "I hate it when we are at outs," she confessed.

"So do I!" He cupped her face and kissed her. After a bit he said soft and low, "Am I welcome in your bedchamber again, my lady?"

"Yes," she said husky voiced.

He scooped her up and carried her upstairs to her room, where he got rid of her gown in short order, without destroying it this time or ruining his own attire, and tumbled her into bed.

A little while later, moving in her with his eyes fixed on hers, his weight on his elbows and his hands cupping her face, he said, "I love you, Ava. Never forget that."

"I love you, too," she said, blinking tears from her eyes. He caught one tear with his thumb and bent his head to catch the other with his tongue on her cheek.

"Don't cry, my darling!"

"I can't help it!" she said, sniffing. "I'm so happy!"

He smiled and kissed her. "Me too," he murmured.

If only we can remain so. We have weathered the first storm, but will there be more to come? He feared two such volatile souls were destined for a stormy passage, but he swore he would do everything he could to keep them on course. His fear of repeating the horrors of his parents' marriage, even without its horrific conclusion, had kept him from taking a wife. But with Ava, it would be different. It had to be different. He loved her so much. She loved him, or so she said. She was not his mother; he was not his father. Their marriage would be different.

Chapter Twenty-One

"My dear, I would not have recognized you! But then it is many years since I was wont to circulate in society. You were just a little girl when I saw you last."

Startled, Ava dragged her gaze from her charge who was executing the Boulanger with a thin, pimply young man and looked around into the haggard face of a middle-aged lady dressed in a gown that was severely out of date.

"You don't know who I am, do you?" she accused and rattled on with a false note of sweetness that set Ava's teeth on edge. "I am a friend of your mama. Surely, she has mentioned me to you? Lady Mostyn?"

Ava rose hastily and dropped a curtsy. A lady who was a friend of her mother's deserved respect, and the lady's name did ring vague bells. "Of course, Lady Mostyn. I'm afraid Mama has not come back to town yet. She is recuperating from a bout of illness. She will be sorry not be able to renew her acquaintance with you."

The lady smiled. But it didn't reach her eyes, which had a cold, bleak look to them. Her cheeks were sunken and lined, and her mouth was thin lipped and bracketed by deep lines on either side. It suddenly struck Ava how sad this woman was, and something tickled in the back of her head. There was some tragedy, wasn't there? Whatever it was, the details eluded her. Perhaps she never knew. After all, her mother's friends were of little interest to a child.

"May I sit?" the lady said, suiting action to words, and Ava perforce sat as well. "I wanted to congratulate you on your marriage, my dear. We are neighbors, you know."

"We are?"

"Oh yes. Our estates lie just north of Ravenshaw, on the coast."

"I see," said Ava, not seeing at all. "Do I take it this is your first visit to town for a while?"

"It is. I find things much changed in many respects, but in others, nothing has changed at all. The rumor mill still churns relentlessly, doesn't it?"

"Yes," Ava said, for what else could she say to such a truism?

"When I read about your marriage, I had to come and see for myself. I must say I am surprised your family consented to it." The smile that went with that made Ava's skin prickle.

Ever forthright, Ava said calmly, "Why is that, ma'am?"

The woman looked at her inscrutably for a minute or two and Ava fidgeted, acutely uncomfortable for a reason she couldn't put her finger on.

"You don't know, do you? They didn't tell you."

Ava flushed; her temper flicked. "Enough hints, my lady. You clearly have something to say. Please say it."

The other woman's smile this time was bitter. "You don't know the monster you've married."

"What?" Ava stiffened in defense of Jerome. "I don't know what you're referring to, and I will not listen to any disparagement of my husband!"

"Has you fooled, does he? But then he was always a consummate seducer of innocents. His father was another, cut from the same cloth. The apple doesn't fall far from the tree."

Ava stared at her, aghast. "You must be mistaken, madam, whatever you have heard—"

"My knowledge is not secondhand, my dear. I know what your precious husband did to my girl! My innocent little Charis. You ask him about Charis Dunsenay and see what he says, what lies he will tell you. Seduced her he did and then refused to do the right thing by her. Broke her heart, poor lamb. They found her body at the base of the cliffs. He's a murderer!" She spat the words at Ava with such venom that Ava flinched, her heart hammering wildly in her chest.

Lady Mostyn stared at Ava for a moment and then, as if satisfied with what she saw, she rose and said sweetly, "Do give my regards to your dear mama," and walked away, leaving Ava shattered.

Ava sat staring blindly in front of her, her mind in turmoil and her heart racing. Her initial reaction to deny that any of it was true was stopped by the fatal recall of that blasted gossip column in *The Chronicle*. *Lady-killer*—did they mean it literally? She tried to push the thought away. Of course not. Jerome hadn't killed anyone. But then she remembered Mama's distraught behavior when she learned of Ava's betrothal to Jerome. "Leopards don't change their spots" was what she said. But could Mama have truly believed such a dreadful thing of Jerome? And Robert? No, Rob had not believed it, or he would never have let her marriage to Jerome go forward. So it must be a pack of lies. But how could Mama have been so taken in? Mama had certainly jumped to the conclusion that Jerome had ruined her. Seduced her, presumably—which was not unreasonable, as it was generally the gentleman that did the ruining. *But no!* She refused to believe such horrible things about him.

She was jerked out of her stupor by Sophie's return to her side and forced to behave like a sensible creature for a few minutes. She was deputizing for Letty tonight who was suffering from fatigue. And Jerome had disappeared into the card room with Pendrell over an hour ago. If only he had been here when that dreadful woman approached her. *But then she probably wouldn't have done so, would she?*

Her object had clearly been to upset Ava. The malice in her eyes and the bitter satisfaction in them when she realized she had succeeded! Ava straightened her shoulders, her stubborn streak coming to the fore. She would not allow the horrible creature to cut up her peace. It was clear that the tragedy of whatever happened to her daughter had turned her mind. She was a bitter woman and perhaps mad because of it.

She would speak to Jerome about it, but not here. She would wait until they were alone, and she would not accuse him of anything. If there was any truth to any of it, if something had happened to this Charis person—well, there were two sides to every story, and she would hear Jerome's first before she started laying blame for any of it at his door.

And there, am I not behaving like a grownup? Waiting instead of impetuously blurting things out, jumping to conclusions. She smiled to herself, proud of her demonstration of patience. She could pretend for a few hours that horrible woman had not destroyed her happiness. *I am quite good at dissembling after all.*

JEROME KNEW THE moment he returned to her side that there was something wrong. Ava had that glassy-eyed, brittle look, and her laugh was a shade too loud, as if forced. It had fooled him once, but not now. He knew her too well for that. But the middle of a ball wasn't the place to find out what or who had upset her.

It wasn't until they had returned Sophie to her home that he was able to put his arms around his wife and ask her what was wrong. Since she visibly flinched when he touched her, he knew it was serious, and he felt both a pang and a spurt of anger that someone had hurt her.

"What is it, sweetheart?" he asked.

She tried to smile and failed. Shaking her head, she said quietly, "Wait until we get home."

So, he was forced to wait until they were finally alone in the library, where she led him. Which had him very alarmed. This was serious.

She stopped before the fireplace, her hands clasped tightly at her waist over her green satin-and-net ball gown. She turned resolutely toward him and said quietly, "Tell me about Charis Dunsenay."

He stifled a groan. *I knew this moment would come, didn't I?* How could he have fooled himself that she wouldn't hear something about it from some malicious or indeed innocent source? He had a moment to regret not telling her himself. But he had hoped against hope that the past would stay buried. After all, Rob hadn't told her, and he could have. But he had chosen to protect her—as Jerome had—from something that would hurt her. And he had to acknowledge he'd been protecting himself as well. *Have I been a coward? Probably. Almost certainly.*

She was holding herself very still, and he marveled at the change in her. Normally she would be impatient, demanding explanations. But here she stood, still and waiting, her expression carefully controlled. Only her clenched hands gave away her inner agitation.

"Come and sit down," he said gently, holding out his hand to her.

She hesitated a moment and then put her hand in his and let him lead her to the couch where they sat, and he kept hold of her hand. He needed the anchor of her touch while he searched for the right way to tell her something which had haunted him for eight years.

"Charis Dunsenay is—was—the daughter of Lord and Lady Mostyn. She was eighteen when I knew her, not yet out."

Ava's indrawn breath was audible, and her hand jerked in his hold at this; he tightened his grip to prevent her pulling away.

"I was invited to their estate for some hunting with a party of others in the summer of 1812. I was twenty-six. Ravenshaw wasn't habitable at that time. I generally didn't visit it except to meet with my steward and would stay in the local hostelry if I did." He paused, trying to steady his pulse. Recalling the events of that summer brought him out in a cold sweat and made him feel physically ill.

He breathed and went on doggedly. "Charis was an excellent rider to hounds and her father let her join us for the hunt. It became rapidly obvious to me that she was"—he paused, looking for the right word—"interested in me." He flushed uncomfortably. "In those days, it was not uncommon for young women to attempt to attach me, and I'd adopted a rather ruthless method of dealing with it. That is what gave me such a dangerous reputation."

Ava was watching him steadily and said quietly, "It never stopped, did it?. I've seen them throw themselves at you over the past two years."

His lips twisted in a grimace. "Not as much as when I was younger. My method was supposed to discourage them. It seemed to have the opposite effect. The more dangerous I was said to be, the more they tried." He sighed and rubbed his face with one hand. "Charis was quite bold, and I didn't realize how young she was at first. I thought she must have been at least twenty."

"Was she pretty?"

"Very." He swallowed. "A petite, blue-eyed blonde."

"Oh!" Ava's calm expression cracked, and she flicked wide troubled eyes at him.

"The house party stretched over two weeks, and despite not being officially out, Charis was allowed to mix with the guests as if she were. She had ample time to—pursue me." He grimaced. "I confess I didn't discourage her. It was obvious to me that her campaign had her parents' approval, if not outright contrivance. Her father's and my estates run parallel. A marriage between me and Charis would bring the two together and enhance them both. What I didn't know at the time was how dire his financial situation was."

"So they targeted you?"

"Yes, I believe so, although it is a hard thing to prove, and given what happened later—but I'm getting ahead of the tale." He took a breath and plowed on. "At the end of the two weeks the other guests departed, but I had been persuaded to stay on one more night. That night, I woke to find Charis in my bed, naked."

Ava jerked. "Were you drunk?"

"Not particularly. I'd had some wine with dinner and a couple of glasses of port I think, afterward, but no, I wasn't drunk."

"Did you kiss her?" Ava's voice had a hollow sound, and he tightened his grip on her hand.

"Not then, but I had earlier." He paused again, recalling his feelings on waking to find the young woman in his bed. "It was then that I fully realized the lengths my hosts were prepared to go to, to trap me. It was imperative I got Charis out of my bedchamber as quickly as possible, but of course the whole thing had been planned down to the last detail, and I was barely awake and aware of what was going on before her father charged into the room full of righteous indignation, demanding that I make an honest woman of his innocent daughter." He shook his head.

"I was angry—furious, in fact—and I refused. I dressed, packed my bags, and left the house that night to stay the rest of the night at the local inn. I knew I was in trouble, for the other guests had seen ample evidence of a flirtation between myself and Charis. I'd let my anger blind me to the realities of the situation. Dunsenay only had to reveal that I had seduced his daughter— and no one would believe I hadn't in the circumstances—and my reputation as a gentleman would be ruined. Realizing this, I returned the next morning to tell Dunsenay I would marry Charis, only to find the house in an uproar, for Charis had vanished in the night."

"Oh! What happened to her?" Ava was by now caught up in the story with him, her hand clutching his tightly.

"Dunsenay and I immediately set out to try to find her. We split up. He went north, and I went south along the coast. His property, like mine, reaches to the sea. He was convinced she would have gone to the shore. She loved the sea."

He stopped and closed his eyes.

"I found her." These were the memories he had fought so hard to suppress. "She was standing on the edge of the cliff overlooking the sea. I called to her, and at first she didn't hear me, I think, over the wind and the sound of the sea. She was wearing a cloak over her thin gown, but she was cold, visibly shivering. I dismounted from my horse and approached her. She heard me then and turned to look at me. Her face was pale, and I knew she had been crying.

"A shout behind me alerted me to the fact that her father had arrived. She took a step back then, and I made a grab for her cloak. She was standing right on the edge and—I don't know exactly what happened—I think the earth crumbled under her feet. Her arms flailed, and I tried to grab her, but she went over with a cry. I—" He stopped, his voice suspended by the tight horror in his throat.

Ava made a noise and grabbed his hand tighter.

"I'll never forget the look of terror on her face as long as I live. She fell into the sea. It was high tide, and the waves swallowed her. Her body was dashed onto the rocks. I saw it tossed around like a rag doll in the foaming water." He gasped in memory.

"I had to wait until the tide retreated to retrieve her body. Her father was distraught, and ten days later he shot himself in his study. It was then that I found out how much debt he was in." Jerome rubbed his face tiredly. "I was to be their means of escape from debt. Instead, they lost their daughter, and he was threatened with debtors' prison. Rather than face that, and I am guessing clouded with grief and perhaps guilt, he took his own life, leaving his wife alone and miserable."

"Oh, Jerome!" Ava wrapped her arms around him, and he sagged with relief at her reception of the tale that had haunted him for eight years, guilt pressing him down with an at times unbearable weight.

"That must have been dreadful," said Ava, her face buried in his jacket.

"It was," he admitted over her head. His arms tightened around her and Ava nuzzled closer. "Who told you about Charis Dunsenay?" he asked, his heartbeat slowing slightly with relief at her reaction. And the relief of telling her the truth.

"Her mother, Lady Mostyn."

"She is in town?" he said, startled. *Why the hell would she come all this way? And why now?*

Ava pulled back to look up at him. "Yes, she heard about our marriage and seems to have traveled all the way to London to tell me that you murdered her daughter." She swallowed. "I didn't believe her, of course, but it was an awful shock. Mama apparently knew about it, which means Rob must, too. Why didn't anyone tell me?"

"They were trying to protect you. Rob taxed me with the story your mother had told him, and I told him what I've just told you." He recalled Robert's reception of the tale and the relief he had felt then, too, when Rob hugged him like a brother.

"No wonder Mama was so horrified. But once Rob knew the truth, why didn't he tell her?"

"I don't know. Perhaps he did tell her, she didn't believe it?"

"Why didn't *you* tell *me*?" Her voice had a note of indignation that made him wince.

"I should have." He stroked a finger down her cheek. "I was afraid to. I thought you would hate me for my part in it. I'm not blameless, Ava. I didn't kill her outright, but her death can be attributed to my actions." *And I failed to save her when she lost her balance. If I had been quicker to catch her . . .* They were thoughts and recriminations that had haunted him for years.

Ava shook her head. "It wasn't your fault! It was an accident. She fell. You tried to save her." Her hand gripped the lapel of his jacket.

"She wouldn't have been standing on that cliff edge if it

weren't for me." *It is my fault, no matter how one tries to justify it.*

"Nonsense, she pursued you!" Ava's hot defense of him sent a burst of warmth through his chest.

"At her parents' behest." *Which was true . . .*

"Exactly! If anyone is to blame it is them for putting her in such a position. They used her for their own ends. It's appalling!" *Agreed . . .*

"I suppose if you put it that way . . ." *But it seemed such a horrendous thing for parents to do.*

"Did you not see it that way?" Ava insisted.

"I have always been too consumed with guilt and horror to think too deeply on it." His throat tightened. He had simply known it was his fault. *All of it.* "She was only eighteen!" His voice cracked in anguish. Ava touched his face and kissed him. His arms clenched around her convulsively. "Oh, Ava," he whispered. "I love you so damned much!" He swallowed the thickness in his throat, his fear that she would reject him for his part in this tragedy receding.

She smiled up at him. "I love you. Did you really think I could credit you were a murderer? Never!" She hugged him close. "Never!" she said against his jacket. Warmth curled into his chest and his love for this wonderful woman swelled and grew. *How can I ever be worthy of her?* His arms tightened round her. *Ava! Sweet Ava!*

"My darling," he murmured against her hair. "Come to bed?" he asked husky voiced.

She nodded, and they went up to her room, where they removed each other's clothing between kisses and caresses and tumbled into bed in a tangle of limbs and heat.

Later Jerome held his sleeping wife in his arms and thanked God for the gift of her. For the first time in eight years, some of the guilt that had oppressed his soul felt lightened. Ava's unequivocal acceptance of his version of events, her fierce defense of him, filled up the aching void inside him more than he deserved.

Oh Ava, I love you so much!

Perhaps now he could begin to put the past behind him and truly embrace the good fortune that marriage to this wonderful woman had brought him. Hope for their future made his heart soar with joy and trepidation. *Do I dare to believe we can be happy together forever?*

Chapter Twenty-Two

TWO WEEKS LATER, Jerome and Ava returned to the house from their customary morning ride in Hyde Park. Ava set her feet on the stairs, saying, "I shall just go up to change. I promised Mama I would visit her this morning. She is quite prostrate from traveling."

Jerome smiled to watch her running up the stairs, his heart full with adoration for his wife, and turned to hand his hat and coat to Skelton, who said quietly, "My lord, there is a gentleman to speak with you. I put him and his companions in the front parlor."

The expression on Skelton's face told Jerome his butler didn't approve of these visitors, and he said mildly, "Thank you, Skelton."

He opened the parlor door and surveyed its occupants. One was seated in an armchair, the other two stood before the unlit fireplace with their hands behind their backs. The seated man was dressed with an elegant propriety that indicated a superior status compared to his companions, whose attire was worn and greasy. Skelton had not seen fit to take any of the visitors' hats.

Jerome shut the door as the seated gentleman rose from his seat, and he advanced into the room.

"You wished to speak with me?" he asked, puzzled and with a

vague prickle of alarm running over his skin at the somber expression on all three men's faces.

The gentleman, who was middle-aged and somewhat corpulent, said, "Jerome DeVere, Marquess of Ravenshaw?"

"Yes," replied Jerome, his heart kicking up.

The other man bowed. "Josiah Forbes, Magistrate, Bow Street." He held out a folded piece of paper with a red seal on it. "My lord, it is my sad duty to inform you—"

Jerome took the paper from him and inspected the seal. *His Majesty, King George IV.* He broke the seal and scanned the paper as the other man continued to speak.

"I have a warrant for your arrest for the murder of the Honorable Miss Charis Dunsenay on the 11th of July, 1812."

Reading the same words on the paper, Jerome's head reeled. *This couldn't be happening!*

"No." he said, shaking his head. "Miss Dunsenay's death was an accident. I tried to save her as she fell." He stared into the impassive face of the magistrate before him.

"That will be a matter for the court to decide, my lord. If you will accompany me?"

Jerome swallowed, his brain whirling. "I gather you mean to detain me? May I have a few moments to collect some of my effects?"

The magistrate bowed again. "Of course, my lord. We will await your pleasure."

Jerome nodded and left the room. He headed first to the library where he scrawled three notes, which he handed to Skelton to arrange for delivery. "Please ask Leyton to pack a valise for me, with sufficient clothing for an extended stay. I will be away for a number of nights. I am not sure how many at this juncture."

Skelton raised his eyebrows but bowed and said, "Of course, my lord."

Jerome then took the stairs two at a time to Ava's bedchamber. He found her with her maid and said kindly to the girl,

"Please leave us. I need to speak with Her Ladyship." The girl bobbed a curtsy and left, and Ava turned to him, her eyes wide.

"What is it?"

He took her hands and said carefully, "I have received a warrant for my arrest—"

"What? What for?" Ava's face paled.

"The murder of Charis Dunsenay."

"No! No! How—?"

"I can only assume that Lady Mostyn, not satisfied with her attempt to wreak havoc between us, has decided to bring an action against me. There are a magistrate and two Bow Street Runners below to cart me off to Newgate—"

"No!" shrieked Ava, her hands clutching at him, tears streaking down her cheeks.

"It isn't so bad as it seems, love. I am wealthy and can pay for comforts in prison. And I have influential friends. This matter will be dealt with swiftly." He pulled her close and hugged her. "Now I need you to be strong for me. Can you do that?"

She nodded, clinging to him, her tears soaking his jacket.

"Good. Now listen, I need you to go to Letty and tell her to secure the services of Sir William Garrow on my behalf. He is a first-rate barrister, former politician, and judge and a man of principle. I am confident he will extricate me from this situation with all speed. Get him to come to me at Newgate, and we will see the wheels put in motion to deal with this situation. I have already sent notes to Rob, Pendrell, and Ashford. They will do what they can on my behalf. I will be with you again very soon, love, do not doubt it."

"Jerome!" she clung to him. "You are innocent, and so I shall tell anyone who dares to say otherwise!"

He smiled, his throat tight with love for her. "I know, love!" He kissed her then. Several kisses and tight hugs later, he left her to collect his valise, stop by the library to get himself some paper, pens, ink, and reading matter, and rejoin Mr. Forbes and his men, dressed in his overcoat and hat.

Ava followed him down and out into the street, where he took a final farewell of her under the embarrassed eyes of the magistrate and stepped up into the hackney that would transport him to Newgate prison.

AVA WATCHED THE carriage disappear from her sight down the street and turned with determination to request her carriage immediately. Twenty minutes later, she burst in upon her sister-in-law with the news of Jerome's arrest.

Letty, who had been lying on a chaise longue in her dressing room, sat up in alarm at Ava's stormy advent and, once in possession of the facts, said with calm practicality, "We shall visit Sir William immediately. Fortunately, I know him, which is why Jerome suggested you come to me to request his assistance. I must say he is an excellent barrister; his record of wins is extremely high. And in this case, the outcome cannot be in doubt, for Jerome is innocent and there is not sufficient evidence that the charge could be proven in any case. Do not despair, my love, we shall prevail."

The ladies met with Sir William Garrow at his home in Great George Street. The man was sixty but still hale and vigorous, Ava was pleased to note, and having heard their story, he was very willing to wait upon the marquess at Newgate.

JEROME'S CELL AT Newgate was on the top floor and had a window, a fireplace, and a bed with a real mattress and bed-clothes, so he was far more fortunate than most of the inmates of that hellhole. He was also blessed with a table and two chairs and candles for light. He was located in the central block above the keeper's house, which was much less noisome than the other parts of the prison and boasted four larger than normal cells with fireplaces like his and windows.

He was not so foolish as to think that his bedding was free of the vermin that infested the place and reflected that his clothes would need to be fumigated or, more likely, burnt when he left the prison. Or he could gift them to the inmates? That was probably the best idea.

The room was stone walled with a wooden floor and painted ceiling. There was even a rug on the floor. Really, if it weren't for the great iron door with its grid and the bars on the windows behind the casements, he could almost fancy himself in a room in an ordinary inn.

He had been conducted to his cell by the keeper himself with much bowing and scraping—the man had pocketed immediately the sum Jerome handed across for the privilege of being housed in this superior room. He had barely settled into his new abode when he received a visit from Sir William Garrow.

The barrister was shown into the room by the keeper who received another *douceur* for the service.

"Sir William." Jerome held out his hand to the barrister, who was a tall, well-made man who looked younger than his sixty years. "My wife obeyed my instructions immediately, I take it. Thank you for attending me here. Please take a seat." He indicated the guest chair and took the other himself.

As Sir William lowered himself into the chair, he said, "Indeed, I was most delighted to receive a call from your wife and sister. I am, as I gather you apprehend, quite well acquainted with your sister and her husband. And I believe we may have spoken briefly in Parliament when I was a sitting member over my cruelty-to-horses bill that you were so kind as to support."

"We did, although I did not know if you would remember."

"I do remember, my lord." Sir William smiled and settled into his chair, taking out a traveling desk from a case that he had brought with him. He arranged this on his lap and uncapped the inkwell. Dipping his pen, he wrote something across the top of the piece of paper before him.

"Now, my lord, your good ladies furnished me with brief particulars of your case. However, I need to hear the whole story from you. By the way, before I came here, I stopped in at Bow Street and ascertained that Sir Nicholas Connyngham Tindal will be representing Lady Mostyn as the prosecutor. Normally I would not be able to obtain a copy of the charges against you, but given your special status as a peer, an exception was made. Naturally, because of your elevated position, the matter will be heard before the House of Lords, as soon as may be convenient to their lordships."

"Thank you." Jerome inclined his head and felt a wash of relief flood his chest, and the tight, sick feeling he'd had in his stomach since he was first apprised of the warrant for his arrest eased.

"Now, my lord, your story if you please."

So Jerome proceeded to tell him. While he spoke, Garrow made notes and occasionally asked for clarification of a point. At the end of it, the barrister sat back with a grin of satisfaction which Jerome thought was a heartening sign.

"My lord, I venture to say that you have nothing to worry about. We shall have you out of here in a trice. The only witness to this terrible tragedy besides yourself is the late Lord Mostyn. The case will be thrown out for lack of evidence and a verdict of accidental death given, mark my words. There is ample evidence that the Dunsenays connived to trap you into compromising their daughter. No doubt the prosecution will bring forth such witnesses to corroborate your flirtation with the girl. But never fear, I shall turn them to account."

"You cheer me immensely with this news, Sir William." Jerome sat back in some relief.

Garrow began to pack his traveling desk away and stood to shake Jerome's hand. "A pleasure, my lord. I look forward to defending this case with the greatest enthusiasm. It quite takes me back to my younger days."

Jerome rose to shake his hand and see him to the door, where a guard unlocked the heavy iron door and let Sir William out.

As the door shut on him again, Jerome turned away to the window from which he could see the street, for the cells were arranged along the outer wall of the building. *How long will I be incarcerated for?* He had asked Rob and his friends to urge that the matter be dealt with as soon as possible. Rob would go straight to Attorney General Brougham and Prime Minister Liverpool, to have the matter brought before the house as soon as possible.

His friends would naturally speak on his behalf as character witnesses. Indeed, it was hardly needed; he was known to almost the entire membership of the house. They knew the good and the bad of him, but his newly married status should be a point in his favor. It could be shown that whatever unsteadiness of character he may have shown in his youth, he had, of later years, demonstrated more moderation. Although there was that cursed article in *The Chronicle* . . .

He heaved a sigh and lay down on the bed, suddenly bone weary even though he had done little beyond riding with Ava that morning. Thoughts of Ava brought an ache of longing to his chest. *I miss her so.*

Chapter Twenty-Three

ALL IN ALL, Jerome spent eight nights in Newgate before being summoned to attend the House of Lords, during which time Ava, in defiance of his instructions, visited him twice.

The first occasion was on the second day.

"Ava!" He sprang up from his chair, where he was sitting before the table under the window, writing.

"Jerome!" She flew into his arms and hugged him, and he lifted her slightly off her feet in an exuberant hug and kiss, so delighted to see her that he forgot for a moment the impropriety of her visiting him here.

"My love," he murmured against her hair.

"Oh, Jerome, I've missed you so!" she said tearfully.

"And I have missed you, my darling, but you really shouldn't be here. It's not seemly."

"I don't care about that. Everything is so horrid without you. And people are saying the meanest things! It is all too dreadful. Poor Sophie is suffering too because of it, and I was afraid Letty would be angry about it, but she has been a tower of strength."

"Letty is the very best," he said quietly. "I never fully appreciated her until this year. Come sit on the bed with me and tell me everything that is going on. But I warn you, the bedclothes may contain passengers who will want to ride home with you."

"Urgh!" Ava wrinkled her nose but sat anyway. "Lady Mostyn has been stoking the fires, and gossip is rife. Whenever I enter a room, people stop talking! It's awful. Most people are keeping their distance from me. A few have given me the cut direct, but the majority are waiting to see what the outcome of the trial is before cutting ties with me completely. But I will remember who stood my friend and who did not. Robert has been marvelous. He has considerable influence, you know, and his steadfast support of your innocence has been wonderful. You know how starched up he can be?"

Jerome nodded with a smile.

"Well, he has been coming the Grand Duke with everyone and that has given them pause. And then there is Mama. She has been absolutely magnificent. She quarreled dreadfully with Lady Mostyn. For you must know, I told Mama what you told me, and Rob backed me up. We were able to convince her that she had been duped by Lady Mostyn. Rob had tried to tell her earlier what you had told him, but she wouldn't listen then. And, of course, Rob told Ashford and Pendrell as well. So, the three of them are standing buff for you. And Rey as well, for what it's worth."

"I'm obliged to him," he said sardonically, not particularly heartened to hear that Ava was in contact with Lannister.

"You mustn't mind that I spoke to him. I had to tell him the truth for I could not bear him to think there was anything in the rumors. They are quite outlandish, you know."

"What *are* the rumors?" he asked, bracing himself.

"There are any number and each more lurid than the last. The latest is that Charis was with child, and she confronted you on the cliff, and you threw her off!" Ava's indignation at this horrendous lie would have been comical if the situation weren't so dire. *How are we ever to recover from this scandal?*

"I am so sorry you are being subjected to this. Perhaps it would be better to stay home and not go out in society?"

"What, and let them think you are guilty? Never!" said Ava,

her eyes flashing blue fire.

"Oh, my darling, I do love you," he said with a besotted grin and kissed her. A little while later he said unsteadily, "You must leave, sweetheart. I appreciate your visit more than you can know, but you shouldn't be here. Promise me you won't come here again. I am confident I won't be detained for long."

"I shall visit you as often as is needful," she said firmly, with a martial light in her eye. "No one will keep me from my husband's side."

He considered arguing with her and decided not to, for there was another point he wanted to make instead. "Very well, my love, but I hope that you are being discreet in your dealings with Lannister, for the last thing we need is for the gossips to link your name with his in anything clandestine with me locked up. You do see how that would look, don't you?"

She screwed her face up and nodded. "It's horrid and completely untrue, but yes, I do see. I will be careful, I promise."

HE ALSO RECEIVED visits from Robert, Ashford, and Pendrell, who all assured him of their support.

When Rob came to see him, one look at the man's face was enough to tell him how much strain he was under, and Jerome winced with guilt.

"I'm so sorry, Rob," he said.

"Nonsense! This is not your fault. It's that wretched woman's malice."

"But you're not sleeping!"

Robert's face twisted in a tired smile. "That's not down to you, old chap. My son and heir is going through a period of not sleeping. And I confess on top of that, my little brother is causing me some anxiety."

"Kenrick?"

Rob rubbed his eyes and nodded. "Be glad you don't have siblings to cause you grief! I thank God for Heather and Hereward. They at least never give me any gray hairs. As for Ingrid, I dread the day she is released from the schoolroom. I'll be white haired in a week once we launch her on the *ton!* She will make Ava look like an angel."

"Ava is an angel!" said Jerome, bristling instantly in Ava's defense.

Rob smiled tiredly. "I will say marriage seems to suit her. Perhaps the secret to managing Ingrid will be to get her married as soon as possible. Then she will be someone else's problem!"

"What's Rick done?" asked Jerome, glad to be talking of something other than his own problems.

"Ruined a young lady and refused to do the honorable thing! I'm so angry with him—there is only so much even my credit can withstand. The Layne name is getting rapidly tarnished."

Jerome winced. "Who—?" The door opening cut off his inquiry in mid-stream as Emrys and Deo came in, and the conversation reverted to his situation.

Jerome sustained a second visit from Sir William on the seventh day of his incarceration to inform him that his case would be heard in the House of Lords in two days' time, and to brief him on his strategy for the defense.

"You will no doubt be forced to make a statement and questioned by the prosecution, who will attempt to twist your words to convict you. I straightly advise you to stick to the facts as you know them. Do not allow the prosecution to cozen you into surmises or speculation. I will do the rest. I am confident of full exoneration."

Ava's second visit was on the heels of Garrow's and principally to assure him that he was certain to be successful. At least that was her avowed reason. He wondered how much of it was to reassure herself. Holding her close, he took solace from her unwavering belief in him and swore that once he was free of this terrible consequence of his past actions, he would spend the rest of his life trying to be worthy of this wonderful woman who, despite all this shame and scandal, seemed proud to call herself his wife.

Thus, Jerome arrived at the House of Lords in a hackney, accompanied by two Bow Street Runners—who were acutely uncomfortable escorting a peer of the realm—and entered the halls of Westminster with a heart that beat too fast and, despite Sir William's encouraging words, a sick pit of fear in his stomach.

He was as immaculately dressed for the occasion as his circumstances allowed. And if his linen wasn't as crisp as he would like, he hoped none but the most discerning eyes would notice. Even so, *he* knew, and it dented his confidence. Then he thought of Ava, and he set his shoulders back and lifted his head. Her love would sustain him through this, and then they would be reunited once more and able to put this terrible episode behind them.

He walked into the chamber with, if not quite his usual nonchalant air, then at least pride in his bearing and the knowledge that, linen or no, he was still one of the best-dressed men in the room.

The buzz of conversation in the room was loud, for the space was full. It was a long, high-ceilinged chamber with six magnificent gold chandeliers and half-circle clerestory windows along the outside wall to afford light. The lower three quarters of the walls were dressed in red brocade wallpaper and red hangings hung over the entrances at the front of the room and behind the King's Throne, which was the focal point of the room's design.

Rows of seats lined the walls, and platforms down either side provided a second tier of seating. The upper portion of the walls and ceiling were painted cream, so the overall effect was of red, cream, and gold opulence, accented by wood paneling on the high dado line below the windows and in the red upholstered pews upon which the lords sat. Several rows of these also occupied the center of the room, and at the rear, behind them, the table at which the bewigged learned gentlemen of the bar sat or stood.

It was to one end of this large table that Jerome was guided to take his seat beside Sir William, robed in black, with his long wig upon his head. At the other end was Sir Nicholas Connyngham Tindal with his client, Lady Mostyn, who was the only woman in the room. Between them were sundry fellows in smaller wigs, whom Jerome surmised to be attorneys or clerks of court as they were all busily scribbling.

Lady Mostyn stiffened at the sight of him and glared malevolently at him. He stared back, unsmiling, determined that she would not provoke him into revealing shame or guilt. He inclined his head in acknowledgment of her and then took his seat.

The house quietened, and after some preliminaries the case got under way. The charges were read out, and the prosecution made the opening address. Lady Mostyn did not speak, leaving the address to her counsel.

In his conclusion to his opening remarks, Tindal said, "I put it to you, my lords, that this man, whose reputation as a libertine is well known to you all," he waved in Jerome's direction with disdain, "did willfully and maliciously seduce an innocent young girl of only eighteen summers, and when caught compromising her, refuse to do the right thing by her. Not content with that, he then, upon discovering her alone and frightened on the edge of a dangerous cliff, did throw her from said cliff into the sea and only afterward claim that she fell. This stain upon the peerage is a murderer in cold blood, so lost to all gentlemanly instincts that when given the opportunity to absolve his sin, he did refuse and place an innocent young girl in utmost peril. I therefore ask you, my lords, in good conscience, that you find him guilty of murder and sentence him to hang."

He paused at this point while murmurs ran around the house. Jerome sat through this barrage of lies with his head up and attempted to look as unconcerned as possible.

"I shall now call my witnesses," went on Tindal. "Is Lord Barrington in the house?"

"Aye," said Barrington. A middle-aged man, short of stature

and with a tendency to corpulence, rose in his seat.

"Will you step forward, my lord, and answer a few questions?" requested Tindal.

"Happy to, sir," said Barrington, leaving his seat in the pews to join them at the table. Barrington was sworn in.

"My lord, were you a guest of Lord and Lady Mostyn in July of 1812 at their estate in Northumberland?"

"I was."

"And was this man, the Marquess of Ravenshaw, also a guest at that time?"

"He was." Barrington threw Jerome a dark look from under his graying brows.

"And did you note during your stay any contact between Miss Charis Dunsenay and the Marquess?"

"I should say so," said Barrington with a hearty chuckle. "The little minx set her cap at him from the start."

It was at this point that Sir William rose and said, "Do you affirm that Miss Dunsenay encouraged my client's attentions?"

"Well, yes. It was obvious she was mightily taken with him, but then, that was nothing new. All the females in London were on the scramble for him."

"Thank you, Lord Barrington." Sir William sat and made a note.

Tindal, somewhat discomposed by Sir William's interruption, continued his questioning. "And what, in your opinion, was the marquess's reaction to Miss Dunsenay's interest?"

"He flirted with her blatantly. We all saw it and commented," said Barrington.

"Thank you, my lord, that is all. Unless my learned friend has any more questions?"

Sir William rose. "Thank you, Sir Nicholas. As a matter of fact, I do." He cleared his throat and turned his gaze upon Lord Barrington. "My lord, how much opportunity did my client have to pursue a flirtation with a girl not out in society? Surely Miss Dunsenay was too young to be mingling with a party of male guests, even if the event was at her home."

"She had plenty. She was included in the hunt and sat down to dinner with us. In fact, I'm surprised to know that she was only eighteen. We all assumed she was older."

"So, in your opinion, Lord Barrington, would you think it reasonable that the marquess thought the girl was a young woman of perhaps twenty?"

"Yes, perfectly reasonable."

"Thank you, my lord, that is all."

Barrington bowed and returned to his seat.

Tindal glared at Sir William, who smiled blandly back at him, and he called his second witness, Lord Revesby, who was also a guest of the Dunsenays that July. Lord Revesby's testimony backed up Barrington's and Sir William asked him the same questions and got the same answers.

Tindal's third witness was Lady Mostyn. The lady's performance was masterly. Dabbing tears from her ravaged cheeks, she denounced Ravenshaw as a libertine, a scoundrel, and a murderer.

Her bitter tirade was brought to an abrupt close by Sir William rising and addressing her stridently. "Madam, I put to you that everything you have said is balderdash!"

The lady stiffened in shock. But before she could say anything, he barreled on.

"Is it true that your eighteen-year-old daughter, who was not out yet in society, was permitted to participate in the events of the house party at which these gentlemen and my client were present?"

"My Charis was an accomplished horsewoman; she always rode to hounds with her father since she was twelve."

"And was she accompanied on these forays by a chaperone?"

"She was accompanied by her father. She needed no chaperone."

"And is it true that she sat down to dinner with a table full of gentlemen?"

"And myself, yes."

"And how exactly was the marquess allegedly meant to have compromised your daughter, Lady Mostyn?"

"There is nothing alleged about it! He did. My husband found them in bed together!"

This bald statement sent a shock wave of murmurs around the room and Jerome willed himself not to blush guiltily.

"And when was this, Lady Mostyn?"

"On the evening of the 11th of July, 1812," she said, swallowing and dabbing at her cheeks again. "It was the last time I saw her alive." Her voice dissolved into sobs.

"So did you see your daughter in bed with the marquess?"

The lady sniffed and blew her nose. "No. But my husband told me of it and the conversation he had with Ravenshaw and the fact that Ravenshaw refused to marry my poor innocent girl."

"That is hearsay, Lady Mostyn, and not permitted as evidence. Your Lordships must disregard it. Lady Mostyn, is it true that your husband is dead, is it not?"

"Yes."

"And he shot himself ten days after Charis's death, am I correct?"

"Yes. He was so distraught over Charis—"

"Then the only witnesses to this *compromising*, other than my client, are dead—your daughter and your husband. Is that correct?"

Lady Mostyn looked to her counsel.

"Is that correct, Lady Mostyn?" pressed Sir William. "Were any servants present?" he asked.

"N-no. There were no servants present. To my knowledge, only my husband and my daughter."

"I see. My lords, I suggest to you that you consider several points here in this case: firstly, that there is no independent eyewitness to the events purported to have occurred. Secondly, that the young lady in question behaved with unbecoming boldness as witnessed by Lords Barrington and Revesby, with the connivance and positive encouragement of her parents, to entrap my client who is—or rather was, until recently—one of London's most eligible bachelors. And Lord Ravenshaw is a wealthy man. This may seem irrelevant to the case until it is revealed that at the time these heinous events took place, Lord Mostyn was in serious debt." He paused to let this sink in with his audience, who were all riveted to his discourse.

Lady Mostyn whimpered at this and wiped her eyes.

Tindal rose and said, "There is one more point I would like to make in closing out the case for the prosecution, my lords. I wish to apprise you of facts that have come to light recently in relation to the present Marquess of Ravenshaw's mother—" Jerome heard this with alarm, his heart rate increasing and a sweat breaking out on his forehead.

"How is this relevant to the case?" asked Sir William.

"If you will allow me a moment, I will explain," returned Tindal with a supercilious air. "The late Marchioness of Ravenshaw was prone to ill health. And—strange fancies."

"I repeat of what relevance—"

"If you will allow me to continue!" Tindal said with some asperity. "Her Ladyship's condition was a sad trial to her husband. On several occasions he contemplated having her committed to an institution where her condition could be treated." Jerome's hands clenched on the arms of his chair, wondering wildly where this was going. "But his compassion for his wife stayed his hand." Tindal paused. "It is a well-known fact that the marchioness fell to her death from the balcony of her bedchamber window at the height of a terrible storm. It should also be noted that it was a full moon that night. The coroner gave a verdict of accidental death under the, ah—persuasion of the former marquess. in order that the lady could be buried in hallowed ground."

Sir William Garrow slapped his hand upon the table and said loudly, "If my friend at the bar could get to the point of his peroration, perhaps we could see the relevance of this piece of hearsay to the case at hand?" A quite murmur went round the room.

"It is not hearsay, Sir William." He produced a slender leatherbound book and held it aloft. "This is the late marchioness's diary. A perusal of it will make it quite clear that Lady Ravenshaw suffered from delusions, that she was subject to fits of melancholy, and that she had persuaded herself that her husband was an evil man bent upon her destruction. In short, Lady Ravenshaw was mad. And it was only her husband's kindness and forbearance that stood between her and Bedlam."

Jerome clenched his teeth and looked at Sir William, who was frowning at Tindal in bewilderment.

"I shall quote a short passage," continued Tindal, perching his glasses upon his nose and opening the volume to a marked page. He cleared his throat and began to read. *"Gareth means to have me locked up. The laudanum brings me no relief from my nightmares. I cannot go on."*

He looked up from the page and lowered the book, removing his spectacles. "That entry was dated the very day that Lady Ravenshaw took her own life by flinging herself from the balcony of her bedchamber. The woman committed self murder. She was therefore, by definition, insane."

He looked across at Jerome and said calmly, "It is a well-known fact that insanity is hereditary. I ask you gentlemen to consider that the marquess may be subject to the same illness of the mind as his mother. After all, not so long ago he was found asleep under a tree in Hyde Park. And a witness saw him the previous night hugging that tree. Is that the behavior of a sane man? I put it to you, gentlemen, it was that illness that caused him to be so lost to honor as to refuse to do right by Miss Dunsenay and to subsequently push her into the sea. The man is a murderer. There is no question of that. The only real question is: Was he of sound mind when he did it?"

The effect of this on the house was electric, a loud buzz springing up. Jerome sat stunned. How had Tindal come by his mother's diary? Could he be right? Had he been wrong in his assumptions that it was his father's hand that killed his mother? Could she indeed have jumped? He had not been home at all that year, choosing to stay at school rather than come home in the holidays. He was dizzy with the possibility, as his life appeared to be unraveling in front of him.

Chapter Twenty-Four

S IR WILLIAM SPRANG to his feet. "My learned friend is deranged! On what *possible* grounds can you bring such a charge? You have provided no evidence whatsoever that my client's mind is unsound! His mother's death and its possible cause have no relevance at all to this case! My Lord Chancellor, I implore you to restore order and common sense to these proceedings and have done with these flights of fantasy!"

Lord Eldon, the Lord Chancellor, shifted uncomfortably on the woolsack and cleared his throat. "I believe I must support Sir William Garrow's position on this. If Sir Nicholas is unable to produce more concrete evidence of his claims, a suggestion that the 7th Marquess of Ravenshaw is deranged is preposterous."

Tindal's pleased expression faded, and he nodded reluctant acquiescence. "As the Lord Chancellor pleases." He sat down.

Sir William shuffled his papers and gathered himself after this curfuffle, and clearing his throat, he said, "I think it is time we heard from my client, what actually occurred during that house party and on the evening of the 11th and the early morning of the 12th of July. My Lord Ravenshaw, will you stand and tell their lordships what happened?" The susurration of murmurs in the house ceased as bodies moved to get a plain view of the accused.

Jerome pulled himself together with an effort and stood to

face the house. His legs felt shaky, but he fancied it didn't show in his demeanor. He took his oath and commenced his story. Sir William had coached him in this, and he kept his voice steady as he pushed away the events of the last few minutes and relayed his first meeting with Charis Dunsenay, his impression that she was older than her actual years, and he admitted to striking up a flirtation with her.

"She was a very pretty young woman, my lords, and in those days—I was twenty-six at the time—I will admit, I liked pretty women, and in general I might be permitted to say with no false modesty that they liked me. Although I also knew that their liking had as much to do with my title and wealth as it did to any other attributes I have. Miss Dunsenay was bold well beyond her years, and I was surprised at the latitude her parents allowed her.

"To put it bluntly, my lords, it wasn't long before I realized they were throwing her at me. She was very willing, too. I do not wish to blacken the young lady's name more than it already is by these sordid circumstances, as I believe she was motivated by an infatuation for me. You see our estates march together, and it is quite likely she had seen and heard of me before we met formally at her parents' home.

"The other guests had departed the property on the morning of the 11th, but I was persuaded to stay one more night. It was on that night that I woke from a sound sleep to find Miss Dunsenay naked in my bed." This statement caused loud murmurs, and the occasional stifled laugh.

"I was not drunk, my lords. I'd had a glass or two of wine with dinner and a couple of ports. Those who know me well will attest to the fact that is not enough to make me drunk. I also did not—I must repeat most emphatically, did *not*—make any assignation with Miss Dunsenay or invite her to my bedroom. I was shocked and dismayed to find her there. Particularly in her state of undress. Before I could take any action, Lord Mostyn burst in upon us and accused me of ruining his daughter. And he demanded that I do the right thing and marry her." He paused to gather himself.

"My lords, I confess at this point I did behave in an ungentlemanly manner, because it was plain to me that the Dunsenays had used their daughter to entrap me. This was motivated, I now believe—although I didn't know this at the time—by Dunsenay's financial distress. My lords, those of you who have found yourselves the target of ambitious debutantes may lend me some sympathy here. I succeeded to my father's title and wealth at the age of seventeen. From that age I was beset by ambitious women desiring to marry my wealth and title. I became cynical and hardhearted toward women who employed tactics to entrap me, and believe me I was subjected to many attempts, although this was the most blatant.

"That is a long-winded way of saying that on this occasion, I allowed my temper to get the better of me. I refused Dunsenay's demand, packed my bags, and left the house to spend the remainder of the night at a local hostelry. My house at that time was not habitable. However, upon reflection in the morning, I realized the error I had made. I had behaved in a most ungentlemanly fashion. I had contravened every precept of honor I had been raised with and returned to Dunsenay's house to say that I would, in fact, marry Miss Dunsenay." He stopped again and gathered himself for the final part.

"When I arrived, I learned that Miss Dunsenay had left the house at some point in the night and not returned. Her parents were naturally concerned for her safety. Her father and I then left to go in search of her. Dunsenay said that she loved the coast and would likely have gone there.

"We headed there and split up. I found her standing on the cliff's edge, looking at the water. I called out to her, and she turned toward me. I dismounted from my horse and approached her. She was visibly shivering. There had been rain in the night. Her cloak was wet and there was a strong breeze coming off the sea.

"I have thought long and hard about my recall of the next

sequence of events, for it all happened very quickly, and the circumstances were very emotionally charged. To the best of my ability to remember, this is what happened:

"I approached her and reassured her that I would marry her. I apologized for my temper the previous evening, and I asked for her forgiveness. As I got closer, I could see she was crying. I was about to take her in my arms and comfort her when a cry behind me alerted me to her father's presence. I turned to see him, and when I looked back—she must have taken a step back, for the cliff suddenly gave way beneath her feet. I lunged for her to grab her, but she had lost her balance and—"

He stopped again, swamped with remembered horror. "I will never forget her look of terror as she fell backward into thin air. Her scream is etched on my memory forever. Her body plunged into the raging sea below. It was tossed about by the waves and dashed upon the rocks. I had to wait until low tide to retrieve her lifeless body.

"That, my lords, is what happened. I do not claim to be entirely blameless in these proceedings, but I swear I did *not* murder Charis Dunsenay. I tried to save her."

A moan from Lady Mostyn, who had collapsed in her chair, broke the silence that ensued when he stopped speaking.

Sir William rose to his feet and said quietly, "My lords, I put it to you that this is a true account of what happened on the night of the 11th and the morning of the 12th of July 1812, and that my client is not a murderer. He was entrapped by his hosts in a plot to force him to marry their daughter in order to save Dunsenay from debt. I also put it to you that Miss Charis Dunsenay's death was a tragic accident, which my client failed to avert despite his best efforts. I further put it to you that there is insufficient evidence to convict my client of murder in any case, as the only witnesses to the alleged crime are both dead. In support of my client's veracity, I will now call the Duke of Troubridge, a gentleman of exemplary character, well known to you all. The duke is also my client's brother-in-law, as Ravenshaw is married to his sister, Lady Ava."

Robert rose from his seat and approached the table, where he gave his oath.

"My lord duke," said Sir William, "how long have you known my client?"

"Since we were fifteen, Sir William."

"And would you say he was a man of honor?"

"I would, my lord, of the highest degree."

"Do you believe his account of these events?"

"I do, my lord. If I did not, I would never have allowed him to marry my sister."

"Thank you, Your Grace." He bowed to Robert, who bowed back and resumed his seat.

Sir William tidied his papers and said simply, "The case for the defense rests, gentlemen. Lord Chancellor, I would move that the house now take a vote as to the guilt or innocence of my client of the crime for which he stands accused, bearing in mind all the points I have raised that discredit this case in the eyes of the law."

Chapter Twenty-Five

JEROME SANK BACK into the hot water of the bath and closed his eyes on a groan. Ava knelt behind the head of the bath and put her hands on his shoulders, her fingers digging into the taut muscles there. It was all over. He had been acquitted, exonerated of all blame for Charis Dunsenay's death by a unanimous vote of the house.

But the damage to his reputation and honor was done and could never be undone. His shame was known to all the world now. No longer a dark secret he kept buried inside. There ought to be some relief in that, but paradoxically, he felt a burning need to strive even harder for the perfection that was always just out of reach. Because now he had things to atone for in the eyes of society. His tainted roots were known and would be the fodder of gossip for months, if not years, to come. *Will I ever live it down?*

Ava's lips grazed his stubbled cheek, and she whispered, "You're home now, my love. Let it go."

He sighed and reached a wet hand to grasp one of hers on his shoulder. "I have so much to be grateful for: you, and Rob, Garrow—he was magnificent! You should have seen his performance. I couldn't have asked for a better defense."

"You were exonerated because you spoke the truth! You were not guilty. It would have been a complete miscarriage of justice for the lords to have pronounced any other verdict."

He smiled at her impassioned tone, and turned his head to capture her mouth in a kiss, which she gave willingly, and he tugged at her arms to bring her around to the side of the tub.

"Want to join me?" he asked, his body stirring. They had been apart for over a week, the longest separation since their wedding.

"I think," she said, dropping her voice to a husky purr and plunging a hand into the warm water, "I want to pleasure my husband." Her hand landed on his stiffening member and gripped firmly.

Jerome groaned again with a different kind of pleasure, and he tugged her closer for a deep kiss. "Come here," he said, wrapping wet arms around her and pulling her over the edge of the tub.

She shrieked on a laugh as he pulled her into the water, gown and all. "Jerome!"

The light muslin fabric splayed around her as she rearranged her knees on either side of his hips. He got his hand under her gown and found her flesh with his fingers, stroking and coaxing as he kissed her with ravenous hunger. Her hips undulated in the water, responding to his touch, and she moaned, her expression of pleasure almost undoing him. She was so beautiful, his wife, his Ava. So precious. His heart swelled, lifting his spirits from their melancholy thoughts.

She moved to engage their bodies, and he let her, as eager as she for the bliss of union. As she slid down his length with another moan of satisfaction, she leaned forward to kiss him, her mouth taking as much as giving. He found he didn't mind being dominated by his little wife. Ava might be small of stature but she was large of spirit and strength, and he was as proud of her lioness courage as he loved her generous heart and spirit.

She rode him with fierce delight and brought them both to that pinnacle of shattering pleasure in moments, sloshing water on the floor, heedless of the mess they were making. Their groans intermingled with their gasping breaths, clutching hands and clinging mouths, as the moment enveloped them in a brief, but transformative fusion of the soul.

At least that was how it felt for him, as he came gradually back to himself, relaxing into the water and bringing her beautiful, flushed face with sparkling eyes into focus. She collapsed forward onto his chest and moaned softly, "I've missed you so much!"

He wrapped his arms around her tightly and kissed her golden curls, falling in disarray around her shoulders. "I missed you too, so very much, my darling."

⤜⤛

IN THE AFTERMATH of the trial, Jerome had demanded that Tindal hand over his mother's diary to him, which the man did with some embarrassment. He learned from Tindal that Lady Mostyn had bribed a servant to search his mother's room for anything of interest and that was how the diary came into her possession. Which finally explained the loose floorboard in her bedchamber. He put the document in the top drawer of his desk unopened. He was not equal to reading it. Yet. He would perhaps take it to Letty and they could read it together. But not yet.

Jerome returned to his usual pursuits with renewed vigor however, determined to put the past behind him, and found to his surprise that the majority of men accepted him back into their ranks with no trouble at all.

He was engaged with a party of sporting gentlemen at the Daffy Club one night, when the celebrated whip and fellow member of the Four Horse Club, Sir Henry Peyton, joined them with his friend and fellow club member, Mr. Annesley. The club had been experiencing difficulties of late with disagreements among the membership as to its rules, and Peyton bemoaned the fact that he rather thought they would have to disband. "Buxton was saying so to me the other day," he said gloomily, raising his glass.

"If there were a way to bring in some new membership," mused Annesley, tracing circles in the spilled liquid on the table, "the dissenting voices might be drowned out."

"Hm," murmured Peyton, contemplating his now empty glass. "What if we were to put on a demonstration of the art, show our mettle?"

Annesley sat up. "Now there's a thought! But why not make it interesting: a race, so that bets might be placed. That will surely draw attention."

"True," said Peyton. "I'll put up my hand for that. Who shall dare to try to best me?"

Jerome, who had listened to this exchange with mild interest, could no more resist that challenge than he could stop breathing; his competitive spirit spurred to the fore. "I will, Sir Henry. Name the distance and over what ground and I engage to beat you by— the distance of half a mile or two minutes!"

"Done!" said Sir Henry, his merry eyes lighting up. And thus it was that the two men were engaged to race a week hence from Hyde Park Corner to Hounslow Heath, a distance of just over twelve miles, at ten o'clock in the morning when much of the route would be heavily snarled with traffic, requiring the drivers to exert every ounce of their skill to negotiate the course safely and at speed. News of the race spread, and it was entered into the betting books at White's and Brooks's. Whether it was Jerome's recent notoriety that fueled the interest, or just the *ton*'s attraction to a closely matched race by two acknowledged whips, there was scarcely a sporting gentleman in London who did not take an interest in the race.

AND WHILE JEROME was settling back into his social milieu, Ava was navigating the choppy waters left in the wake of Lady Mostyn's bitter malice. Ladies, she discovered, were far less forgiving, and she was in a constant state of vigilance to defend Jerome's honor. Mama, Sarah, and Letty were staunch allies in this endeavor, and the four women battled bravely through, refusing to kowtow to the attempts to cut them down. The dowager duchess was not without influence, and gradually their united front began to pay dividends, winning over such high sticklers as Mrs. Drummond-Burrell and Lady Cowper.

And in the middle of it all, there was the scandal over Rick and Miss Cecelia Woodrow. Cecelia had been a debutante the same year as Ava. Both girls were pretty, petite blondes and Cecelia was an heiress to boot. They had often been bracketed together. Miss Woodrow had been engaged to the Earl of Tavistock, but for whatever reason, the engagement came to nothing, tainting her reputation somewhat in the process. Ava had felt for her when her engagement faltered, but all the same she wasn't sure that she was best pleased to have her favorite brother's name linked with Miss Woodrow's. Now there was this scandal hanging over her and Rick. Thus, Ava was surprised, and a little troubled, at opening an envelope over breakfast to find a gold filigree invitation inside.

"Oh, no!" she said.

"What is it, my love?" asked Jerome, looking up from his paper. She passed the invitation across to him.

His eyebrows rose as he perused it. "'You are cordially invited to the wedding of'—. Well, Rob got him to the sticking point after all."

"It would seem so," she said with a frown.

"You're not happy, love?"

"I'm not sure that she is right for Rick," she confessed. "I don't think he is ready for marriage yet. They could both be miserable."

"You never know. It might be the making of him."

She sniffed skeptically. "Rick isn't one to settle down, and she—" She cut herself off from saying anything uncharitable, but it burned inside her. Miss Woodrow struck her as not mature enough for Rick. As much as she adored her scapegrace brother, she privately thought he needed someone who would stabilize him. Miss Woodrow seemed too young and unformed to give him the ballast he needed. Unless he loved her, of course. She resolved to speak to him and ascertain his feelings on the matter.

However, the opportunity wasn't afforded to her until the wedding breakfast, held at Layne House, which was rather too late. She watched him with Cecelia, trying to gauge his feelings, but he wasn't giving anything away. He was so tall and lean and she so petite, they appeared as a rather odd couple to Ava's way of thinking. Rick treated Cecelia with careful courtesy and Ava noticed how Cecelia's eyes followed him with a kind of mournful longing when he moved away from her. *This isn't good!*

Ava managed to corner him while his new wife was dancing and he was propping the wall with a glass of champagne.

"Are you happy?" she asked bluntly.

"Why wouldn't I be?" he asked with his usual lazy smile, but she wasn't fooled.

"You were forced into this. It's not what you wanted. Did she trap you?"

Ricked stiffened and then his shoulders relaxed as he shifted position. "Of course not."

"Rob told me you refused initially to do the right thing by her."

His generous mouth tightened. Then he said quietly. "It wasn't me, Ava. I'm not the one who ruined her."

Ava stared up at him aghast. "They why—?"

"There was nothing else to be done!" he said tightly and swallowed the rest of his champagne. He pushed off the wall and wandered away in his characteristically loping stride.

She had no other chance to question him further, and she stood beside Jerome as they farewelled the couple who were leaving London for Cecelia's Bedford Estate, where presumably they would remain until the scandal died down.

Meanwhile, her own battles, combatting the aftermath of Jerome's trial, soon swamped Ava again.

The fight took its toll on Ava, a fact she kept from Jerome who, as far as she was concerned, had had enough to bear, and she was feeling rather low as a consequence, when she received a missive from Rey that threw her into a dilemma.

My Dear Ava,

I am reluctant to ask this of you, for I know the antipathy with which your husband regards me, but I am in flat despair and have no one but your fair self to whom I can turn for succor.

Would you grant me an hour of your time to unburden my soul?

If you are able, I would meet you at Grillon's dining room at eight o'clock. Naturally, you should come veiled to protect your reputation.

Your friend always,
Reynard Fairbanks

Ava's heart clenched in sympathy for her friend and she debated what to do. *Tell Jerome and beg for permission?* As a dutiful wife that was what she should do. No, a truly dutiful wife would ignore Rey's request altogether. But everything in her rebelled at those two courses of action. While she had acquiesced to Jerome's request to keep Rey at a distance, she still thought it unreasonable of him to ask her give up a friendship that meant so much to her, simply because he feared the gossip that would ensue.

Since his arrest and trial and its aftermath, she had a better understanding of why he might be more sensitive to what people might think or say than she had hitherto realized. But even so, she knew that only the direst of circumstances would have prompted Rey to request to speak to her. The notion of letting down the man who had risked life and limb for her on more than one occasion sat ill with her. She owed him a debt she could never repay, for if he hadn't taken her to Ravenshaw, she feared that Jerome would have married the countess after all, and her life would have been ruined.

After wrestling with herself for an hour, she decided that she would keep the appointment and leave a note for Jerome telling him what she was doing. He had gone to Ascot for the races and wouldn't be back until late. In all probability, she would be home before him in any case and could then explain her lapse in person, asking forgiveness after the fact. He would be angry, she was sure, but she was also confident she could placate him; after all, he did love her so.

Thoughts of how much her husband loved her threw her into a pleasant daydream for a while, and only when she looked at the clock did she realize she needed to dress to keep her appointment with Rey. So she scribbled a note to Jerome and left it on the mantle of his bedchamber, where she was confident he would see it when he returned, as he would wish to bathe and change when he reached home. She then rang for her maid, and also for the footman, whom she requested to find her a hackney carriage for half past seven.

She chose the most understated of her evening gowns, a plain white muslin ornamented with Mechlin lace and instructed her maid to pin a white mantilla to her curls that she could pull down over her face. If she found this strange, the girl didn't comment, and dressed and cloaked, Ava descended the stairs to take the hackney to Grillon's in Albemarle Street just off Bond Street.

Once there, she discovered Rey had secured a private parlor. Shown to this room by a sniffy waiter who clearly thought this veiled young lady, meeting a gentleman of Lannister's reputation in a private parlor, was no better than she ought to be.

Closing the door on the disapproving waiter, she turned and put back her veil and surveyed her friend. To say he looked haggard was an understatement. He had lost weight since she last saw him. There were dark circles beneath his eyes and no trace of his usual, slightly ironic humor in his eyes. Instead, they were dull and despairing.

"Oh, Rey!" She flew across the room to him and enveloped him in a hug.

"You came," he said thickly against her curls, giving her a squeeze back.

"Of course! Did you think I would fail you?"

"I thought your husband would object," he admitted, letting her go and stepping back.

"Well, he doesn't know yet. I left him a note."

"Somewhat dangerous, my dear?"

She shrugged. "He's at Ascot. I'll likely be home before he is, and I will confess all then and face his wrath." She dimpled. "I'm confident I can soothe him." She sat down on the settee and patted it. "Tell me what the matter is, for I can tell it is bad."

He swallowed visibly and sat beside her. "The worst," he admitted, and proceeded to unburden his heart.

Chapter Twenty-Six

JEROME RETURNED FROM Ascot just after nine, to learn that Her Ladyship had gone out in a hackney about an hour and half ago, which extraordinary piece of news made his skin prickle in foreboding. Going up to his room, he took only moments to find her note.

My Dearest Jerome,

I beg you will temper your anger, for I am breaking my promise to you. But the circumstances are, I believe, extenuating. I have taken a hackney and am wearing a veil, so no one will know me. You need not fear any more gossip will be heaped upon us.

I have heeded a request from Rey to meet him, for the poor man is in great distress. I know you find this upsetting, and I am truly sorry to cause you distress, but I owe him a great debt and I cannot in all conscience let him down when he has always been my staunchest champion and friend. I do not expect to be out late and will speak with you upon this matter anon.

Your loving wife,
Ava

The anger boiled up so swiftly it took his breath, fury so white-hot he couldn't contain it. He had thought he had successfully dealt with the events of a few weeks ago and was getting on with his life happily. Congress between himself and Ava had been both passionate and contented, wrapped up in a warm blanket of mutual love and affection.

This! This threw a cannonball into his fantasy of wedded bliss. He knocked the ornaments on the mantelpiece off with a roar and a sweep of one hand. Which did little to relieve his feelings. He went through to her room, hunting for the correspondence from Lannister that had sent her flying to his side. His hands were shaking by the time he found it stuffed into the top drawer of her writing desk.

Having mastered its contents, he sank down on the bed with weakened knees. He felt gutted. Jealousy roiled through his stomach, making him feel physically sick. *What game is Lannister playing?* He had thought the man had more honor than this, but clearly his original assessment of him was more accurate than he had been brought to believe more recently. But whatever Lannister's motives in contravening his request that Ava keep her distance from him, it was Ava's breaking of her promise that ate at his soul. Her willingness—nay eagerness—to fly to this man's side whenever he asked it of her in defiance of her husband's request that she not do so.

She professed to love Jerome, and yet—all his old insecurities came bubbling to the surface, and he wondered in despair how he could ever have fooled himself into thinking he could have a happy marriage. *I am not fit for it. I don't deserve it.*

A step on the stairs made him sit up as the door opened and Ava stood there in a plain white muslin gown beneath a blue satin cloak. Her golden curls tumbled around her shoulders beneath a white mantilla, thrown back from her face.

"Jerome!" She smiled, but it was weak, for she saw the paper in his hand. "You got my note?"

"I did." His voice was husky. He cleared his throat.

She came into the room and shut the door. Then she crossed the room and dropped to her knees before him, clasping her hands. "I know you're upset. I promise you, there is nothing to worry about. No one will ever know I met with Rey tonight. The waiter thought I was a high-class light-skirts, and his notions of propriety were offended, but he had no inkling of my identity, I assure you."

"That's a small consolation, I suppose," he said bitterly. "You broke your promise to me, Ava."

"I know," she said composedly, "but I didn't seek to hide it from you and even if you had not discovered my note, I planned to confess the whole to you once you came home. If you had been here when I received Rey's note, I would have spoken to you about it."

"Would you?" His face pulled tight in a grimace of a smile. "We will never know, will we? I suspect it is too much to assume you would, in that circumstance, have asked me to relieve you of your promise?"

She looked down a moment and then up, squaring her shoulders. "I would have asked for your understanding of why I needed to break it." He closed his eyes, battling with himself. Her voice came to him, quiet and steady. "I would ask you to trust me."

He opened his eyes. "I do trust you, Ava. I will admit that at one point in time I doubted, I wondered—I—"

"If you trust me, what is the problem?" she asked.

He shook his head, unable to articulate the hot ball of emotions in his chest.

"Jerome, his sister died!" she said softly. "He has no one else. No family to share his grief. He just wanted a hug!"

Jerome stared into her eyes and his heart turned over in his chest. Jealousy and compassion battled inside him. Part of him wanted to tear Lannister apart for daring to ask *his wife* for a hug, and part of him felt an unaccustomed surge of sympathy and compassion for the other man. After an inward struggle, he said hoarsely, "God, I'm sorry, Ava. I'm a monster of selfishness." He put his arms around her bringing her into his chest. "I didn't even know he had a sister," his lips pressed against her curls.

"She had been ill for a long time. She never came to London."

He nodded. "I see. I'm sorry," he repeated. His chest was aching. He hated that Lannister could command hugs from Ava. Yet it was her open-hearted warmth that he loved so much. But he wanted it all for himself. Which was both unreasonable and selfish. The old prickle of self-loathing tore at him. He was so very far from perfect.

She cupped his face in her hands and smiled mistily at him. "No. I'm sorry to have upset you so. After everything you've had to deal with . . ."

In his fragile state, her sympathy tipped him over the edge. Jerome felt tears sting his eyes and the tight ball of pain inside his chest that he had been keeping bound down ever since his arrest for Charis's murder, suddenly exploded, and he gasped on a sob that wouldn't be suppressed.

Ava rose up on her knees with an exclamation. "Oh, Jerome!" She clasped his head to her bosom as he clung to her and cried. He had not shed a tear throughout the whole process of his time in prison and the trial. And now it all came boiling out in a flood of white-hot pain. It hurt so damned much he had trouble breathing through the storm of tears. He couldn't remember crying like this in years. Even after Charis's death, he hadn't cried like this. He had shed a few bitter tears of regret, but then he'd packed it all away, pushed it down, tried to forget it.

All the regrets, the failures, the mistakes. All the loneliness of his boyhood, spent in a gloomy, half-empty house that was full of bad memories, with a mother who was ill more often than she was well, and periodic visits from a man whose temper terrified him. All that pain layered on year after year, and consolidated into a hardened ball of self-loathing, hidden beneath a façade that fooled the world into thinking he was perfect.

It all came unraveled in this moment of weakness as he wept in his wife's arms like a little boy. His tears soaked the bodice of her gown, as the warmth of her generous bosom cushioned his face and his sobs gradually abated, leaving him feeling hollow and slightly sick.

He sat up, wiping his face with his palms and found Ava offering him a handkerchief from her reticule. He took the dainty bit of white cloth and lace and blew his nose, wiped his face and sniffed.

"I'm so sorry," he said thickly.

Ava sat back on her heels and glared at him. "Don't you dare! Don't you dare apologize for feeling! I was wondering when you were going to crack. You've been so strong!"

She leaned in and wrapped her arms round his neck. "I love you so much!" she whispered and kissed him.

"Oh Ava, I don't deserve you!" he said brokenly.

"Yes, you do!" she kissed him again and he kissed her back fiercely.

"God, I love you," he muttered and dragged her down onto his bed.

"And I love you," she responded between feverish kisses as their hands tore at each other's clothes.

His mouth landed on her bared breast and took the nipple with a deep, almost punishing pull that made her arch off the bed with a moan, as his hands scrabbled beneath her skirts to reach the soft weeping flesh between her legs. His fingers plunged inside her, his thumb swirling on her clitoris, his mouth laving and punishing that poor nipple until the surrounding breast was red with the scratch of his bristled chin and the ravaging of his lips and teeth.

"Give me this," he whispered, his fingers curling inside her. "Come for me!"

She arched up with another moan and shattered. With a groan of satisfaction, he kissed her. "At least I can make you do that," he said, his voice hoarse with emotion.

She blinked up at him and frowned. "Jerome, it's not a competition. A fight. You don't have to defeat me. I'm not the enemy."

He stared down into her flushed face, her curls in disarray around her head. The lace veil had come off and was lying on the pillow. Her gown was open at the front, baring her breasts to the waist. She lay beneath him, vanquished. And it was a hollow victory. He withdrew his fingers as a cold wash of horror ran through his body. Suddenly, a picture of himself he'd never seen before presented itself to him. *Is that how others see me? Is that how I am? Someone who must win at all costs?*

He felt sick. Rolling onto his back he stared blindly at the bed canopy overhead. But he wasn't seeing that. He was seeing Tindal reading from his mother's diary, trying to prove that she was mad and so was he. He'd failed. But the parallel had hit him hard and gone deep. A sword thrust to the heart that Jerome had blocked until this moment. His relentless drive for perfection. The win at all costs. *Was it a form of madness?*

"Jerome?" Ava sat up on one elbow to look down at him, her expression alarmed at whatever she saw on his face.

He got up off the bed. "There is something I need to show you," he said, heading into his room. He went to his desk and drew out the diary that he hadn't looked at and brought it back into her room, where he found her sitting on the edge of the bed. She had tidied up her bodice, but her hair was loose and tangled.

"What is it?" she said.

He sat down beside her, the little book felt heavy in his hands. "I didn't tell you this. But during the trial, Tindal tried to suggest that my mother was mad and"—he swallowed—"that I was too."

She gasped and said indignantly, "You are not!"

He smiled weakly at her valiant defense and squeezed her hand.

"The gambit failed, no one thought I was mad, and once Garrow was able to present his argument and Robert gave me a character reference, it was put to the vote and I was exonerated."

She nodded. "Yes, you told me." She touched the book. "What is this?"

"It's the evidence Tindal used to try to prove my mother was insane and killed herself. It's her diary."

"Where did he get it?"

"Lady Mostyn paid one of her servants to break into the house and search it for, I'm not sure what she expected to find, but they found this—I believe under a floorboard in my mother's room. I had no idea of its existence until Tindal produced it in the trial. Afterward I demanded he surrender it to me."

"That woman—!" exclaimed Ava. "If anyone is mad I think it's her! Her mind has been turned by grief and a desire for revenge."

"Indeed," he said heavily.

"Have you read it?" she asked softly, covering his hand with hers.

"No. I couldn't face it after the trial. I just shoved it in my desk drawer. I planned to take it to Letty and read it with her."

"You should do that," she said firmly.

He chewed his lip, and took a breath. "You're right. I had convinced myself that my father had a hand in her death, but Tindal's words have made me wonder if I was wrong. If perhaps she jumped after all. I—" He shook his head. "I don't know what to think."

"Should we take it to Letty now?" she asked.

He glanced at the clock. "It's after nine. Even if she is home it's hardly the time to be paying calls—"

"Will you be able to sleep with this playing on your mind?"

"I don't know." He admitted reluctantly. "It's my race in the morning. I had planned an early night—with you." He smiled and squeezed her hand again.

She rose and said briskly. "Come on. We will pay her call. If she isn't home, we will try tomorrow—after your race."

He nodded and rose. And thus they arrived at Grosvenor Square twenty minutes later and were admitted by Her Lady-ship's surprised butler. He led them upstairs to her dressing room, where she had retired for the night. Letty was lying on her chaise longue, reading a book by candlelight, a rug over her knees. At sight of Jerome and Ava she threw book and rug aside in alarm and rose.

"Good heavens what is it? Is someone ill? Dead?"

"Nothing like that, my dear," said Jerome kissing her cheek.

Letty invited them to sit, and Jerome explained about their mother's diary and held it out to her.

Letty took it gingerly. "I'm not sure if I *want* to know," she said, looking at the little book as if it might bite.

"I have mixed feelings, too," admitted Jerome. "But I feel compelled to find out. What if we're wrong about him?"

"You can't tell me he was a good man Jerome. I *remember* his rages."

"But it is possible that Mama's mind could have been overset by his behavior?"

"Entirely possible," she admitted and sighed. Opening to the first page, she patted the seat beside her and he transferred to it to read along with her.

The first entry, in a curling, sloping hand, was dated some three months prior to her death, and while there were gaps between entries, it was easy to piece together the tenor of her days from her notes, which focused primarily upon her ailments or troubles with the servants. It was clear that Lord Gareth wasn't in residence for these earlier entries and that she longed for word from her children. Which made Jerome wince. While he had written, it had been infrequently. He glanced at Letty and saw her bite her lip, for to his knowledge she had not written at all after she left home.

Then there was a gap of several weeks. It became evident that she had been ill and was only then recovering, though taking rather more laudanum than she should to numb the pains in her head.

> *I have begun to have fancies, brought on by the laudanum. I am sure that Eliza's ghost is haunting me.*

"Who is Eliza?" asked Jerome, pointing to the page.

"I've no idea," said Letty with a frown.

A cold shiver ran over Jerome's skin, and his vision narrowed in an alarming way as something tickled at the back of his mind, but, like a black whisp of smoke, it evaporated when he tried to grasp it.

Nothing more was said of Eliza for several pages and then it was clear that the marquess was home for their mother stated baldly:

I tried to lock him out, but he obtained the key. He would have his argument of me and my submission. My face still throbs. I took the laudanum tonight, after he was done.

"That!" said Letty stabbing the page. "That is what I remember. If she ever argued with him, he would strike her across the face."

Jerome nodded. "Did he ever hit you?"

"No. You?"

"He took a hand to me a time or two and a crop to me once. But honestly, it was no more than other boys suffered. It was the way he treated her that haunted me. I should never have left her alone that summer. If I'd been home—"

"Jerome, you were twelve!" He rubbed his eyes wearily. "I think we have our answer Jerome. If he didn't physically throw her off that damned balcony, he drove her to jump, just to get away from him!" said Letty fuming.

"Surely you're right. And if the laudanum was giving her hallucinations—" said Ava leaning forward.

"Yes, this Eliza, whoever she was—" Letty flicked over the next few pages scanning, and her finger stopped. "Eliza Stubbs! Now why is that familiar? I'll swear I've heard the name, but—"

Jerome felt himself sway as his vision turned black round the edges again and his skin turned ice cold. He heard Ava's voice calling his name urgently, but it was muffled as if from a long way off.

"Jerome!" Ava knelt before him, her hands on his arms shaking him. "God what is wrong with him?" she wailed. "Jerome!"

The jumbled fragments of memory flickering in his mind made little sense initially, all he was conscious of was puzzlement, followed by a creeping sense of terror. Then his adult mind clicked into place and he dropped his head into his hands and said muffledly, "He killed her. I—I think I saw it!"

"Killed who?" asked Letty sharply.

"Saw what?" cried Ava.

He lifted his head and looked at Letty. "Could she have been a housemaid? Eliza Stubbs? Young, pretty, with red hair coming out of a mob cap?"

"Oh my God!" Letty stared at him horrified. "She was the nursery maid. She helped Nanny Mercer. She disappeared one day, and eventually I think they said she had gone home to her family. I—" She frowned in an effort of memory. "How old were you?" She shook her head counting on her fingers. "You must have been two, maybe? Not any older. I was eleven. How do you even remember—"

"I don't really. Just fragments that make no sense. I wouldn't have comprehended what I was seeing."

"What did you see?"

"Our father with his hands around her throat." He swallowed. "God, I feel sick." He closed his eyes and breathed. Letty got up and came back in a moment.

"Here, drink this." She held out a glass. He took it and tossed off the brandy, letting it settle his stomach.

She sat down and put an arm around him. "We may never know the details, but it's clear that Mama found out and she was trying to get up the courage to confront him about it. That must have been what happened."

"And he killed her, too?" He rubbed his face. "God, I'm glad he's dead. If I'd known—" He shuddered. "Part of me did know. I always knew there was something. But I could never grasp it. I had night terrors as a boy—"

"Yes, you did! I remember that!" said Letty. "Poor lad, what a horrible thing to carry. Gosh, I feel guilty for leaving you behind. If I'd known, I'd have dragged you out of there." She wiped her eyes, smiling at him sadly. "I'm so sorry, little brother."

He shook his head. "Not your fault, Letty." He shook his head again, trying to shake off the flood of energy in his body. He felt as if he were a geyser about to explode.

He rose. "We had better go. I've got a race in the morning. Are you all right?"

Letty nodded. "Better than you I suspect."

He bent down and kissed her cheek. "I wish John were here for you now."

Letty sighed. "I wish he were, too. I shall write to him."

"Have you heard back from him? Does he know about the baby?"

"Yes." She smiled, a hand going to her belly. "Yes, he does, and he is very pleased and wishing he hadn't gone."

Jerome picked up the diary and he and Ava left.

⟫⟫⟩⟨⟨⟨

ENTERING AVA'S ROOM, he tossed the dairy on her desk and drew her into his arms. They had said little to each other in the carriage, his mind occupied with trying to work through everything the evening had revealed. And she seemed to understand that and held his hand in silence.

"Ava," he murmured against her hair now.

"Yes?"

"I need you, and I don't think I can be gentle."

She raised her face to him and he kissed her, pulling her tight against him. His body was shaking. "Ava?" he whispered.

"Yes, Jerome," she said pulling at his neckcloth. Clothing went flying, and in moments they fell on the bed in a tangle of naked limbs, exchanging fierce kisses. She wrapped a leg round his hip and he found the place to enter her body with a hard deep stroke, pulling her tight against him. Rolling her onto her back, he thrust rapidly. She moved with him, her breathing as ragged as his.

His body shuddered as he drove them higher, the pleasure tightening to a pinpoint of searing flame that stubbornly refused to release no matter how much he tried. His muscles worked and sweat broke out on his skin, his breath came in gasping pants, everything wound tighter and tighter until he was sure something would break.

And it finally did, in an explosion of pleasure that almost made him weep. He collapsed slowly in the aftermath, his body boneless, his pulse thudding, his breath coming slowly back to normal, the sweat cooling on his skin.

Eventually he moved enough to pull the coverlet over them and he sank into a dark oblivion with her arms around him.

He woke with a start some little while later, his skin prickling with latent horror. He rolled away from Ava, careful not to disturb her. Getting out of bed he picked up the diary, crept into his own bedchamber, where he put on a robe and slippers, and then he quietly walked downstairs to the library. He built up the banked fire and sat down to read the whole book. It was after three in the morning when he finished, and he sat staring into the fire for a long time before he finally got up and went to his desk where he drafted a letter to Kelham. He folded, sealed, and addressed it and set it on the table in the hallway where it would be collected for delivery. Then he walked upstairs slowly to his bedchamber where he lay down on the coverlet, still in his dressing gown, and stared at the ceiling until dawn.

Chapter Twenty-Seven

W HEN AVA WOKE in the morning, her bed was empty, she assumed Jerome had risen early to attend his race.

She worried that he must be tired. She was tired, and yesterday he had been subjected to shock after shock. But Jerome was a consummate driver. She supposed she would have to trust his innate abilities to shine through, no matter the circumstances.

Even so, she spent an uneasy morning waiting for his return. She didn't expect him back realistically before two, given that the duration of the race would be at least an hour and there would then be celebrations to be had among the spectators before the combatants and their compatriots returned to London.

JEROME ARRIVED AT the meeting place for the race with a headache and gritty eyes from lack of sleep, compounded by a heaviness in his heart from yesterday's revelations and insights. His internal turmoil he hid behind a smile and a wave to the crowd of people who had gathered to see the start of the race and broke into spontaneous applause upon his arrival.

He shook his opponent's hand. Peyton appeared as fresh as a

nosegay. Grinning, he shook Jerome's hand vigorously and said, "This is something like, eh? We will give 'em a show."

"We will!" Jerome returned with a smile that felt tight across his cheekbones. "I'll be waiting for you at the finish line!" he said loud enough for the crowd to hear as both men turned to climb into their vehicles once more and proceed to the starting line.

"Ha!" returned Peyton good-naturedly. "We'll see about that, my lord!"

Jerome was conscious as he waited for the starting signal, holding his restive horses in line, of an unaccustomed anxiety that made his pulse beat erratically. Normally he relished these sorts of competitions, confident in his own ability to best all commers. But the events of yesterday played on his mind. His insight about his competitive nature undermined his confidence. He wasn't at his best, and he knew it.

The adjudicator called a countdown of three and dropped a handkerchief to signal the start of the race, and his horses leaped forward as he let out the reins. The traffic was heavy in this part of London, and it was some time before he and his opponent could get a clear enough run to put on any show of speed. But as the carts, carriages, and horses thinned, and the houses fell away, he was able to urge his team into a trot and then a canter. Settling into the rhythm of the race, his nerves steadied, and he began to gain a slight edge over Peyton. The road was wide enough at this point for them to drive abreast for the moment, as there were no vehicles coming the other way. But there was a bend coming up and one of them would have to give ground to the other. He coaxed his team to a burst of speed to take the lead and force Peyton to drop back as he feather-edged the corner, with a coach coming the other way. His curricle's wheels came within inches of scraping the coach's and the driver swore at him.

Jerome grinned. He was getting his eye in and his confidence lifted. *I can do this!* He urged the team faster into the straight ahead and established a comfortable lead. Another bend in the road forced him to slow a trifle, but he was still going at quite a clip when he rounded the bend and found a lumbering coach just pulling back onto the road. He was going too fast to pull up behind it and was forced to go around.

Which pushed him onto the other side of the road. The wheels hit a rut and jerked the whole vehicle sideways. The horses panicked and took off, and before he could pull them back, he found himself suddenly airborne, headed for a thicket of brambles. He expected a prickly and unpleasant landing. What he got was searing pain as his body landed with force on something hard and jagged. His head bounced and he knew no more.

AVA WAS STARTLED when a commotion in the front hall just after twelve brought her out of the first-floor parlor to the sight of a bloodied and broken body on a stretcher being borne into the house by two men.

Her head swam, and she clutched the banister, a cry caught in her throat.

"Jerome!" She tumbled down the stairs toward the tableaux, only to be swept aside as the men prepared to carry her husband up the stairs to his bedchamber, escorted by a footman.

"What happened?" she asked, bewildered. "Has a doctor been sent for? Skelton?" she turned the butler.

"Yes, my lady, I sent one of the footmen straightaway."

A dapper man stepped forward at this point and introduced himself with a bow. "Lady Ava, my deepest sympathies for this shock. I am Sir Henry Peyton."

"Yes, I know who you are," she said through numb lips. "What happened?"

"I didn't see the accident occur, my lady. I was a few lengths behind your husband's curricle and a bend in the road obscured it from my sight. But I heard it. It appears His Lordship miscalculated when he attempted to overtake a coach. A rut in the road caused the wheels to go awry, and the whole equipage tipped and fell into quite a deep ditch by the side of the road. His Lordship's body was catapulted out of the curricle and into a briar patch containing some hidden rocks. He received some scratches and bangs, which account for much of the blood on his exposed skin. But he has also sustained several injuries, I fear, including a nasty jagged tear to the cheek. I believe he may also have broken several bones. We kept him as still as possible during the journey back, but the pain was sufficient to keep him unconscious for the duration, which is a kind of mercy, I suppose."

"I see. Thank you," she said. "If you will excuse me, I must attend to him—"

"Of course." He bowed and stepped away.

She turned to find the housekeeper, Mrs. Grundy, standing by the newel post, her face slack with shock.

"Mrs. Grundy, I require hot water and plenty of bandages, as well as the arnica and spermaceti cream, to His Lordship's room immediately." She turned back to Skelton. "Send the doctor up as soon as he arrives."

"I will, my lady,"

Ava ran up the stairs to her husband's room where she found Leyton carefully disrobing Jerome's prone and still unconscious body.

The sight was ghastly, and terror gripped her. He was covered in blood, and his skin, where it could be seen, was deathly pale. The wound to his cheek was bleeding still, and she moved immediately to seize the bowl of water on the dresser and dip a cloth into it to clean away the blood from the wound.

She was barely aware that she was muttering things beneath her breath. Mostly "Don't die, please don't die!"

By the time the doctor arrived, Leyton and Ava had contrived to disrobe Jerome and remove the worst of the blood from his person, and he had still not regained consciousness. Ava was so terrified she was shaking. Her magnificent husband had never looked so—reduced! Pale, vulnerable, broken! His beautiful face ruined. Her heart ached, and her stomach churned with worry as she waited in silence for the doctor's verdict.

The man, infuriatingly, took his time examining Jerome thoroughly. Ava wanted to scream at him to tell her that Jerome would be all right. But she kept her impulses in check, clenched her hands tightly together, and waited.

Finally, the portly little balding doctor stood back and said, "My lady, your husband has a number of serious injuries. The first, and I fear the most dangerous, is a severe concussion, suffered by a blow to the head. You see this lump here?" He pointed to the side of Jerome's head.

She bent and observed a swelling that had turned an ugly purple on his temple. She nodded.

"That is why he has remained unconscious for so long and is the most worrying aspect of all his wounds. We will not know until he comes around how much damage may have been sustained to his brain."

Ava stifled a whimper and swallowed, nodding her understanding but unable to trust her voice to speak.

"The second most worrisome injury is this nasty gash to his face. It would seem your husband collided with some sharp rocks at considerable speed and slid across their surface, acquiring both the blow to the head and this gash, as well as sundry scratches from some wickedly sharp plant."

"Yes," she managed around the lump in her throat. "That is what the gentleman who brought him home said. That he was catapulted from his curricle and landed in a briar patch, which concealed some rocks."

The doctor nodded with a little smile, clearly pleased with his reconstruction of events from the evidence before him.

"As to his other injuries, I believe he will probably have a cracked rib or two and he has a broken collarbone. His other limbs appear to be intact, although he has suffered some bruising from the force of impact."

Ava sagged a little in relief at this testimony.

"However, it is possible that there has been internal damage to organs that we cannot see. If there is such injury, symptoms will manifest in the coming days."

"What symptoms, doctor?" she asked, her voice trembling.

"Blood in the urine, pain, vomiting, difficulties breathing, all of these would be signs of internal bleeding or damage to organs, for which we can do little."

Ava blinked rapidly, her heart squeezing in panic. She took a breath, trying to calm herself. *I can't afford to give into my terror. Jerome needs me.*

"Fortunately, your husband seems to be a fine specimen, in excellent health. Provided his wounds are kept clean and bandages changed daily, he should make a full recovery from those wounds. The question, as I said earlier, is the extent of the damage to his head. And only time will tell that."

"How—how much time?" she asked shakily.

"The next twenty-four hours are critical. The sooner he wakes, the better for the prognosis. That said, I shall take advantage of his comatose state to set his collarbone with a sling, bandage his ribs, and stitch the wound on his face. I require a piece of linen for the sling, about two feet square, and bandages."

"Of course!" Ava turned to Mrs. Grundy, who had brought the bandages herself along with the ointments Ava had requested.

She nodded to Ava with a quick bob and said, "I'll fetch the linen straight, my lady."

To Ava's massive relief, Jerome came around as soon as the doctor touched his arm. Leyton had cut him out of his clothes to minimize moving him and had been so careful and gentle, he did not disturb the patient. But the doctor's touch provoked a groan and fluttering of the eyes.

Ava, standing on the opposite side of the bed from the doctor, took Jerome's left hand—it was his right clavicle that was broken—and bent over so that she brought her face into line with his eyes. "Jerome? My love—?"

He blinked at her for a moment and then a smile broke out

across his face, swiftly replaced by a wince as the movement pulled at the wound on his cheek. "Ava!"

Relief made her sob as she raised his hand to her lips and kissed it, tears coursing down her cheeks and wetting his fingers.

"You're a very lucky man, Your Lordship," said the doctor, observing these encouraging signs.

"Banged myself up a bit, I think," said Jerome, wincing as the doctor manipulated his arm into position.

"You have. I'm going to make you more comfortable with this sling. You've broken your collarbone and, I suspect, some ribs. Once I've done that, I'm going to stitch your face. You have a nasty gash on your cheek."

"I thought I could feel something. How bad is it? Will it scar?"

"I'm afraid so, yes."

Ava squeezed his hand and said with a tender smile, "You will look quite piratical I'm sure, my love."

He glanced at her but said nothing.

"Does your head hurt?"

"Like the devil," admitted Jerome.

The doctor frowned down at him as he folded the square of linen that Mrs. Grundy had just brought him diagonally and then slid it around Jerome's bent arm and tied the ends behind his neck. "There, that should hold it still. You will need to sleep propped up and with a pillow beneath your arm to keep it steady until the bones knit. About six to eight weeks. Now let's have a look at that head of yours."

He took Jerome's chin in his fingers and held up one finger on his other hand. "Track my finger with your eyes," he said, his gaze fixed on Jerome's. He moved the finger back and forth and observed Jerome's efforts to track it.

"Hm. Your pupils are a little dilated, but you were able to track. That is good. Your head will ache for several days, I suspect. You sustained quite a blow. Do you feel dizzy?"

"I don't think so."

"Well, you'll be staying in bed for a few days, anyway. Do

you have any sharp or dull pain in your abdomen or back?"

"I can't tell. To be honest, everything feels like it hurts at the moment."

"Well, monitor it. If the pain gets worse, let me know. Nausea?"

"I bit, but that might be my head," admitted Jerome with a grimace.

"Yes, likely, but if you start to vomit, let me know. Any breathlessness?"

"I can't breathe deeply because of the ribs. You're right, at least one is broken. I can feel it."

The doctor nodded.

"It is important that your wounds are dressed and kept clean to avoid fever. Let's bandage your ribs and then I'll get to that face."

⟫⟫⟩✕⟨⟪⟪

WITH A BANDAGE around his rib cage and his upper body propped against pillows, his arm at rest in its sling, Jerome braced himself for the stitches. He had sustained wounds before and been stitched, so he knew what to expect, but the notion of his face being scarred bothered him more than he wanted to admit. *Am I so vain?* It seemed he was.

His cheek was raw pain, and hot throbs of it pulsed through his already aching head, making his stomach roll ominously. He felt wretched. How could he have made such a dreadful error while driving? *Because I was tired and not myself!*

When it was over, he was fed some drops of laudanum for pain and slipped into an uneasy doze.

His next sensations were of heat. He was burning up. Had he died and gone to hell for his sins? He felt awful enough to be in hell. His whole body ached and stung from a dozen small wounds and the big one on his cheek. His collarbone ached. His ribs throbbed.

A cool cloth on his forehead brought some momentary relief and a soft, "There my darling, is that better?" *Ava.* Tears of gratitude stung his eyes. *My sweet, darling Ava.*

He twitched his right hand, looking for her. He couldn't open his eyes, they felt leaden. Then her small hand was in his, squeezing gently, and he sighed, slipping into another doze.

⇥⟫⟪⇤

AVA SPENT A terrified night by his side as his temperature spiked and his body became bathed in sweat. She wiped him constantly with wet cloths to keep him cool and prayed harder than she had ever done in her life.

By morning, the fever seemed to have abated, and he slept through until midafternoon, enabling her to seek her bed for a few hours of sleep. When she returned from her nap, she was pleased to see Jerome's eyes open as she approached the bed.

Leyton had stayed with him while she was sleeping, and he rose when she entered and bowed. "He's just woken, my lady," he said quietly. "Do you require anything?"

"No, you go and rest. I'll take over now." She smiled at him gratefully, and he took his leave of Jerome, who thanked him.

She approached the bed and drew up a chair to take his hand. "How do you feel?"

"Somewhat better. Everything aches, but my head is pounding less, and I'm hungry."

"Oh, that is excellent news! I shall ring for a tray for you."

Chapter Twenty-Eight

London, three weeks later

AVA CAME IN from her morning ride and went straight up to Jerome's room to see how he fared. He was lying against the pillows with his face turned away. At first, she thought he was asleep and approached quietly. The sling kept his arm and collarbone fixed in position to encourage healing, but even so, she knew it caused him pain. The inflammation in his face was slowly reducing as the wound healed.

He turned his head as she approached the bed and stared at her, almost as if he didn't recognize her. Her heart flipped in alarm.

"Jerome?" She came closer and bent to kiss his forehead. "How do you feel?"

"No different. Why do you keep asking? Nothing has changed," he said irritably.

"I'm sorry," she said, her heart wrung by his obvious distress. "Can I fetch you anything?"

"No." He turned his face away.

"Do you wish to sleep?"

"No!" He let out a breath. "I'm sorry. I've done nothing but sleep. I'm sick of this bed."

"The doctor said—"

"I know what the doctor said!"

She bit her lip, stifling the desire to rip back at him. He was impossible in this mood.

"Would you like me to read to you?"

He hesitated and then said softly. "Yes, thank you. I can't seem to read without getting a headache yet. I would appreciate that."

She smiled. "Just let me change. I'll be right back."

He nodded and as she turned away, he caught her hand with his free one and squeezed it. "I'm sorry, I'm being a beast."

She smiled wryly. "I know, but it's because you *feel* beastly."

Ten minutes later she was back with a copy of *Waverley* and settled carefully on the side of the bed to read to him, resting the book on her lap and holding his free hand in hers.

She looked up after a bit and found his eyes closed.

"Don't stop," he said, still with his eyes closed. "I'm listening. The light just makes my eyes ache."

She kept on until Leyton arrived with morning tea. She took the tray from him while he helped Jerome sit up in the bed. Jerome wouldn't suffer anyone to touch him but Leyton. As much as she wanted to help, she knew better than to try. Instead, she busied herself with the tea things, preparing him a cup of tea just as he liked it and optimistically putting a biscuit on the saucer in the hope that he would eat it. Setting it on the bedside table in easy reach, she sat down carefully and sipped her own cup while Leyton tidied up and left them alone.

"I saw Emrys in the park. Annis is recovering well. I am going to visit her this afternoon and see the baby. They have settled on Annabelle for a name. He is so proud, you would think it's his first instead of his fourth child!"

Jerome smiled; it was only half a smile as the healing wound pulled his mouth down on the right side. "He'll be unbearable."

"He wants to come and see you when you're up to it."

He nodded slowly but didn't say anything. His eyes fell to the teacup in his hand, and he took a sip.

"Rob and Deo too. They're all worried about you," she said

quietly. *And so am I!*

"Hm." He sipped his tea.

She stifled a sigh, finished her tea, and resumed reading. He finished his tea but didn't eat the biscuit, settled back against the pillows, and closed his eyes. She eventually stopped reading when she could tell by his breathing that he had fallen asleep. She sat looking at him as silent tears rolled down her cheeks. He was so unlike his usual energetic self. So quiet and withdrawn, so bruised and battered. Her heart ached just looking at him.

She left him quietly, ate her luncheon in solitary state, and spent the afternoon visiting her former governess with her new baby.

She held the little scrap in her arms while the babe slept and wondered if she would have one of these to call her own one day. It would seem a logical consequence of the physical expressions of love between herself and Jerome, but in his current condition, it would likely be a while before such conjugal bliss was resumed.

She pushed aside her own gloomy thoughts and entered into Annis's genuine joy in motherhood. It was late for her; she was almost thirty.

"Emrys scandalized the midwife by insisting on being present for the whole thing. Wild horses couldn't have kept him out," said Annis with a fond smile. "For which I was actually grateful, because he was extremely useful wiping my brow, holding my hands, breathing with me. I thought he might be upset to see me screaming in agony, but he was eminently practical about it. He knew what to do far better than I did. It pays to have an experienced husband," she said, biting into a biscuit.

"Good heavens," said Ava, revising her view of the viscount, whom she had always considered to be amiable but slightly buffle-headed. *How might Jerome be? Will I get the chance to find out?* She supposed there was no reason why she shouldn't, but one never knew after all.

When she returned to the house, she found Jerome sitting up playing checkers with Leyton, which made her smile.

"Sarah has invited me to the theatre tonight, but I needn't go," she said.

"No. Do go, I'll be fine here," he said with his new lopsided smile. "My head is aching less, and I daresay I'll go to sleep early."

"Are you sure?" she asked anxiously.

He nodded. "You've been dancing attendance on me for weeks. Go and enjoy yourself for a few hours. I'll be fine here with Leyton, I assure you. We may play a round or two of cards after dinner."

She smiled and nodded at Leyton. "Don't let him fleece you. He never loses, you know."

"I know, my lady. I'll be careful."

"Leyton has quite a talent for cards, Ava. I wouldn't bet on his losing. And in any case, I doubt I'm at my best at the moment."

"Well, don't overdo it," she scolded gently, and kissed his forehead. Leyton had the tact to turn away and give them some privacy, and she attempted a kiss on the lips, but he evaded her again. *It has been like this since the accident.* She thought it must be because of the wound hurting him and tried not to mind.

The Troubridge coach collected her at eight o'clock, and she joined Sarah, Robert, and Sarah's sister Deborah. Ava hadn't seen much of Deborah in the past few weeks, but she watched her now with new knowledge and wondered. But of course, she couldn't say anything. Rey had sworn her to secrecy, and she would never break her word to him. But still, she wondered.

"How is your husband faring?" asked Deborah, once they were seated together in the box, under cover of the murmured conversation of the audience and the sounds of the orchestra tuning up.

"On the mend," said Ava brightly, and plied her fan. It was warm in the theatre already.

"Nevertheless, you're concerned," said Deborah shrewdly. She placed a hand on Ava's arm and said with genuine empathy, "It must be a difficult time for you. Males, active ones in particular, are never good patients."

Ava smiled in relief. "So true. You've had experience?"

"Lots!" said Deborah with an expressive grimace. "With three small, very active brothers always getting into scrapes. And the male of the species always suffers more from a head cold or other trivial ailment than a female. Or at any rate, they would have us think so," she said with a smile. "I also help with Papa's parish-ioners. Sarah and I would visit the sick regularly and offer what relief we could. Ruth and Mary go with me now, and Hepzibah is getting old enough to go too, if I can just keep her still long enough to dress her properly. The wives are often grateful for someone to do the washing or prepare a meal, when juggling a sick spouse and multiple children, along with their other chores. And of course, if it is the wife who is ill, the menfolk need all the help they can get. Single fathers even more so."

Ava listened, fascinated by a world she knew nothing of, and her conscience pricked her. Of course, as a lady she should be embracing charitable works, but most of the ladies she knew certainly didn't get their hands dirty doing actual work them-selves. They inspected orphanages and gave money and gifts. Some took up causes, and those of an evangelical turn preached salvation. Mama occasionally spoke of the evangelical work she had been forced to do when she lived with her uncle, a Methodist minister. It had given her a deep distaste of such approaches to supporting the poor, and she took a more practical stance on such things, but even so, Mama had not done any actual manual labor.

Rey had described Deborah as an angel. It seemed he had meant it literally—a ministering angel to her father's parishioners at least. A stronger contrast with Rey's dissolute life would be hard to find. *The angel and the devil, indeed.*

Ava enjoyed the play but was glad to get home, for she couldn't help but worry about Jerome. He was never far from her thoughts. She went straight to his room and entered quietly. A branch of candles burned beside the bed, throwing shadows on the wall and revealing his slumbering figure beneath the covers.

He lay on his back, the arm in its sling lay across his bared chest and his face was turned away from the light, exposing the scarred cheek, with its divots and still inflamed flesh, the stitches still in the skin.

She crept to the bed and stood watching him, her heart full of love and anguish for him. She slipped off her cloak, gown, shoes, stockings, petticoats, and corset, and dressed only in her shift, she moved to the far side of the bed and slipped between the sheets, careful not to disturb him.

Despite her care, though, he woke and blinked at her as she turned toward him.

"Ava!" his voice was low and husky with sleep. "Did you enjoy the play?"

"Yes, but I would have rather been here with you," she confessed, sitting up and leaning on an elbow. "How was your evening?"

"Well enough," he said.

She reached out a hand to touch his face, and the movement disturbed the equilibrium of the mattress, and he winced as his arm moved involuntarily.

"Oh! I'm sorry!" she said, withdrawing her hand.

"It's all right," he said, closing his eyes.

She lay back down and watched him for some time. Eventually he said, with his eyes still closed, "Ava, please stop staring at me."

"How do you know I am?"

"I can feel you. Look, it might be better if you went to your own bed."

She jerked and caught her breath at the stab of hurt. "O-of course if you'd rather—"

"I would." His tone was flat and tired.

She climbed out of bed, gathered up her discarded clothes and said softly, "Good night then."

He grunted in response, and she went to the door to her own room blinking back tears.

Chapter Twenty-Nine

EIGHT WEEKS AFTER Jerome's accident, the season was over, and summer was making life in the metropolis unbearable. Jerome was mobile, but unable to pursue many of his favorite activities with his arm still in a sling.

Over breakfast one morning, Ava said, "I was thinking we should go to The Castle. We can't stay here. It's dreadful and not good for you."

"You go. It will do you good to have a break. You have been hovering about me for weeks. You must be heartily sick of it by now."

He paused and pushed his half-eaten plate away. His appetite had never fully recovered after the accident, which worried her. He rubbed his face with his left hand. A gesture she had noticed was becoming more regular, as if he couldn't resist touching the scar.

"No, I will not leave you here!" she protested.

"I'm perfectly able to care for myself with Leyton's assistance now. There is no need for you to remain here—"

"No! I will not have you say you would rather have Leyton care for you than me!" She threw down her napkin and rose, coming around to his side of the table. "Please don't push me away!"

He eased back from the table and sighed. "I'm sorry. I'm a beast."

"No, you are not!" she said, leaning in to kiss him. He let her do it, but he didn't respond, which alarmed her more than all the rest. He had kept her from his bed while he was healing on the grounds that he feared her presence would endanger his healing bones. But his increasing distance from her terrified her. He seemed bent on pushing her away.

"Jerome, what is wrong?"

"Nothing! Everything!" he burst out, rising to his feet and heading for the door. "The truth is I cannot abide myself, if you must have it! This—this imposed idleness is killing me!"

And he left the room, shutting the door with a decided snap.

Ava plopped down in his vacated chair, sank her head in her hands and gave into the urge to cry that had been plaguing her for days. Jerome had become increasingly impossible as his body healed. His lowness of spirits and irritability were understandable, and she made allowances for it, but it was so hard when he behaved like this. Like he hated her when all she was trying to do was love him and care for him.

She wiped her eyes and rose determinedly. She would speak to the doctor. Surely Jerome must be healed enough to begin exercising a little soon? She understood perfectly that urge to move—a good walk or ride was always the antidote she sought herself if her spirits were low. And such an outlet was denied him. No wonder he was behaving like a bear with a sore head.

THE ACCIDENT AND the scarring of his face on the back of the revelations about his parents had plunged Jerome into a bout of melancholy that he could not seem to shift. He was aware that he was treating Ava abominably and couldn't seem to stop. Her care, her love, rubbed him raw at the same time it comforted him.

For he couldn't shake the conviction that he was unworthy of her love. And every time he looked in the mirror he was convinced he was right. His inner ugliness that he had long sought to hide from the world was now writ large upon his face for all to see. And surely Ava must see it too. Yet she had remained steadfast in her devotion and her love, and every gesture of care buried him in ever deeper layers of guilt.

But in the last few days, he had been granted the ability to begin resuming his physical routine. The doctor had lifted his moratorium on exercise and was now encouraging him to resume some activity. Getting his body moving again brought him significant relief and helped him to not only feel better, but to realize two things. One was that he was being an absolute ass toward Ava and he owed her a massive apology. And the second was that he was determined to go to Ravenshaw. The matter he had written to Kelham about had produced no result as yet, and he knew he needed to go there himself and sort the matter out for once and for all. Otherwise he feared being held hostage to these nightmares for the rest of his life. He must lay the ghosts of his past to rest.

But firstly he needed to apologize to his wife. With his arm now free of its sling, he felt reasonably whole again, and as long as he didn't look in a mirror he could forget for a few minutes that his face was a pitiable ruin of his former handsome self. It had been a shock to realize how much that mattered to him. But it did.

His instinct was to hide himself away, but such behavior was the act of a coward. How could Ava be proud of a coward? For her sake, he dressed with his usual care, which he had eschewed for the last several weeks, and left the house to walk to Bond Street where he had several commissions he wished to execute.

AVA WAS OUT saying farewell to Annis and Emrys, who were packing up their brood and taking them to the seaside for the summer the following day, and did not return to the house until late afternoon. Skelton greeted her with a grin, which she found a little odd. He tended to be of somewhat sober disposition as a rule. She trod upstairs to her room to change for dinner and opening the door stood transfixed at the sight within.

The room was full of flowers. The variegated colors and scents mingled in the air and quite overwhelmed her. She entered the room slowly, noting each vase and wreath that had been used to decorate the room like a bower. She turned to the bed and saw a long, slender red velvet box sitting on the pillow, atop a folded sheet of paper. She sat down on the edge of the bed and reached for the slip of paper. Pulling it from beneath the box, she unfolded it and read.

My dearest Ava,

I have behaved abominably toward you for the last several weeks, and I do not know how to make amends for my ill-mannered treatment of you.

You are a saint to have put up with my ill temper, when you have extended toward me nothing but love and care. You have stood staunchly by my side through all the dramas that have unfolded and fought valiantly to uphold my honor. You have shown, as always, your true colors of loyalty and kindness, of selfless love and affection.

And to my never-ending shame, I do not feel worthy of your love and loyalty, for I have demonstrated the ugliness of my soul in the way I have behaved in my surliness, my moodiness, and bad temper. I have been in the grip of a melancholy humor that would not let me go. But that is no excuse for my loathsomeness toward you. How you tolerate me I do not know.

I hardly dare to ask for your forgiveness for I do not deserve it.

I can only pledge to try to do better in the future and beg you not to give up on me. There are demons that plague me still,

*but I have resolved to conquer them. With you at my side I am
confident of doing so. I confess, my darling, I do not know how
I would go on without you.*

*Please know that I love you with all my heart and soul, and
I would give my life to make you happy. I hate myself most
deeply for causing you pain.*

Jerome

Ava sat on the bed wiping tears off her cheeks as she read and
reread the letter. What came through to her most strongly was
his pain, and it made her heart ache to relive it. She sniffed and
kissed the paper, whispering, "Oh, Jerome, my love!"

She heard a faint sound and turned to the door of his room
where Jerome stood looking at her, and the ravaged expression
on his face sent her across the room into his arms.

"Jerome!" she flung her arms around him.

"I'm so sorry, Ava," he said, his arms pulling her tight against
him and burying his face in her hair. "Can you forgive me?"

"There is nothing to forgive, love," she said softly, her hand
coming up to stroke his scarred cheek. He flinched under her
touch and closed his eyes.

"I'm sorry," he whispered.

They stood for several moments in silence, just hugging each
other tight. And then he said, "I've decided to go to Ravenshaw.
Do you want to come with me or go to The Castle?"

"I'll come with you, of course. Why do you want to go?" she
asked.

"I have to confront my ghosts. I've spent my life running
away from things. It's time I turned and faced them." He cupped
her face and kissed her. "With you I can do anything."

She laughed. It came out a bit broken in the middle, for the
emotions welling up didn't know whether to become a laugh or a
cry.

He glanced at the bed, "Did you look at your present?"

She shook her head. "I was more interested in the letter."

"Have a look," he said, guiding her gently towards the bed. She sat, reached for the box, and opened the lid. Nestled in white satin was a gold pendant of heart pierced by an arrow.

"That is what happened to me when I saw you descend the stairs at Lady Castlereagh's ball. You were wearing jonquil silk and looked like golden joy and sunlight to me. I've loved you ever since, Ava. But it has taken me a long time to accept that someone so wonderful as you could love a man like me." He dropped to his knees by the bed and took her hands. "I don't deserve it and I don't know how to be good enough for you, but please let me try?"

"Jerome, stop!" she said through the tears falling on her cheeks. "I'm no angel. Have you forgotten how often I have been in a scrape, and how willful and selfish I can be? I am not a saint Jerome, far from it. I've just discovered that when you love someone and they need you, you rise the occasion, that's all." She freed her hands to cup his face and kiss him. "I'm not going anywhere. I'm you wife, for better or worse, remember?"

He nodded. "I remember."

"Good," she said softly. "Then you can worship me with your body in my bower of flowers please, because it's been weeks and I've *missed* you!"

"Oh, Ava." He rose and pulled her up with him. In a few moments of flurried removal of clothing they were down on the bed and he was worshipping with deep enthusiasm to her even deeper satisfaction.

⟫⟫⟫⟪⟪⟪

THEY TRAVELED BY coach, four days of a kind of foggy bliss, wrapped up in each other, and Jerome tried to not think about what awaited him at Ravenshaw. But as they drew closer he found the shadows and ghosts creeping forward in his mind more and more.

Ava squeezed his hand, dragging him back to the present and said gently, "Memories?"

He nodded. "Yes, sorry—"

"Don't! Don't apologize. You have a lot to deal with. I understand."

He took a breath and let it out slowly. "Thank you."

⇒⟫⟪⟸

WHEN THEY DREW up finally in the curving driveway of the large gray stone house where Jerome had been born and spent most of his childhood, he was surprised to see Kelham standing at the foot of the front steps shaking the hand of a big, dark-haired fellow, dressed in a dark-brown suit, which was clearly the fellow's Sunday best but far from fashionable elegance. *One of the tenants or a contractor working on the house?* Repairs had continued in Jerome's absence.

He opened the carriage door and leaped out, turning to help Ava down.

"My lord!" Kelham said coming towards him. The other fellow hung back but didn't leave. "You couldn't have received my letter—I only sent it yesterday."

"You're right, I didn't. We left London four days ago. Ava, this is Kelham my steward, and an excellent fellow he is too. Kelham, may I introduce my wife, Lady Ravenshaw?"

Kelham flushed at his praise and bowed to Ava. "Your Ladyship, I am honored to meet you." He turned back to Jerome. "My lord, you should have let us know you were coming. The McClellans will be at sixes and sevens with Her Ladyship here and nothing set to rights."

"Oh, don't mind me," said Ava quickly. "I know the house is still under repair."

"Your Ladyship is most gracious," said Kelham with a another bow.

Jerome nodded at the fellow in the brown suit. Something in the cast of his features made Jerome think he should know who the man was. "Who is our guest?" he asked Kelham.

"Well, he was what I wrote to you about, my lord. You told me look into what happened to Eliza Stubbs." Jerome felt Ava stiffen beside him. "This fellow claims to be her son, Jeremiah Stubbs. It seems when Miss Stubbs left Ravenshaw in '89, she was with child. She went home to her parents and gave birth to Jeremiah."

Jerome put a hand out to grasp the carriage door as a wave of relief washed through him. "So he didn't kill her after all," he said softly.

"It seems not, my lord."

Jerome grabbed Kelham's hand and wrung it. "Thank you, my dear chap. You have relieved my mind enormously." He trod over to the other fellow, Jeremiah Stubbs, and held out his hand. As he did so, he recognized the man's heritage in his face. The same dark hair, curved brows, and curl of the lips. This man was his half-brother. The resemblance was unmistakable.

"I'm Ravenshaw," Jerome said firmly and with a smile. "I'm pleased to make your acquaintance, brother."

Stubbs flushed and said gruffly, "Your Lordship is kind to acknowledge me. I didn't expect that. Mother always held to it my father was a lord, but she never told me who. Wasn't until I got his letter," he nodded at Kelham, "that I realized what might be in the wind."

Jerome noted that the man's diction was, if not precisely that of a gentleman, not rough. He began thinking immediately of what he could do for the fellow. "Come into the house, we have much to discuss," he said. "And meet my wife, Lady Ravenshaw." He waved Ava over and introduced them.

Ava smiled and said warmly, "I'm delighted to meet you."

"We have an older sister, you know," said Jerome, leading the way into the large entry hall. "McClellan, get Mrs. McClellan to send up refreshments please."

"Aye, my lord," said the butler with a smile.

"We do?" said Jeremiah with an odd note in his voice.

"Yes. Leticia, but we call her Letty. She's married to the Earl DeCrecy." Jerome clapped him on the arm. "It'll take a bit of getting used to. But never fear, little brother. I'll help you."

The younger man grinned at that, because he was a few inches taller and broader than Jerome. "I'll try to be an apt pupil, my lord."

"Jerome," said the Marquess of Ravenshaw firmly.

AVA TURNED TO Jerome in the big bed Mrs. McClellan and the housemaids had hastily made ready for them and said, "Did you know you had a half brother?"

"No. Not an inkling. You know I thought I'd witnessed my father killing Eliza Stubbs. It is clear from her diary that Mama thought he had too. Perhaps he meant to and relented. I'll never know. My memories are fragmented and through the eyes of a child too young to comprehend what he was seeing. I was just left with this nameless dread deep inside. A feeling of—of inadequacy, as if I had failed at something I never understood. I know now it drove my relentless pursuit of perfection, my desire to win at any cost. When the accident scarred my face, it brought it all up again. I felt like my internal ugliness was there on my face for everyone to see. That was why I was so unbearable. I was unbearable to myself. I'm so sorry."

She stroked his cheek and murmured, "You will never be ugly to me, Jerome. For I know the best of you, and I love you so much it hurts. You have nothing to apologize for. I will always love you, even when you don't love yourself. In fact, especially then. Because that is when you need it most."

"Oh, Ava!" He buried his face in her neck and she felt the warmth of his breath. "I promise you, my love, that I will spend the rest of my life trying to be worthy of you."

"Tush!" She pulled back and forced him to look at her. "You *are* worthy of me! So much more than you give yourself credit for. Just because you have a moment of self-doubt that doesn't nullify all the good things you do! All the things you are so very good at! You have worked hard to be the best Jerome. Don't denigrate that effort!"

He smiled, his new lopsided smile and cupped her face. "I love you, Ava."

"I love you!" she said. "Show me how much you love me, Jerome."

He propped himself up on his elbows and murmured, "With my body I thee worship . . ." and she stroked his scarred cheek.

Those were the words she had latched onto at the wedding. She had been a girl when they got married. She was a woman now and a wife. She smiled and returned his kiss with a deep one of her own, trying to wordlessly convey to him how much he meant to her, how much she would sacrifice for his happiness and peace of mind. And how very much she wanted him.

His kisses deepened, became more passionate, but with an added dimension of care and tenderness. She felt precious and oh so loved, wrapped up in his arms. His lips traced kisses over her skin, tasting her, loving her. She returned them as she twisted her head to find his skin to caress with her mouth, tracing patterns over his skin beneath with her hungry mouth.

His hands cupped her breasts and he bent his head to suckle the nipples with tender long pulls of his mouth and laves of his tongue.

He rolled her under him as her hands ran over his back and chest. Their mouths sought each other as he sought to join their bodies, his hand finding the right place between her legs.

"Ava!" he murmured, breathless, all his need in his voice.

"Yes, yes!" she urged him, desperate for the joining.

Their bodies came together with the ease of familiarity, and the added edge of banked desire. She arched up into him as he bore down. And everything happened in a heated rush as they sought and found the missing piece of themselves in each other. The rising tide of unstoppable desire took them over the edge in an explosion of passionate love that left them both floating in a haze of blissful happiness.

With Ava's head resting on his chest, as he lay on his back, Jerome knew at last that the gnawing ache of inadequacy, shame, and guilt that drove him was eased by the love of the woman he adored. It might never be fully extinguished, that sense of not being enough. He would always want to win and be the best. But he now knew that if he didn't always succeed, it wasn't the end of the world. *Because Ava loves me just as I am.*

Epilogue

Ravenshaw, Christmas 1820

AVA SURVEYED THE drawing room with satisfaction. It was full to bursting with family and friends gathered to celebrate Christmas. It had taken a lot of work, but the gardens had been transformed into a riot of color.

The house renovations had been completed, along with a complete redecoration of the rooms, to Ava's design. The objective was to banish the shadows of the past. The portrait of the sixth Marquess of Ravenshaw had been exiled to the attics. Jerome had wanted to burn it, but Ava stopped him. "Your descendants will want to know about your father. He is a part of the family history; you can't erase him. Time will heal the wounds." He'd agreed reluctantly.

Ava moved among her guests, content to see her husband across the room, deep in conversation with his friends and his half brother Jeremiah, who had been welcomed into the family despite the blemish on his birth. The addition had been welcomed by her brother, Ashford, and Pendrell. The four men were as brothers and they could do no less than sponsor Jeremiah's introduction into society. It ruffled a few feathers, but the Laynes were gaining a reputation for doing the unconventional, and only the most stickle-backed refused to receive the dark-haired giant with the unmistakable stamp of the DeVere good looks. And she finally felt grown up enough to be a sister to the other men's wives. Even her former governess, Annis.

Letty had birthed her baby safely. A boy at last. Her husband John was home now and delighted to welcome his heir. Ashford was, of course, a doting father to the new addition to his house, Isabel. And Emily was big and nearing her time.

Ava placed a hand on her own belly where she suspected might reside the next Marquess of Ravenshaw and caught Jerome's eye as she did it. His expression froze a moment before he plunged across the room to her.

"Are you?" he asked quietly.

"I'm not certain yet, but possibly," she admitted with a wide smile. And her husband kissed her, in front of all their family and friends.

Her mother and sisters, catching the news, came around her like a flock of geese and Ava laughed for sheer joy. "I don't know yet! Really, I will tell you all when I am certain."

Her sisters-in-law, the Misses Watson, clustered together by the window listening to Miss Ruth read to them from a book of poems, watched quietly by her brother Hereward. And Kenrick lounged at his ease beside his wife, also big with child. Ava had reluctantly revised her opinion of her newest sister-in-law. Deborah was missing, but Ava smiled, knowing that at last her dear friend Rey had his happily ever after, too. The nursery upstairs was full of babies and children, and the drawing room bursting with happiness.

My cup runneth over!

About the Author

Wren St. Claire has wanted to write since she was twelve and discovered her mother's Georgette Heyer collection. Wren St. Claire lives in Brisbane with one confused Mini Schnauzer and six mad, Bengal cats. She writes steamy historical romance, where the heroes spoil the heroines and readers get to tag along for the ride, enjoying a roller coaster of emotions. Wren has a master's degree in Egyptology and used to lead tours to Egypt up until the revolution during the Arab Spring in 2011.